CRYSTAL LAKE PUBLIC LIBRARY
3 2306 00734 0345
P9-DEE-503
JE - - '16

ALSO BY WHITNEY TERRELL

The Huntsman

The King of Kings County

THE GOOD LIEUTENANT

PROPERTY OF CLPL

THE GOOD LIEUTENANT

WHITNEY TERRELL

FARRAR, STRAUS AND GIROUX   NEW YORK

Farrar, Straus and Giroux
18 West 18th Street, New York 10011

Copyright © 2016 by Whitney Terrell
All rights reserved
Printed in the United States of America
First edition, 2016

Library of Congress Cataloging-in-Publication Data
Names: Terrell, Whitney, author.
Title: The good lieutenant : a novel / Whitney Terrell.
Description: First edition. | New York : Farrar, Straus and Giroux, 2016.
Identifiers: LCCN 2015035380 | ISBN 9780374164737 (hardback) |
ISBN 9780374712556 (e-book).
Subjects: | BISAC: FICTION / Literary. | GSAFD: Love stories.
Classification: LCC PS3570.E692 G66 2016 | DDC 813/.54—dc23
LC record available at http://lccn.loc.gov/2015035380

Designed by Abby Kagan

Our books may be purchased in bulk for promotional, educational, or business use. Please contact your local bookseller or the Macmillan Corporate and Premium Sales Department at 1-800-221-7945, extension 5442, or by e-mail at MacmillanSpecialMarkets@macmillan.com.

www.fsgbooks.com
www.twitter.com/fsgbooks • www.facebook.com/fsgbooks

1 3 5 7 9 10 8 6 4 2

TO GAYLE, MOSS, AND MILES—
YOU'VE ALWAYS BEEN THERE, FROM
START TO FINISH. ALL MY LOVE.

AND

TO W.F.

PART ONE

THE FIELD

1

The target's house was surprisingly palatial: three stories, winged and modular, its tan concrete balconies adorned with geometric, beveled corners, so that the whole seemed to have been cast from a mold. A stone wall circled it, covered with a matching taupe coat of mortar worked into a pattern of diamonds and grooved lines. Even after Lieutenant Emma Fowler directed her Humvee through the front gate, she still believed that she had not decided unequivocally to let Captain Masterson off the hook for all the illegal crap he'd pulled to find this place. Especially since that crap might well have been the reason her platoon sergeant, Carl Beale, was dead. She had merely come to scope the situation out. Make sure she was not endangering Lieutenant Pulowski or her platoon unnecessarily. Make sure that she could live with allowing Masterson's whole bullshit-o-rama to stay intact. She'd expected this to be difficult but, somehow, during the hour it had taken them to convoy here from Camp Tolerance—the target's house was deep in the Iraqi backcountry, west of Baghdad—the mere fact of driving in her own Humvee with Pulowski had made her feel as if, for the first time in months, they were together, and their old selves had come back. Inside the compound, she counted her soldiers as they chest-bumped the scorching summer air, feeling more than just relief. Yes, the war was fucked up. Yes, left and right you could see examples of people completely botching things in the worst way. Of people who refused to step up. But Pulowski and Crawford, Dykstra and Waldorf, the rest of the platoon—they had not fucked it up. They had not quit. They had not bitched and whined. They had acted in good faith.

She felt as if she had needed only that one gesture of good faith. Seeing Pulowski touch the broken shackle Beale had welded to his Humvee on the ride out, listening to him speak a memory of the sergeant, even after they'd gone all *Survivor* on each other over the past three weeks—*especially* after she'd cornered Pulowski in her trailer and, like some camera-hog New Jersey housewife, decided it would be helpful if she said the *worst possible things* to his face—as Jimenez might've put it, the moment had some serious *bueno* to it, the kind you didn't feel every day. Better than tribal council, anyway.

As for the recovery of Beale's body, after all this effort, it appeared completely matter-of-fact. She talked to Masterson about it at a broken picnic table in the rear of the compound. "Faisal says the body's in the field out back," he said. "We'll just search it in sections, like we're looking for a weapons cache." He fanned his fingers on an aerial photo he'd pinned down with his pliers. "We form a straight line, walk it through. Take a couple hours, maybe. Faisal says he used to play here when he was a kid. There's a well or something out there. Claims it's hard to find, but I doubt it."

The field was beyond the compound wall. Inside were non-incriminating beds of rosebushes, a toolshed, a half-swept terrace. The broken poles and stays of . . . a badminton net? She'd worried how badly Masterson might've hurt his interpreter to get this intel. Now she worried he hadn't hurt him enough. "You find the owner?"

"Nobody's here," Masterson said. "But this patrol's rotation began at three a.m. So, Lieutenant, I know this particular mission is important to you. I know you are eager to have this happen. I know you've been waiting a long time . . ."

"But you've got some tired men."

"To say the least."

"So what do you want from me?"

"I got a dozen guys here," Masterson said. "We add your platoon, we can sweep this field in an hour." He pointed to a road on the map, a black worm at the end of the field's shaded gray. "Then we'll have the Bradleys pick us up and take us home."

"That's on the opposite side of the field," Fowler said.

"That's right."

She understood what he was asking then. With the twelve men he'd brought, Masterson would have to go down one side of the field and then come back up the other in order to cover the entire area. But if Fowler added her guys to the mix, they might sweep it in a single pass. "*I* can go," she said. "But I've got those cameras we talked about with me. Plus a signal officer." She avoided Pulowski's name, bending her tone to suggest that this being was far beneath Masterson's attention. "You don't want him out there. And if he stays, I need my team in here for security."

"Who is this guy, somebody's brother?" Masterson was fitting his body armor back on. When Fowler didn't respond, he sighed. "All right, have it your way, Lieutenant. We do these cache searches every day. We got to stay out an extra couple hours, so be it. Why don't you have your signal guy put a camera up while we're working, at least?"

5

Harris was her real brother's name. She thought about him as she and Pulowski crow-hopped the tubs of camera gear into the target's empty house. Harris in his yellow tie and moleskin coat, his lower lip poked out, concentrating, the last time they'd met before she deployed, at an actual skating rink with actual pastel skaters painted on the boards, a memory no more or less incongruous than the hocus-pocus things that Harris had actually said. *Let somebody else worry about what's supposed to be true. That way you can figure out what you really believe.* Now, with Pulowski above her, sweating and sharp-edged as usual, wiping his beaked nose, as they heaved the last tub up a ladder to the roof, she would've said that it had never been about what she believed. She'd only wanted to believe *with* someone else. That was the *bueno* in the Humvee, and that was what it felt like now, as she and Pulowski scuttled together to the roof's edge, his face smeared with two days' growth of beard but open to her again. Seeing her. Like the last piece to a puzzle she'd been struggling her whole life to complete. From there, they could see the toylike, humped bridge that marked the midpoint of Route Valentine, the distant railroad tracks, the tawny, rough edges of the canals, their silent banks of reeds. The field behind the house appeared to be several acres square, roughly the size of a section back in Kansas. The palm forest loomed on either side, and a mix of darker, orange-tinted wheat stalks and the paper-white clumps of plain grass ran away from them, slightly downhill, in a rolling series of bumps. Beale was there. This did not make the field feel ominous. Not in the way that an empty alley in Muthanna might. She heard the hard, dry hum of grasshoppers, the almost comic—given the usual tension of their patrols—desolation of the place. But she felt the strange, giddy lightness you sometimes got when you pulled off the interstate after a long drive, piled out of the car, and squatted behind a tree to pee: amazement at the stillness going on here, the stubborn persistence of life, always continuing, away from the rush of things. "Man, it was like some kind of ghost town coming in here. You wanna talk depopulation"—Pulowski snapped a picture of the field—"it's like the Iraqi version of Kansas. Maybe we should just evac whoever's left to Salina, give them a chicken farm, and call it good. Holy shit, what's this?"

Pulowski wandered over to a weirdly shaped object in the center of the flat roof. His neck was so skinny up above his collar that his helmet resembled a tapered mushroom cap, and his white hips flashed between his belt and body armor. "You clear that?" she asked one of Masterson's men as Pulowski poked his head inside.

"Yeah, we went through everything."

"It's a fucking spaceship," Pulowski called excitedly.

"What do you mean, a spaceship?"

"I mean like some guy built a spaceship here, you know? Like to play in. It's kinda weird, right?" Pulowski had clambered inside the structure, which looked more like a vegetable steamer with its metal panels folded in.

"Probably a lookout post, is what it seems to me," Fowler said.

She waited through a fussy, rustling silence, which was the sound of Pulowski worrying. "So what are *we* looking for here?" he said, climbing out.

Fowler hunkered down along the edge of the roof. "The note you gave me," she said. "It was good. We think the guy who wrote it also took Beale. This is his house. Beale's body is supposed to be out back."

"Why didn't you say that before we left?"

She'd expected this question. She'd decided that if she couldn't explain what she'd done to get this information from

Masterson's interpreter, Faisal Amar, then she should ditch the whole scheme. "I had to push the envelope a little. Captain Hartz wouldn't have understood. And even if he had, he wouldn't have let me come out here."

"Push the envelope? What the hell does that mean?"

"It means him." Fowler nodded down at Faisal Amar. She'd located him in the yard below, lying on his side, cuffed, like a trash bag that somebody had tossed out for collection. "That guy's in bad shape. Masterson's been having a party with him."

"So this is like, what, violence-bad? Bash-on-an-Iraqi-bad?"

When Fowler nodded, Pulowski covered his face with his hands and started laughing and pacing across the roof. "Oh, shit, that is too perfect. I told you Masterson was a fucking stooge. You didn't listen to me!"

She tilted her head to the side. "It's worse than that. If you want to trace it all the way back, it's probably Masterson's fault that Beale got taken in the first place. He's been fucking up big-time out here. The good news is, it also means that whatever's happening here, whatever happened to Beale"—she nodded at the field—"it's not on you."

Pulowski did not seem in any way willing to classify the interpreter's crumpled body as good news. "So if we find Beale," he said. "You think that's actually going to make this whole thing somehow *less* of a joke?"

"That's what I'm hoping," she said.

"Hoping?"

"That's what I believe. We get our guy back. No matter what happened, no matter how jacked up it was, that's the only way to make things right."

Pulowski did not reply to this. She could remember feeling this way the first few months she'd worked recovery: trying to convince herself that the war was like a practical joke, one that couldn't actually fool her so long as she was around someone who already knew the punch line. Like Pulowski.

Or now, in Pulowski's case, like her.

She watched as he hefted a goobered-up antenna from one of his Tupperware tubs and, spooling out Ethernet wire as he went, set it on the edge of the roof. She went over and crouched next to him and grabbed his hand and put the palm of it against her lips. It wasn't something she'd planned. But it felt right. Somebody looking would've thought that he was telling her to stop. But she kissed him in the folds of his palm.

"All right," he said, blushing. He might have seemed just a little bit happier. She noticed that he didn't wipe the kiss away. "Let's get on with it."

The Yagi antenna on the roof beamed the video back to Pulowski's laptop at about sixteen frames per second (normal television was thirty), and so as the camera panned across the field, there was at each pass a certain level of trailing distortion, a moment when squares of color would flare up, a single pixel bolting out to supernova size, and the swarming calculations underneath the image—the Chebyshev filters, the anti-aliasing equations, the algorithms constantly drilling away at wave sample after wave sample—would be revealed in unnaturally perfect geometric shapes. After a few adjustments, however, the body armor of the soldiers who'd stayed behind pressed Pulowski's shoulders, their fingers reaching out to brush the screen. They marked the shadows separating the wheat field from its bordering reeds, identified the wall that defined the house's garden, its terra-cotta top, and the iron gate whose chain they'd cut, at Faisal Amar's suggestion, in order to enter the back field. They could see, on each pass of the camera, the ragged line of Masterson's platoon—accompanied by Fowler—as they walked down the left side of the field. At the controls, Pulowski felt increasingly magnanimous. Without him, the field would have remained a mystery. A fragment of someone else's dream. Now he presented it to them as a gift. The Syscolite interface had an animated circle of buttons in its upper left corner. These controlled the camera's pan, tilt, and zoom, and Pulowski allowed the men to play with it, breaking the camera out of its preset sweep and aiming at something specific: a patch of reed, a crinkle of paper blowing across the roadway, a pile of bricks. They did this not because they saw something interesting but only to prove that, safely hunkered down inside the compound wall, they had the power to see whatever they wished to see.

After this, the mood of Fowler's platoon eased. Expecting a test, they'd been granted recess. Dykstra, the jowly sergeant from Philly, pulled MREs from the back of his Humvee, snipped their brown foil covers, like he was back behind his ancestral Wawa counter slicing Boar's Head, while others did a *Sports-Center* recap of the Muthanna intersection bombing two months back. "Dude, you would not believe that shit," a soldier named Jimenez said. He was about Pulowski's height but rubbery, swaying on the outside of his boots, as if he was used to doing something more interesting with his feet. The bright emerald wingtips of a dragon wove up from his shirt collar and circled his neck. "Man, it was like some kind of fucking medical show cleaning that shit up. Giant fucking disaster. You know? I mean, we've seen plenty of wrecks and shit. One guy gets hit with an IED, that's plenty nasty. But you got two dudes? Standing around a dump truck packed with a thousand pounds of dynamite and some gravel? It's cold, man. Fucking cold. And at night, man? At night, man, you hear these fucking rats—"

"Damn, man . . . that was—I don't even want you to mention

that nastiness while I'm eating," Crawford said. He was the youngest of the group and he made a frightened face, eyes wide and bulging behind his gold-rimmed glasses, mouth covered daintily with a paper napkin, which he'd folded neatly in his skinny, graceful hands.

"Eeek, eek, eek," Jimenez said, his fingers fribbling along the table.

"No!" Crawford dropped his napkin and clapped his hands over his ears.

"Hey, hey, hey," Jimenez said, tapping Pulowski's shoulder, a dirty love band flopping on his wrist. "You ever seen anything like that?"

"I've been to the Muthanna intersection," he said. It was where they'd lost Beale. "You know that."

"That bomb was like a point-blank blast, man, except with *gravel.*"

Then, on Pulowski's laptop screen, a dog appeared in completely clear silhouette, ears up, gazing back at the house and the camera there as if aware of them.

"You see that?" Pulowski said. He was panning the camera, trying to center on the animal again. "Dogs are usually with people, right?"

"Naw, naw, there's dogs all over the place. Just keep it on the sweep." Crawford stood and began to stretch as if preparing to take his leave.

"Wait a second, wait a second—where are you going?"

"The LT's order is we stay here," Crawford said. "Inside the wall."

"What for?" Pulowski said. "What's the point of going to the trouble to put this camera up if we're not going to do anything about what we see?"

"You tell me, man," Crawford said.

Pulowski paused. He looked up from the familiar rectangle of the laptop, its chrome highlights, the pleasing dry waffle of its keys, to Crawford's glossy brown cheeks.

"Why did she have us stay inside the compound, then?" he asked. "It would've been faster if we'd all been out there doing a sweep."

Crawford didn't respond to this.

Pulowski looked up at the surrounding faces of Fowler's platoon. Whatever interest or pleasure they'd shown when he'd originally fired up the camera had dissipated, and their expressions were blank, unfocused—not that far different than they'd been when he'd reported the loss of Sergeant Beale, just seventy-two hours ago. A nice little air pocket of unhappy.

In the center of it was him. He was the reason they'd stayed in.

"Okay, fine. I'm the idiot signal guy. I don't know anything about field operations. I don't know whether it means anything to see a dog out there or not. So I'm just asking for an opinion."

"Could be one thing, could be another," Crawford said.

"Don't you think we should go check it out? Or at least alert them?"

"They ain't got any coms," Crawford said.

"All right," he said. "Let's do it."

"Sorry, sir?" Crawford said.

Who the fuck is this idiot? Pulowski thought, listening to himself. *What kind of moron leaves a protected compound when he doesn't have to?* It was a deep violation of the signal officer's code. And yet, strangely enough, as soon as he spoke, he felt great. Not brave. Not smart. Just great. His hands had stopped shaking. He could handle fifteen minutes of stupidity if Fowler was genuinely at risk. "I said we're going out. I'm the ranking officer here. Lieutenant Fowler, *your* lieutenant, is out there in the field. She's got no perspective on this. She can't see the terrain. How difficult is it to just drive down there and take a peek with a Humvee?"

When Masterson's foot patrol started into the field—a line of thirteen soldiers holding their arms out for spacing—Fowler stood next to the captain and brushed his fingertips. They were nearly black, the dirt ground into deep half-moons beneath his fingernails, and he wore several days' growth of beard. But the spackled, deformed skin between his glasses and his chin seemed less drawn and fearful, a tiny flicker of his frat-boy cheekiness coming back, and though she believed he deserved his fear, she also found its absence a relief. On either side of them were soldiers with metal detectors strapped to their forearms, waving their black disks over the furrows. "Worth a try," Masterson said. "If he's got a gun down there, they'll get a beep. Faisal says he hears they put the body down in a well or something. For what *that's* worth. Says he's not sure he can find the actual place. But if Beale's been down there since, what, Tuesday?"

Masterson waved a hand in front of his face and she realized that he was trying to warn her that the body might stink. She breathed in deeply through her nose, but all she could smell were the smells of the living: Masterson's perspiration, which was sharper and more acrid than her own. The sweet ammonia of the dip the soldier beside them was chewing. "You trust him?" she said, nodding to Faisal.

The interpreter was upright now and walking several spots over in the line, hands cuffed behind his back. His lithe, handsome features appeared mushy, like a smashed melon, and there were scabbed patches on his scalp where he was missing chunks of hair. He wore his familiar rotten suit jacket over a gold Lakers jersey. No body armor.

"Hell, no," Masterson said cheerfully. "But I've tried to make it clear to him that it would be a bad idea to lie."

"You think he did it?"

"Killed your soldier?" Masterson grinned. "No, no—he was with me that day, I checked my battle journal."

"But he could have been involved."

"It's the usual crazy Iraqi business. You ask one question, you get a thousand and one answers."

"And the current one is?"

"The current one is that a couple guys 'showed up' at his house with Beale's body. Asked Faisal for a place to hide the goddamn thing, and he sent them here."

"He was already dead?"

"If you believe Faisal."

"That's a relief." Fowler said the words, but she did not in fact feel this. As soon as she'd seen the interpreter's wounds, the good feeling she'd had back in the Humvee with Pulowski had started to fade. "My guys were real upset about the possibilities."

"The possibilities of what?"

"The possibilities of what might happen to a guy who's left alone with a bunch of Iraqis. To do whatever they want."

"Which are?"

"Which are bad enough to make my guys really pissed. We were mostly fobbits, you know. Before we lost Beale at that intersection, these guys were happy as hell to be working inside the wire, putting up walls for the general's bowling alley."

"So that's how you got them to step up, huh?" Masterson said.

"It definitely helped," Fowler said. She squinted, staring at the gauzy far end of the field. "I'm not going to say I didn't use that information motivationally."

They found nothing on the first pass. They'd gone down the wrong side of the field, Faisal claimed, weaving more and more Arabic into his sentences, though she knew his English was perfectly good—explaining that he hadn't been in the field since he was ten. Then that he'd only been in it when it was dark. When he started in on his third explanation, one of Masterson's soldiers drove a rifle butt into his ribs.

There was a canal at the field's end, broached by a single corrugated drainage pipe. Masterson wobbled heel-toe back over the culvert, consulted with the Bradleys waiting there, then returned, snapping his chin strap back in place, and signaled his men to head back up the field's east side. "How's your kid brother doing?" he asked.

"My who?"

A fishhook twisted in her gut, but then Masterson's smile relieved her—just fucking around. A crinkle of amusement. "We just got a call from your signal guy."

Oh, Jesus, Fowler thought.

"Says he's got a mad dog to check out up ahead of us."

"Is he in trouble?"

"No, no—a little unauthorized air usage, but no. I said we'd meet them there."

She tried to scrub her face of meaning, aware of his scrutiny off to her left side, the nosy wetness of his curiosity. "So you take shit seriously, don't you?" he said. "Fucking tell Fowler you've got a tip, and she calls out the cavalry."

A strange dry heat spread over her scalp with this remark, like a powder. It was meant to be a compliment, but the aftertaste was ugly, like she'd done something desperate and needy. "Was I not supposed to?" she said.

The radio chatter was interrupted by a calming, booming bass that Pulowski recognized as belonging to Waldorf, the somber black sergeant who commanded Fowler's second team. "Hey, boys, we got a target. I need Charlie and Delta to go right at him, straight through the field. Dykstra and I are gonna swing around to the tree line, just in case he's got buddies." The rest was broken up by the sudden seasick jolting of the Humvee as Crawford accelerated through the field, and Pulowski, after his helmet ricocheted twice off the Humvee's roof, scrambled to secure both his computer bag and the camera system's wireless receiver, which tumbled and banged around the cabin like a brick in a washing machine. By the time the computer was clamped between his knees, there were several unexpected things happening, all in such a rough jumble that he found it hard to keep track. First, he was impressed by the speed and precision of the platoon, a speed and precision that Fowler—he could see her, or at least the line of soldiers that included her, hurrying up from the bottom of the field—no doubt had taught them. They circled like wolves around the "target," Crawford charging in directly, flanked by the tank-like recovery vehicle they called the Hercules, while the other two Humvees, containing Waldorf and Dykstra, flared out to the right, one of them, apparently, finding a back road on his Blue Force Tracker and punching through the trees—out of sight but still in radio contact—while the other swerved along the field's edge in case the target tried to run away. This was, he supposed, what the camera system really was—a hunting device. A target finder. It had been completely idiotic to imagine that it would be used in any other way.

The real shocker, though, was seeing the target in reality: a shirtless, hobo-type figure in an oversize blue jacket, his front lip lifted rabbitlike over a pair of jutting teeth. He shifted in and out of focus as the Humvee bounded across the furrows of the field like a buoy out at sea—but his presence, at least to Crawford and McWilliams, seemed to change everything, to be like an electric charge, amplifying and overriding reality. "Get down, motherfucker! Get down!" Crawford was shouting. "Wave at the motherfucker, Mickey. Come on, you shithead. Please!" But each time the prow of the Humvee nosed down, there he would be again, like some kind of drifter or clown, flapping his arms at them, waving them away, his urgency mimicking Crawford's urgency, the whole thing tightening up in what seemed like a bad way. Pulowski had wanted there to be a target, he supposed. At least that would prove his case. But now, seeing the target live, he found himself wishing that the Iraqi would escape. He wished desperately to warn him, had to literally cover his mouth to prevent himself from screaming, Watch out! Watch out! We're coming! You have to—

The screaming voice Pulowski heard when he woke up was high-pitched, piercing, but he couldn't figure out where it was coming from. It definitely wasn't Crawford, who was leaning forward in the driver's seat, his body suspended against the thickly woven strap of his shoulder belt, as if he'd been trying to lunge out his side door. He had light, walnut-colored skin and pale olive eyes, and what Pulowski saw in his expression, when he pulled Crawford's body back toward him, wasn't blame or even anger but some sort of outraged plea for sympathy: *You see what I'm doing? Isn't this ridiculous? I can't believe you caught me doing such a stupid thing!* and then when Pulowski propped himself up on an elbow, and he saw that the dash, the steering column, and the heavy metal cabin that held the vehicle's electronics had swallowed up Crawford's legs and that behind him McWilliams, the gunner, had no right ear or cheek and the blood from the dark hole that had replaced them was currently staining his pants at the knee. For a moment, Pulowski gathered himself and tried to push himself free, his thighs flexing, but his left leg was pinned and a bright current of pain flared up his thigh, and then finally he quit screaming and lay back into the quiet wilderness of the front seat.

"You think you can get out?" he said to Crawford. The door on Crawford's side was missing.

Crawford clenched his jaw so tightly that the ridged skin of his lips disappeared and his mouth seemed only a nubby seam. The gold-framed glasses that he wore beneath his goggles had fractured and swiveled down along his cheek and he thrashed against the shoulder belt, lunging toward the open door, and the field beyond, in a way that reminded Pulowski of a fish flopping on dirt, or on a parking lot, on some completely foreign piece of asphalt, the water miles and miles away.

"Okay, I get it, I get it. Chill out for a second." Pulowski tried to open the door on his side of the Humvee but it wouldn't budge. He couldn't crawl over Crawford to get out. So finally he jabbed at the broken windshield, clearing away bits of glass as best he could with what appeared to have once been an air-conditioning vent, then stared out over the exploded engine, the axle, the soft, four-foot-deep hole where the bomb had been. Beyond it, he saw the Iraqi who'd waved at them. He was maybe twenty yards off and lay facedown in the dirt, his feet toward Pulowski, as if he'd been spun around by the shock wave. He was alive—that Pulowski could clearly see. He was crawling on his belly, moving with a painful, almost ridiculous slowness, his jacket covered with chaff and one of his legs folded sideways over the other at a wrong angle, like an insect's. "Hey!" Pulowski shouted. “Somebody! There’s a guy here moving. He’s still alive! He’s trying to go someplace!” Then Pulowski heard the crunching sound of boots running across a chaff-strewn field and, at the same moment, saw Fowler approaching with an M4 at her shoulder. “Get down! Get down!” she shouted. And then, in a different tone, “Stop! Stop! Stop moving now!” Her face was familiar beneath her helmet, flushed, darkly tan, the blond-brown wisps of her hair plastered all around, then fading out pale into the curve of her cheek, but her expression was all wrong, blunt and explicit, terrifying in its intensity. “No,” he said. “Wait!” He raised his arms. “Down!” she shouted, and then he huddled quickly behind the ruined dashboard of the Humvee and he heard a flat burst of fire, and when he sat up again, the Iraqi had rolled over onto his side and curled up, as if he’d decided to go to sleep.

Pulowski definitely recognized his face.

When Fowler wrenched open the Humvee’s door, Pulowski struck at her, knocking her hands away, as if he had a train to catch. Fowler did not particularly care. He was alive. That was the cure for the black cape of badness that was swarming around the back of her head. “Settle! Settle!” she said, grabbing him, her thumbs on either side of his sweating nose, fingers curled around his cheeks. “Everything’s gonna be okay.”

“What the hell are you doing?” he said.

“Where’s Crawford?” She was craning her neck, trying to see inside the cab.

“Crawford,” Pulowski bleated. “He’s bad.”

She ran around the Humvee. Crawford’s body was leaning halfway out of the cab, at an angle that seemed impossible not to be causing him pain, and she lifted him back into the seat. He was dead. Standing up, she saw that two of Masterson's soldiers were working slowly back the way they'd come, away from them, out of the field. In the other direction was a rough half circle composed of the vehicles from her platoon: Waldorf's Humvee over by the edge of the field, then Jimenez's, then the Hercules, which also had been hit and had thrown a track but was not on fire. Eggleston, the driver, was pulling Halt, the gunner, from his turret, and Halt, just based on body language, was not injured seriously. "Sergeant, my radio's out here," she shouted. "Can you communicate?" And when Eggleston gave the thumbs-up, she ordered, "You're going to have to run comms for me. Call the TOC, make sure we've got medevac. Call Waldorf on the other side. Follow your own tracks back out. Do you got me?"

So, good: there was that. All this time she was avoiding the sight of the Iraqi's body. The one she'd just shot. It was on Pulowski's side of the Humvee, in the no-man's-land between the Hercules and Masterson's soldiers, and she kept her eyes averted so she wouldn't see the dead Iraqi's face. Instead, she checked on McWilliams—dead—dug out the Humvee's med kit, and circled back to Pulowski, who was shaking his hands loosely in front of his chest, and pried open his ruined door. "You're okay," she said, opening the kit. "It's going to be okay. You couldn't have known what the guy was going to do. It's not your fault, Dix. You can't—"

"Not my fault!" Pulowski hissed.

And now, here, she was granted full, unfettered access to his pale eyes, his direct gaze. She'd made love to him like this, this close, her fingers running over the pores of his skin, his beaky nose, the acne that sometimes rose up around his eyebrows—and her favorite spot, the soft skin beneath his ear, leading down to his boy's neck.

"Do you want it to be? I could think something up."

It all checked out. No spinal damage. Nothing destroyed, except for down below, where the Humvee's dash bit down on his legs. "Try me," Pulowski said.

"You could've sat in back."

"I could've stayed in bed."

"Well, that goes without saying."

"I'm pretty decent in bed. I know you have a hard time admitting it."

"Try me," Fowler said.

"Did you check my junk?"

She was straightening him up, trying to judge the angles on getting him out, and her chin was down in that territory.

"I'm serious. I want to make absolutely sure, when we get out of here, that you check my junk over carefully."

She tugged his belt. "What for?" she asked. "Brass?"

But it didn't work quite exactly right, the old banter thing. The skin tightened shiny along his temples, a simulacrum of amusement, but then, after a couple of seconds, he rolled his head. "What a shit show," he said. "Look at what we did."

"It was the fucking hadji's fault," she said.

"I saw him, the guy you wasted," Pulowski said. "I saw his face. It's the same guy who wrote that note. He was trying to wave us away—"

"He was guilty," Fowler said, though she felt a sickness crawl across her skin like sweat. "He was guilty."

Pulowski backhanded his nose to clear it of snot. "No," he said. "No. If he was a bad guy, he wouldn't have waved us away."

"Pulowski." She'd found the right tone finally. Not a lover's voice, a commander's voice. Masterson's fuckup erasing confidence. "Tie it off. Okay? We got the paperwork on this guy. You found him. You did the right thing—" Without warning, she braced and tried to lift him from the cab. Pulowski stared bug-eyed, as if he were slowly being inflated with air, and then when she tried to tear his leg out from beneath the dash, he began to thrash and claw, making a deep horrible humming sound in his throat, and she had to set him down again, resting her cheek against the sweaty chest of his fatigues. "Okay. We're going to need a better plan."

Pulowski rallied, just marginally. "Ya think?"

She didn't talk after that. The floorboard was wet with blood, and she lifted his right leg so it lay across her back and grabbed his left ankle where it disappeared into the dash. When she touched it, the bone inside was loose and wobbly and Pulowski clawed at her helmet and she grabbed the cuff of his fatigues and jerked hard and the leg came free and she dragged him out into the grass. "Hey! Hey!" she shouted. "Hey! We need some help here. Somebody help me with Pulowski, okay?" But the field was as silent as it had been from the roof of the house, only this time aggressively so, a nullity of silence, bodies moving, sun, grass, but the sound track shut off, and there seemed to be something very private that this nullity was speaking to her, irradiating her like a gamma ray so gently and so confidently that she was frightened of it more than Pulowski's injuries, and so she propped his leg up and cut the pant to his thigh and pulled a Velcro tourniquet from the Humvee's medical kit. The foot and boot were gone and she could see gristle and flayed bone and she put a compress on and held it tight, counting to sixty, and when this failed she strapped the tourniquet above his knee and tightened it, screwing down hard, and then fit the plastic windlass beneath the Velcro strap, and then waved to Eggleston and Halt and pointed back at the house and shouted, "Let's go! Let's go! Follow your vehicle's tracks," and then picked Pulowski up with one arm under his thighs and another under his back and said,

"Come on, Dix, we got to go," and began walking as quickly as she could out of the field, feeling the blood rush to her head, keeping her eyes fixed on the target's house. Twice Pulowski gagged, and she set him down and banged his chest with the ball of her hand and then, muttering in embarrassment, "All right, all right," put her lips over Pulowski's and blew in, hating and clinging to the salt there, the sweat, the staleness of his tongue, his dirty teeth, his awful breath.

2

Ayad's first problem had been the dog. Yellow, the fur mud-stippled along its back, the obscene droop of teats underneath, and, high on her back haunches, a dark foam-line of hair, like an inseam. He'd first spotted her from his lookout on the roof, slinking in through the green reeds that guarded the field's western edge, as if aware that someone was watching. It was dusk by the time he reached the well. He covered it in the way his father had, recentering the plywood board, scooping back the earth that the dog had scraped away, working by feel and memory. He saw the dog's face for the first time, a slash of lemon behind him. He'd charged, shovel raised, only to plunge into the empty night; the third time this happened, he'd rushed immediately back to the hole, caught the dog already digging, but she bolted through the waist-high wheat.

I have a dog problem, he wrote this carefully on a sheet of his father's stationery, and tucked it into his pocket. He left his house by the back door and walked west along a dike-top until it crumbled and descended into a dried slough, a papery, head-high grass whispering past his cheek. He crossed five canals after this, the first a swaying footbridge that he and his brother had used to joust on, the last a brand-new eighteen-inch section of aluminum culvert that had been hammered into the bank. The foot traffic on this familiar path seemed to have increased, the grass worn back in furrows, but the culvert was unfamiliar, and as he crossed it, he began to sweat—cold sweat, high up on his neck—and his insteps curved uneasily over the patterned metal and the guide wire burned his hand. He entered town through a field whose current tenants included a donkey who'd been chained to a steel drum and a long, low-rising esker of slurried trash that curved into a copse of thorn trees. A sign had been propped up against a mud wall that read *Haircuts, kitchen utensils, sinks*. It had hung over the awning of a shop in town for as long as Ayad could remember; its owner, he had heard, was now dead.

Raheem al-Najafi was in his repair shop as usual, talking on his cell phone in the back room, his body hidden by the door frame and one of his scrawny chicken legs stretched out across the opening, the calf bare beneath his tan house shirt.

Ayad slid the paper past the bulky parts books: Nissan, Toyota, Opel. Still talking, Raheem grabbed it, read, and nodded gravely, the solemnity that entered his brown eyes completely at odds with the salesman's grin—tongue poked out in anticipation of a hissing laugh—which he aimed at the speaker of the cell phone, as if the person on the other end could see. Then he disappeared into the back.

There had been a time in Ayad's early teens when he had considered becoming an auto mechanic, going into something like an apprenticeship. This had been before his father died and before his family had frozen up around that death, a situation only worsened by the news that his mother had been awarded a pension by the state, thus eliminating any immediate need to earn money. Back in the old days, then, when his greatest concern had been himself: What would he do? How would *he* earn money?

How would he learn a trade if he could not even go to school? At that time, his father had been in Baghdad frequently at the flat that he kept there (abandoned now, since the outbreak of the war) and his mother would drive in to see him, made up, happy to be going into the city, and Ayad—his brother away in the army, his older sisters married—had stayed for weeks at the house alone, too frightened by the city, by its traffic, by the way it emphasized his disability. So he had started walking into town and squatting at Raheem's shop—the mechanic knew him, had fixed his father's SLE many times before—not speaking, just watching. An undeclared apprenticeship.

It had been both a provocation and a debasement: What was he worth? Or rather, a way of saying to his father: Without you, I have no worth.

Or maybe it had just been an attempt at truth.

But he was not a nothing now; after his brother had valiantly failed to survive the American invasion, Ayad had become his family's oldest living male, and thus the steward of his mother's land, and Raheem was something other than the man who fixed his father's SLE. If not a criminal, then, as a Shi'ite, a man known to have connections, the possessor of a new and undefined authority. The blue sedan that the intruders had been driving when they'd arrived at Ayad's house—it had taken him some time to place it, but Ayad was fairly sure he'd seen it before, parked in Raheem's lot out back.

When he thought that Raheem had been on the phone long enough, he pounded on the bell that the garage owner kept hidden, out of reach, atop his desk. Raheem deliberately—Ayad was familiar with his habit—refused to even budge the sallow curve of his shin as it stuck out across the rear doorway.

Where is this problem with the dog? Raheem's note read when it came back.

This dog wants your friends' gift, he wrote. *This night, every night.* He drew a picture of a dog digging a hole under the moon, surrounded by stalks of wheat.

He slept in the living room of the main house. His only means of communication, the only way he had to confirm his continued existence, was the cell phone his mother had left for him. It was a long, skinny silver Nokia that resembled one of his father's shoehorns. It could text in Arabic but the phone's system of having to push a button one, two, or three times just to summon up a letter of an alphabet made his own true desires, the things he really would have liked to say to his mother—*I'm afraid* or *How long does it take a body to decompose?*—seem even more impossible to communicate. However, he discovered that if he put it on speaker, he could hold the phone in his palm and feel her voice vibrating. Who knew what the hell she was saying? He'd walk the house, sit down at her dresser, stand in his father's closet (the clothes were all still there, his city shoes nicked at the heels), pace out front on one of the no-electricity nights, feeling that great swallowing dark coming on, while her voice buzzed away there in his palm. He could get a fair amount of information from the vibrations: the quick prickling of worry, a buzzing jagged reverb of a rant, the longer, silkier passages when she cried. (Or at least he could imagine these things, which was probably better than understanding what his mother actually had to say.) Mostly, he understood that she was claiming him. They had never gotten along well, but now, at noon and again at six, she'd call and talk to him for a good ten or fifteen minutes that were always surprisingly emotional and satisfying for him. And then he'd lift the headset up and make his own barfing donkey noise into it (this was how Faisal had described his voice after Ayad had once written, *Seriously, how do I sound?*), and that was the signal to hang up.

When he woke, a pale blue-gray light was swimming around the walls, over the furniture. At first Ayad thought he was doing this by himself, beaming the image in out of the past, but he realized that some of the shadow bars that spun, flickered, and recycled over the bare walls were coming from outside. And when he went to the door, he saw the cars of the—what should he call them? insurgents? *takfiri*?—curving around through the side yard, heading back out onto the road through the front gate, having solved his dog problem. And probably also mined the field.

That morning, the dog returned—not to the field but to the old incinerator where he'd been dumping his trash. He noticed a flash of movement just outside the back gate. He walked down through the garden, peeked over the gate, saw the dog limping and whining over the trash, then returned to the kitchen, opened a can of chickpeas (there were fifty such cans, part of his mother's supply stash, shipped in before the roads got bad), carried them back outside, and dumped them in the dirt—a large pile just at the spot where the spacing between the gate bottom and the foot-worn path was the largest. Then little dribs and drabs leading in. At the door to his father's workshop, he left a second can, open but untouched, then returned to the house and the TV.

His mother's family had owned the field. When he was twelve or thirteen, Ayad had been astonished to find this out. It was also his mother's family who'd had the money, the land, the prestige that had allowed her to maintain the (in his view) illusory sense that such a thing as stability was to be expected in the first place. This traced clear back to pre–Ba'ath Party times—or to, as his mother insisted, dangerous-to-mention *original* Ba'ath Party times—a time that seemed to Ayad distant and historical, though he could tell from his mother's ferociously maintained and guarded scrapbooks it was the Polaroid-engulfed, thickly emulsed 1950s. The friendship then had been with Hassan al-Bakr; that was the man whom he'd seen pictures of, sitting in their side yard eating pickled cauliflower, surrounded by his mother's (then his grandmother's) roses and gardenias. And, if you wanted to look at the under-the-bed and inside-the-mattress albums, you could find a photo or two of good old Nuri al-Said.

Whomever it belonged to, the dog had no interest in going back out into the field. He'd tried to lead it out the back gate a few times—this was after he'd gotten a collar on it and manufactured a leash out of some hammock chain—and the dog kept doing this insane, maddening thing of sitting down on its rear end and ducking its head.

So, instead, he had to walk the dog down the fairly abandoned, half-paved, half-dusted-over road outside his house. A lonely line of two-strand phone poles echoed the road above their head. You want to talk about boring? Try taking this landscape seriously after you've spent half an hour watching a DVD of *Beverly Hills Cop* with your neighbor Faisal Amar. Or *Independence Day*. Or *Sex and the City*. No subtitles needed for that. In the past, Ayad had been big on backgrounds, big on the space and feel of other countries, had often walked this road without seeing it at all, head filled with nostalgia for places he'd never been. But now that same yearning pull applied to the road itself, or at least the road as he remembered it. For instance, the small grove of olive and eucalyptus trees just across from the doctor's old place. His family had picnicked here. Horrible, boring, two-bit afternoons, as he'd seen them. A couple plastic chairs, dust-covered bowl of hummus, better replaced by Central Park, or the Vegas Strip. But now when he unfolded his imagination amid the polite churning dapple of its leaves, it was to reassemble the full complement of his family, all together, and bitching less than was strictly accurate. This particular afternoon, he'd been remembering a yellow ball he'd juggled here during a family outing, its surface the perfect combination of soft and sticky. He had caught the ball between a bare, upturned toe and his shin, and hopped on his left foot to show his father—he'd been so desperate for his father's praise back then—and just as he made a ghost of this same turn, he saw the dog running toward him.

The thing he hated, feared, despised, loathed about his deafness was his vulnerability. But in this case, the dog's approach gave him enough time to crouch, catch a glimpse of the oncoming convoy, and then scuttle away into thicker brush so that when the American Humvees blasted by at a hundred kilometers per hour, pushing a hot, dry wind and filling the grove with its dust, he was safely hidden. The dog lay beside him, chin upon her doubled paws, a comically flat deadpan quality to her black-brown eyes as she followed the trucks and then swiveled over to look at him—no change in expression, no movement other than the eyes—as if to say, *What the fuck?* And then she was gone, bolting down the road after the convoy, which was not what he'd expected, quite honestly. He half ran, half walked after her, keeping to the tree line, since, if there was one thing you could say about the Americans, they had good signage:

DANGER

خطر

STAY BACK

ابقى بعيدا

After about ten yards, he saw that the convoy had turned in at his front gate, and he retreated quickly back to the copse. What he wanted to do was warn them: *Yes, the body is here. I don't want it. But watch out—there might be something dangerous in the field.* Against this was his awareness of how difficult, and possibly incriminating, this would be to explain, not to mention his fear of prison and arrest, the simple, unreasoning desire to remain free. After an hour, these contradictory impulses brought him to the canal on the west side of his house, at a point that, by dead reckoning, he figured was roughly perpendicular to the dry well that contained the body. He was crossing on a felled palm trunk when he felt a faint spray of wetness against his skin and he saw the yellow head of the dog swimming below, head up, very earnestly, then disappearing into the field without a look back. He bleated to it quietly. Nothing. He pounded the ground and hissed, and it came to him, tail wagging, ass down on the ground—excited. Probably barking. He saw its throat work. Urging him to come out into the field. There are strangers here! No, no, no. Quiet. Quiet, please. Then, glancing up, he saw trucks coming out the back gate. And then he was on his feet, scrambling, pushing out into the open, giving his broadest, most moronically chipper grin, the one used by American actors whose role was to be humiliated or, most preferably, ignored: *Yes, hello, soldiers? I am not against you! Yes! Please stop! Please wait! There's danger this way!*

3

Subject: re: mobile camera network

Sir,

Request deployment of so-called mobile camera network, if such network should be operational. Destination would be Patrol Base Fortitude, intersection of Route Tender and Route Trap. Request that accompanying technician be familiar with the system.

V/R,
LT Emma Fowler
Echo Company
1st Division
27th Infantry

From: Clarence.McKutcheon@us.army.mil
Subject re: mobile camera network

Lieutenant,

Regret to inform you that cameras are still in the prototype phase. I appreciate your interest in our program and will be happy to comply with your request after a requisite testing period. The estimation from our project manager is one month to six weeks.

V/R,
Major Clarence McKutcheon
HQ Company
1st Division
27th Infantry

Pulowski lay in the meat pod of his trailer, surrounded by forty thousand other meat pods, across the acres and acres of Camp Tolerance, all piped in and nourished by the black goo of the American Forces Network and super-strong AC. Eighteen hours had passed since Fowler had left for the patrol base. Since then he'd showered, hauled his filthy uniform to the laundry, sucked up some meat pod television (*Doctor Who*, over on the Sci-Fi Channel of AFN), but avoided email studiously. So it hadn't been until midnight that he'd seen Fowler's message, or McKutcheon's response. Schlubby, white, with the sloped body of a swimming buoy, and a small fortune in hair plugs beading his forehead, McKutcheon had grown up in Sacramento, majored in communications at Chico State, and done ROTC to pay the tab—this back in the middle nineties, post-Gulf, when the last place anybody imagined going was Iraq. As a Headquarters Company officer, he prepared intel reports for the battalion briefings. He wrote PowerPoints, edited the battalion newsletter, supervised Pulowski's installation of the battalion's VoIP phone network, but most important, he had been Pulowski's guide, his Laurence Fishburne, offering, in the smothered language of the true bureaucrat, two pills—fight, or stay inside in the meat pod farm indefinitely. McKutcheon had also made it clear which choice led to enlightenment, which was how Pulowski's work on the mobile camera system had come up. It was funded under something called the Asymmetric Warfare Initiative. DoD oversight, private matching funds, forty-page progress reports: the true matrix. McKutcheon would get credit from the colonel for bringing in outside dollars. Pulowski would make his own hours, would no longer have to hang around headquarters, would be out of McKutcheon's hair—and, implicitly, would not be at risk of doing something that might actually get him hurt. So he felt embarrassed to be formulating an argument that the cameras should actually be deployed, as if he were disappointing McKutcheon in some crucial way. But the argument was there, so after he'd lain awake awhile longer, he swung his feet onto the plywood floor of his trailer and turned on the light.

The trailer was spotless, floor swept, programming manuals in alphabetical order atop his desk. His laundry wouldn't be back until the following morning, so he dug around under his rack for a T-shirt, grabbed his cell phone, and then went outside.

On the surface, Camp Tolerance—the Dining Facility, the laundry, the long stretch of dirt road that he and everybody else in the battalion walked every day, even the gravel corridor outside his trailer—looked the same as it always had. The rocks glowed faintly in the moonlight. The shadowed ranks of the trailers stretched out as far as he could see to either side, fronted by HESCO barriers and grainy due to the lack of light.

However, the panic caused by Sergeant Beale's abduction still twanged the air, an invisible vacuum, like the hallways of his old house in Clarksville, Tennessee, after his parents had had a fight. His immediate neighbor, Lieutenant Krauss, was a platoon leader with Alpha Company. Normally Krauss liked to leave his door open when he slept, but his door was closed, his trailer dark, which meant he was probably on patrol tonight. Also, Pulowski could hear shouting from the north, directly opposite the door to his trailer and the grated metal steps where he'd sat down to think. As he listened, the voices intensified, then a clear fragment—*Well, get him the fuck in here!*—broke through, and a pale band of headlights flashed along the frontage road outside battalion headquarters. At this time of night, there would be activity there only if a patrol was bringing Iraqis in for questioning. It was cool out, so he tugged the T-shirt on—noting briefly that it didn't seem to fit—keyed McKutcheon's number into his cell phone, and flopped along in his shower sandals to the right. The major would definitely be awake.

"I was thinking about that request from the patrol base," he said when the major answered. "It sort of makes sense, doesn't it? I mean, if the cameras were good enough to deploy yesterday, why not send them out now?"

"Yeah, well, yesterday Fowler hadn't fucked up and lost a guy," McKutcheon said, more drolly than Pulowski would've liked, "*while* she was supposed to be installing those cameras. Speaking of which, you got any information on how that went down?"

Pulowski considered this. He hadn't spoken to McKutcheon since returning from the Muthanna intersection where the attack had taken place. So there was no reason the major would know that he'd had a front-row seat for Beale's abduction. "No," he said.

"You didn't see anything?"

"We got hit. There was a shooter in one of the buildings beside the intersection. The word I got was that Beale got picked off going in." He was walking fairly briskly between the white ranks of trailers that housed the battalion—taking care to avoid Fowler's and, especially, Beale's. As he'd expected, he felt less guilty now that he'd allowed McKutcheon to make the case for doing nothing, rather than making it himself.

"I'm just saying," he continued, "if we'd had a camera at the exact same intersection two months ago, we would've stopped that truck bomb, don't you think? No truck bomb, no dead soldiers. And if there aren't any dead soldiers—*and* we already have a camera set up—then nobody's out at the Muthanna intersection yesterday."

"Maybe," McKutcheon said. "Except that truck *was* stopped two months ago. Fredrickson and Arthur checked the driver's papers *before* the bomb went off."

A small electrified charge lit Pulowski's stomach, a feeling that resembled the spark of despair when he found bad code early in a command—from this fork branched a thousand possible mistakes. "Why would they do that?"

"They let the truck through," McKutcheon said, "because, apparently, we were paying an Iraqi contractor to haul gravel to a construction site inside Muthanna. Spreading a little U.S. taxpayer money around. Somebody must have slipped the driver the right papers. Not to mention filled him in on our entire routine."

"We were paying the bomber?"

"Or at least his boss. Look, you got off of this detail easy, Pulowski. Everything about the Muthanna intersection has been a clusterfuck from start to finish. Setting the cameras up yesterday was strictly a cover-your-ass project for the colonel. It didn't work. He's got a bigger problem on his hands now. If I were you, I'd leave it that way."

He smiled at the comforting Homer Simpson nihilism of McKutcheon's advice. He'd been called in to work intel when Alpha Company lost a tank back in January. The ambush outside Al-Shula. During all these disasters McKutcheon had talked this way.

By then he'd slipped into the battalion's "Cyber Café," which occupied a ramshackle wood shed, and a private showed him to an ancient, clicking Acer computer, set on a long plastic folding table, bookended by a pair of palm trees. It was in the base's smaller public spaces—the toilets, phone banks, and computer clusters—that McKutcheon's philosophy made the most sense. A half dozen soldiers hunkered around him, heads bowed, boots spread wide, postures submissive—already defeated—before happy onscreen cornucopias of bank ads, Web graphics, and interactive news feeds. One had begun to cry, hands clutching the back of his head. All of them were or would soon be involved in the hunt for Beale, and every inch of their unhappiness could be explained and even possibly prevented by his own personal cartoon slogan: Safety Comes in Can't.

He'd invented it in this very room, on similar nights when shit had gone bad and he had sat here trying to email his mother, staring up at a plastic banner mounted by the same geniuses who'd named the cafeteria Camp Chillin':

SAFETY COMES IN CANS
I CAN
WE CAN
YOU CAN

What if somebody, somewhere, had simply argued that the safest thing was *can't*? Even Senator Kerry hadn't quite had the guts. He'd stood there, grim and hatchet-faced at the convention, watching can-do photos of his Vietnam days, and then the swift boats came and took him out. Why? Because 'Nam had been a great big pile of can't. As a signal officer, *can't* was one principle Pulowski never sold short. The other came from a book he'd read for English class at Pitt, whose touchy-feely motto he'd also Homerized: *Do not connect.* Both self-evident truths, nowhere more obvious than in the pleasures of the Cyber Café when shit was truly going bad. The fact that he'd never managed to convince Fowler to see any of that wasn't his responsibility.

At the same time, none of this accounted for how he'd felt when he'd watched Carl Beale disappear into that alley doorway. That was the tidal wave of stupid that he'd been counting on McKutcheon to talk him out of, its oncoming boil cold and gray, carrying with it death and rot, wreck and stink. "So what you're telling me," he said, "is that we have a device that might very well . . . no, no, no . . . would be demonstrably helpful to our soldiers in the field. Americans. People who you and I know personally. And yet you're lying about its readiness because . . . why? Because we're afraid to go outside the wire and set up the thing?"

The phone was dead by then. When he hung up, Pulowski stared for some time at the email on his screen, reading first the text, and then allowing his eyes to swim across the Kelly-green banner flashing at the top of the screen:

E*TRADE—DISCOVER THE POWER OF YOU

Also deeply stupid. Also clearly not a message designed for geeks. It would've been much better if he hadn't worn the shirt. He'd figured out by then why it didn't fit. Every time he stretched the fabric down around his belly button, he could smell Fowler's scent drifting up out of it. Then he cut-and-pasted Colonel Seacourt's email into the top line, CC'd everybody except McKutcheon, and typed:

Sir,

I am the project coordinator for the mobile camera network. There has been a miscommunication between myself and Major McKutcheon.

The camera system has been fully tested and is ready for deployment. I will have it outside the offices of the 16th Engineer Brigade at 0800 hours tomorrow morning, ready for pickup.

Sincerely,

LT Dixon Pulowski

Then he hit send.

Patrol Base Fortitude was no larger than a high school football stadium, set out in a bean field forty miles north of Camp Tolerance, surrounded by blast walls, domed by empty sky. Fowler handed the note to Captain Masterson on the doorstep of the farmhouse that served as his TOC. Her convoy had arrived the night before and she could feel her soldiers watching from the barren infield as she explained how Pulowski had gotten the note, and why it might be a clue to Beale's abduction. It could be nothing, she admitted, but she'd like to talk to his interpreter just to be sure. Masterson listened, forefinger rubbing his tallow cheeks, and then abruptly headed toward the base's motor pool—followed by Fowler, who didn't know what else to do. Once they were out of sight, Masterson veered right toward a concrete hut with sandbagged windows. Out front, his first lieutenant, Anderson, stood quickly from a plastic chair.

"All right." Masterson stopped short of the building's door, which had been fitted with a shiny brass lock. "Trust me, Lieutenant. This is not something you're going to be excited about. The advice I'm giving you is to go home and forget it."

"Yessir," Fowler said. "I just—"

"Do you know where we are, Lieutenant?"

"We're at the intersection of Route Tender and Route Trap."

"Actually, this base is on the border between the Al-Tamimi

tribe, which is Shi'ite, and the Al-Dulaymi tribe, which is Sunni. It's like having an apartment in Watts between the Bloods and the Crips. All those guys at the schoolhouse? Sunni. Except for Faisal, no Shi'ites came. So trust me when I say you have no idea where you are."

Fowler returned this stare bluntly for a few moments, asserting—what, exactly, she wasn't sure. That she was as capable of being overconfident and condescending as Masterson? That she hoped he knew more about the local population than he did about South Central L.A.? Then she said: "Sir, I already requested backup. They're coming out. All I want to do is talk to your interpreter. Is there some problem with that?" As she spoke, she felt a pinch on the insides of her wrists so strong that she rubbed them.

Masterson wrinkled his forehead as if still uncertain what to do with her. He glanced back at Anderson, who was unlocking the building.

"You're free out here, sir," she said, scrambling to register some argument that he might take seriously. "You're free to operate."

"Oh, yeah," Masterson said grimly. "Freedom—that's what we're all about, Lieutenant. The problem is we got too much of it around here."

If this was a joke, or even an unexpectedly intelligent comment, Fowler couldn't tell it from his face. Instead, as Anderson's bald head disappeared into the dark shed, Fowler noticed Masterson fiddling with a roll of black electrical tape that he'd earlier removed from his pocket. He fitted a strip over the stitched FOWLER on her fatigues, tearing it with his teeth, then tossed the roll to his lieutenant as he reemerged. This made the cuffed figure who shuffled along beside Anderson, accompanied by the searing, eye-watering reek of unwashed human flesh, all the more surprising. It was Faisal Amar, the smart-ass interpreter who worked for Delta Company, the young man with the mole and the dusty gray suit. The man she'd come to see. "Faisal has begun working with us in a more *advisory* capacity," Masterson said. "Maybe you'd like to advise him to share his knowledge of what happened to Sergeant Beale yesterday."

Faisal Amar's condition, his dangling arm and tufts of missing hair, embarrassed her more than she'd expected—worse, somehow, than when Beale had hit him three weeks earlier, because the injuries seemed almost meditative. Deliberate rather than passionate. She also disliked the clothes that Masterson's lieutenants had dressed him in, once they'd taken him into custody: scrawny, shifty arms sticking out of a Lakers jersey like a drag queen's, a pair of oversize shower slippers on his crusty feet. But his hostility was clear enough. You saw guys like that at gas stations in Kansas City: pompous, sallow-eyed, acting like they had a secret answer to everything. Real sweeties to women, they were supposed to be. Wondered why their countries looked like shit when they kept trying to blow up everything. After Lieutenant Anderson left, he studied her face, then shrugged at her covered name tag. "I know you," he said.

"Yes, you do," Fowler said, peeling off the tape.

"Three weeks ago you beat me up. Now you lose a soldier. Man, you are on some kind of streak." She got a genuine leer out of his thin face, salt whitening the corners of his mouth: they had bad luck in common. A nice thought. Unless it wasn't bad luck at all that Faisal appeared to be connected to both of these events.

"You remember a lieutenant named Pulowski?"

Here was some bad acting in her opinion: squinting, ceiling examined, eye movements to suggest the ruffle of memory. "Which time is this?"

"He brought you to this man." She showed him the note that Pulowski had given her and pointed to the drawing of the anonymous Iraqi's face. "We think he has information about my missing soldier, Sergeant Beale. We also think you know him and you pretended not to. Why would you do that, Faisal? Why would you lie to us in such an important case?"

"We do hundreds of these, lady," Faisal said, "a million, whatever. Come on. I do not know this person." He craned his neck so he could shout around her, toward the door. "Hey, boss. You got somebody more interesting for me?"

She felt a trigger flipping in her head, lower than her brain—down in the spinal cord, the center of the neck—and she jerked his slim, champagne-flute wrist down and leaned in, her elbows on his knees. "Just read the goddamn paper!" she said. "Read it and tell me the truth about what it says."

Her actions and her words felt thick and meat-headed—as bad as Masterson's riff on Watts—and yet Faisal overopened his eyes and licked his lips to simulate eagerness to please. Then, as he focused on the text, his features shut down, as if a plastic sheet had covered them. No need to translate that. "It is nobody," he said. "This man."

"What I'm curious about," she said, "is when you're going to realize that you might want to start telling the truth. If you think I'm here to save you"—when Faisal made a move to protest, she grabbed his face where Anderson had bruised it—"I'd ask myself, why aren't I being processed? I offered to take you back to Camp Tolerance, but these guys, the one who hit you—"

"Anderson."

"Anderson told me that there wasn't any paperwork on you."

She backed off, waited. Faisal limped to the threshold of his cell and nodded at the door, which she opened. "Three letters," he said. He held up three fingers, his zip-cuffed hands paired beneath his chin, then jumped over the threshold with an odd sideways hop, as if skipping rope. "Three letters, personal testimony from real Iraqis, yes? We take, we fax to Washington, get okay, the bad guys go in here. Hard to get, this testimony. This guy is bad, he did this to me. People know but don't want to say. So I write them—"

"Yeah, I know, you translate Masterson's arrest affidavits," Fowler said, though Faisal's tone caused her to shiver, to notice the sweat cooling beneath her undershirt.

"No, I *make them up*," Faisal said. There was a strangely mechanical element to his speech. "Whoever he wants to shoot, whoever he wants to detain, I make up a story of how they are bad. Like in a movie. So if the captain arrests *me*"—he tapped the socket of his eye, then pointed out across the dusty expanse of the patrol base and made a whooshing sound, fanning out his fingers, as if a flood had covered everything in sight—"everybody, every people he send to jail the past six months, they go free. And these people will come to find him personally. He knows this, so he does not charge me."

"You faked the affidavits," Fowler said.

"What the fuck?" Faisal said. "How else does he catch so many this way?"

Twenty minutes later, Fowler pushed into the last of eight long brown tents that occupied the southern end of the patrol base. Masterson's staff had warned her not to disturb the captain at this time of day, and the farther she wandered down the stifling rows of empty bunks, draped with gear, Kevlars, and sweaty fatigues, the less certain she was that ignoring their warning was a sound tactic. The tent's far end had been sectioned off by a wall of egg crates and she found him there, laid out like a pharaoh, an iPod glowing on his chest, his bare, callused feet atop a plain white sheet. A thick line of black crew cut scalloped low across his forehead, and his skin was acne-pitted, which, when he was awake, gave his features a roughened look but now resembled a putty covering for some other, younger face. "Sir, could I talk to you for a minute?" she asked.

Masterson raised his eyebrows, rubbing the back of his head against his wrists. He'd been a club rugby player at Oklahoma State and, at Fort Riley, a serious lifter, but he'd dropped at least twenty pounds, and now sat up gingerly, as if his skeleton had been riddled with some incurable disease—not a good sign, especially if what Faisal had told her was true. "You'll have to excuse me," he said. He made an effort to lift his head, but this failed, and he belched and quickly aimed his gaze at the floor again. "This is not really my best time of day. We're running these patrols all night. It's a twenty-four-hour operation. I like to be there. So this is really my time to sleep."

There was, for the first time, a hint of apology in his voice—though it was factual, not self-pitying—and by way of answer, since she wasn't leaving, Fowler reached under his makeshift desk, grabbed a wheeled stool, and rolled it between her knees.

"Why'd you have Faisal detained?" she said.

Masterson chuckled as if she'd made a joke, then spat dryly into a wastebasket. "There's a killing field out here along Route Trap. An old field where Faisal used to play soccer as a kid. Yesterday, Anderson finds a body out there with a communiqué pinned to its chest, saying Faisal organized the bombing at the Muthanna intersection."

A large floor fan thrummed in the center of the tent and music tinkled out of Masterson's earbuds as he curled them up. No other accompaniment to tell her whether this story should be believed. "Why, he give you something?" he asked.

"I showed Faisal this," she said, producing the same note Masterson had read that morning. "He wouldn't admit it, but I think he recognized the drawings and the writing. He also had some comments about how he was detained."

If he heard this last remark, Masterson ignored it. Instead, he perched on the edge of his cot, his bare feet flat on the gravel and his head bent, examining the pen-and-ink sketches, their startling facility. "So Pulowski interviews some hadji at the schoolhouse," he said. "The guy draws a couple of weird pictures and then leaves. So what?"

It was a decent question, except that it seemed designed to avoid the subject of Faisal's detention, as if Pulowski's story, up on the surface, were a distraction for some worse and troubling shadow in the depths. "An unidentified Iraqi gave Lieutenant Pulowski this when we linked up with you at the schoolhouse after the kidnapping," she said, reviewing the facts. "He said the guy was . . . friendly. Trying to communicate. So he went to get Faisal, and the minute Faisal walks in, the guy just freaks."

"Why didn't he report this to you at the time?"

Now *her* secrets glided up, black and quiet, beneath the conversation. Pulowski's confession back in her trailer. Her own responsibility for Beale. "I'm just saying, sir, look at the drawing." She pointed to the sketch of the dark angel, engaging in some equal-opportunity misdirection. "That's a person, isn't it? A white guy, not an Iraqi. I'm not saying that *has* to be Sergeant Beale, but given what you've told me about Faisal—"

Masterson glanced up quickly, wolfishly, with a glint of amusement in his eye. "Wasn't Pulowski *with* your missing soldier when he got taken? So, this guy loses a soldier. Then he comes up with a story about how some Iraqi *might* be responsible, but doesn't detain the guy? And you trust this information?"

By then she was no longer sure who was misdirecting whom.

No one had entered the tent since she'd come in, the empty bunks still looming awkwardly at her back, as if Masterson's soldiers felt the same way. She folded her hands and put her boots together, scanning the small space where Masterson lived. There were piles of underwear and brown T-shirts at the end of the bed. Stray Styrofoam containers from the cook shack. She recognized the mess, recognized its similarity to her own trailer, as well as what it meant. Flying off the handle wasn't going to help her here. Not if there weren't any handles left. "Sir," she said, "when I was talking to Faisal, he had a couple of things to say about how he was detained. Could I ask you about them, please?"

"Like what?"

"Like what's going on with your arrest affidavits?"

For a moment Masterson's old arrogance seemed to rise up, and he glowered at Fowler from between his flattened hands, as if she'd failed to consider how dangerous that comment could be. Then he said:

"You've got a lot of balls, Fowler. That's fucking good. You and Beale. You guys ran well together. You were a good team. It's the best thing about you, loyalty. That and balls. I can understand how you'd get all broken up about this thing—"

She and Beale had never run well together as a team.

"I'm not arguing your detainee policy, sir," she lied in return. *Everything* about Masterson's detainee policy was arguable, but she wanted to focus on the worst part, the key. As Faisal had indicated, his company had by far the highest kill and detention rates in the battalion—over 350 Iraqis total. They were *all* supposed to have signed affidavits and approval from a judge advocate general before anybody targeted them. If Masterson was forging his paperwork, however, he could kill or detain innocents. Strangers. Whomever he liked. "But faking arrest affidavits is a totally different thing."

"Who said anything about that?"

"Faisal. According to him, that's why he's on your staff."

If Masterson had blustered at her, if he'd yelled at her as he had back at Fort Riley, she might have left right then. But instead, he tottered to his desk for a bottle of water, rinsed his mouth, and spat, as if the sickness had risen up inside him again.

"You think that's the solution here? Better paperwork?" Masterson had dropped into a squat, his bare feet spread, showing her his back. "Or do you think maybe it's arresting guys who I think are going to kill my men? With or without the paperwork."

There was some minor shred of truth in that. In the long string of choices that had led to Beale's disappearance, filing honest paperwork had turned out to be a hindrance, if not a mistake. "Why don't we talk about your objectives here instead?" Masterson asked. "You're in the Army. We're having a war. You lose a soldier, that's just what happens. That's the game. So I got to figure there's something else at stake."

"I wasn't there to help him," Fowler said.

"Why do you have to take responsibility for that? Isn't it true that you requested backup from the battalion and that backup didn't arrive?"

"Yes," she said.

"You don't think that absolves you?"

"No," she said.

"So we're on the same page, Lieutenant. I sent men to *that same intersection* three months ago. I knew it was poorly defended. I clearly registered my protest but was ordered to do it anyway. I followed orders. The Muthanna intersection was attacked, my men died. I know who did it. To me, that doesn't feel right."

I know who did it. That was the shadow beneath their conversation. Any interpreter had access to sensitive intel. They were always the first and most dangerous candidates for a leak. The problem was that Masterson had hired Faisal *because* he was dishonest, because he could be taught to falsely detain or kill who knew how many hundreds of his countrymen. He'd trained his own traitor. Now he wanted to cover his mistake. "Come on, Fowler. Give yourself a break," he said. "You've done the hard part. You found your target. You're not responsible for me. Leave the rule-book shit to Seacourt and Hartz. I don't see either of them out here fixing anything."

Fowler snorted. The things that they were discussing—murder, torture, her own complicity in the same—were things that she had never imagined considering. Choices she'd always believed she'd know not to make. But the language seemed personable, normal, and when she tipped her head and gazed up at the tent's ceiling, the sun glowed golden through the fabric, as it always did. It was jail if she went along with Masterson and got found out. She did wrong here or she abandoned her only lead on finding Beale. The variable was Pulowski, who might very well turn *her* in if he found out. On the other hand, if he wasn't responsible for what had happened to Beale, he deserved to know he was clean. She trundled over atop the stool and plucked the note from his hand. The two drawings—one of the anonymous Iraqi, the other, she believed, of Beale—were underlined by slanting scratches of Arabic. The one clear thing she'd felt all day had been the guilt of the beaten interpreter, Faisal, when she'd seen him in the shed. It was still there, the feeling of it twining up around her skin, black-rooted, the vines of it—though of course she could not see any such thing in reality—seeming to whisper against her, as if growing out of her own skin. "Whoever wrote this note," she said, "leads us to Beale."

"And Faisal?"

"If Faisal is leaking your intel, he has to have somebody to leak it to, right? Why wouldn't it be this guy? Maybe he got nervous. Maybe he wanted to confess. Maybe that would explain why the guy freaked out when Faisal came in."

Masterson looked at the note, glanced up. "Shit," he said.

"My feeling is, we get this translated, see if it matches what Faisal told Pulowski. If it doesn't, I go get these cameras and stake out this guy's place. And you lean on Faisal to tell us where it is. Which you appear to be doing anyway."

"I knew there was a good reason I let you stay," Masterson said, smiling.

"I am not good," Fowler said. She had not consciously moved the rolling stool that she'd been perched on, so when their knees touched, she was surprised and quickly flinched away. "I'm just improvising."

"Yeah, well," Masterson said, "welcome to the team."

Fowler stood for a time in the sunlight, staring out over the barren infield of the patrol base, the surrounding blast walls and sniper towers, trying to shake off the crawling darkness that she'd felt in Masterson's tent. Then she went to check on her platoon. The tent they'd been assigned had a single hole in its roof, which Masterson had told her had come from a mortar attack, and when she pushed through the front flap, Crawford was crouched in a column of daylight, examining an unplugged air-conditioning unit that looked as if it had been smashed by a giant fist.

"You got a little project there?" she asked.

Crawford peered up at her with his child's unlined skin. "My grandma has one like this. York. Shame to ruin a good AC unit like this."

"You think your grandma can send us hers?"

"I doubt it. She's real attached to it." He was still examining the top of the boxy AC unit, the hole that had been punched in its lid. "They say the shell came through and landed right here. Didn't go off. They all just sat there real quiet, looking at it."

She would've liked to hold or hug Crawford, touch his body gently, the opposite of how she'd handled Faisal, whose smell was still on her fingertips. Instead, she hiked her pants, eased down next to him, and ran her finger around the damaged area, so that their hands touched. He glanced up. She grabbed his forearm, squeezed, as if that were the end of their conversation, as if she understood what he was doing by not asking where she'd been. "Where are your glasses?" she said in a brighter tone.

"Fuck," Crawford said. "They around."

"You had them coming in, didn't you?"

Crawford glanced up, sheepish, pleased.

"Now we're getting somewhere," she said appraisingly. It was well known that Crawford wore his glasses at all times, even in bed. "This is not a situation where you are having philosophical thoughts about an AC unit. This is a situation where you lost your glasses and *because* you lost your glasses, you're afraid to go to sleep."

"I looked around," Crawford said.

"Did you look under things?"

"Nothing to look under, ma'am."

"Is that right?" She was on her hands and knees, peering under one of fifty bunks.

"I ain't been here long enough to get under them."

"You check the guys?" She was already up then, looking. They were all asleep, but the search gave her an excuse to touch them, check them over, which she wanted to do anyway: Dykstra's hammy double chin, Waldorf with his blast goggles strapped around a bicep, Jimenez, Halt, Eggleston, McWilliams with the burned-out butt of a Camel still clutched between his knuckles. She lifted the Camel from McWilliams's fingers and folded his arm back against his chest, and when she did, Crawford's gold glasses tumbled out from beneath his armpit. She carried them over and fit them silently onto Crawford's upturned face, and he immediately curled up on an empty rack, knees against his chest. Then she sat on another. They were a good platoon. It was a sentimental thought, since the main thing she was thankful for was that no one had asked where she'd been, or why she'd spent the morning in a shed in the back corner of the patrol base.

There wasn't any way she could ask their advice, though, and so, after she'd writhed around on her bunk for some twenty minutes, she crossed the gravel infield, entered the farmhouse that served as the patrol base's TOC, and followed Masterson's directions down an airless, stuffy hall to find Faisal Amar's replacement. She drew back a shower curtain that had been hung across an alcove and found a fat, middle-aged man lying there, reading. "I am sorry, can I help you?" he said.

The room was no more than a closet, squalid, hot, and the man lay on his side atop a black foam sleeping pad, a small stack of Arabic paperbacks and an electric light beside his head. She wondered if these had been Faisal's things.

"It's all right, it's okay," Fowler said, reading the embarrassment on the man's face. She averted her eyes until he'd buttoned his shirt. "I was just wondering if you could give something a quick look-see for me?"

"At your service," the fat man said brightly. But when he donned his glasses, he clicked his tongue in disapproval. "Hello, yes, you are the lady who lost the soldier. I'm sorry to hear about you. You are here to kill my friend today?"

"Faisal?" she said. "Is he still your friend?"

The man's face fell at her tone. "No, not anymore."

"Good," she said. "Then translate this."

She left the 'terp with the note and walked back down the hall and logged into the base's single public access computer to check her email, see if her camera request had gone through. Her SOS to Pulowski. The room was hot and stuffy, filled with the scent of food and tobacco spit. She sat for a moment before the computer's shifting screen, her forehead furrowed. She didn't *have* to tell Pulowski what she was doing, so why worry about it? By then the green bar at the bottom of her browser had loaded, and she opened up her in-box, found an email from Pulowski's CO, Major McKutcheon, saying the camera system wasn't ready yet. Then, a few lines down, she found one from Pulowski himself, with his contradictory response to McKutchon's email attached.

Hey LT, Pulowski's email said. *The cameras are ready (see below). You were right about these assholes. Or I was right and you were wrong, then you were right and I was wrong. So at least we covered all the bases. Cheers. I'll be waiting.*

She stood and walked into the back room. The translator had disappeared, leaving behind the note and his translation, written in pencil on a legal pad.

I am Ayad al-Tayyib from Bini Ziad. I am 23. I have a friend who is a translator with the 27th Infantry. His name is Faisal Amar. If I help you, can you guarantee his safety?

The note proved that Faisal had lied about knowing the Iraqi. But it didn't prove he knew anything about Beale. It wouldn't be enough to detain him if she followed protocol and took him back to Camp Tolerance. So she had a choice. Either she allowed Faisal to be questioned by Masterson, which was probably the same as killing him. Or she reported Masterson and risked letting Faisal walk free. Which might mean never finding Beale.

She crouched in the alcove where Faisal Amar had slept, her boots waffling patterns in the sleeping pad. The worst part about listening to Masterson evade responsibility for Faisal Amar was that she'd been reminded of the conversation she and Pulowski had had back in her trailer, when she'd blamed him for what had happened to Beale. Blame was what *she* needed. Stories of blame. Reams of affidavits supporting it. What was the proper gesture when you condemned a man? She touched the books, but couldn't read them. Only a fool would lie down where he'd lain. Then she returned to her computer and typed in: *0800 hours tomorrow. 16th Engineer Brigade HQ. See you then.* Then, after a moment's hesitation, she added, *We got the bastard*, then pressed send.

4

"Can you draw?" Pulowski asked. He opened the notepad Fowler had given him, flopped it onto the table, and drew a stick figure of himself. "Dixon," he said. Then, remembering that the Iraqi across from him couldn't hear—the man's hand flittered up to his ear again as Pulowski spoke—he wrote his name on the pad in English. *DIXON.* He pointed at himself. Then he turned the pad so the man might do the same.

The room that they occupied was in a small rural schoolhouse in the northern sector of their territory, near a town named Bini Ziad. When Fowler's platoon had shown up, a line of civilians, detained by Captain Masterson, whose territory this remained, stretched clear through the school's courtyard and into the road. All of them had to be questioned about Beale and the attack at the intersection. It was a mime show, in Pulowski's opinion, a necessary but pointless routine, and so it felt somehow proper to be interviewing a man in his mid-twenties who, rather than answering his questions, fired off a picture, quickly sketched but done in the proper proportions, a hint of perspective, crosshatched shading, the way a genuine cartoonist might work. It was a self-portrait, no blemish left out, his defects if anything exaggerated, the chin melting away into his neck, the teeth overlarge, possibly the most honest testimony he'd seen all day.

"Very cute," Pulowski said. He held the drawing up beside the man's head as if to judge its likeness. Then he frowned, as if he couldn't see the resemblance.

The man widened his eyes insistently. *Yes, I am that ugly*, he seemed to be saying, if it was possible to derive actual words from the folds and positioning of a face. *Seriously, I'll show you!* He stuck his rabbit teeth out and jabbed at them, then jabbed back at the picture—*See?*—and gave a quick offhand shrug—*Who, me?*—as if he did not intend to let his achievement of this ugliness go to his head.

Pulowski laughed. *Okay, okay*—he nodded—*you win*. Then he pointed to the name *Dixon* on his sketch and tapped the blank space beneath the artist's.

The man shook his head gravely. He flipped the stationery and the sketch over, revealing what appeared to be a formal note, written in Arabic.

"You want me to read this?" Pulowski asked.

The man nodded, though of course there was no way he could have understood. Then he grabbed the note and drew on it again, this time right beneath the text, the small lines scratching and fanning out magically, creating out of the nothing that had been there a face, a body, a pair of wings. Was it . . . what? A male angel. Did they have angels in Islam? Or just virgins? The man pointed eagerly toward the door, as if he wanted someone to read the note, so Pulowski nodded politely and carried it into the hallway.

The main problem Pulowski was experiencing just then was the awareness of his own secret. The fact that he'd abandoned Beale and then lied about it was probably more important than anything the Iraqi had to say. On the other hand, he'd decided that telling the truth about it wouldn't help anybody, least of all Beale. He had reasoned very carefully through all of this during the twenty-four hours that had passed since Beale had charged into the abandoned building in the Muthanna intersection, and Pulowski, rather than follow him, had stood and sprinted away, back into the intersection, unhooked the mic from Waldorf's dashboard, and said, *We got separated from Beale. I have no idea where he might be.* Pulowski's father had been a liar too—as well as a resident surgeon at the Blanchfield Army Community Hospital outside Clarksville. Or at least that was how Pulowski had thought about him when his father had filed for divorce and, two months later, retired from the Army and moved to Naples, Florida. One of the most curious things about that divorce—one that had grown more curious once Pulowski, who'd been sixteen at the time, had gone off to college and developed a better sense of how a divorce might work, not to mention how a man like his father, who was extremely organized, would tend to plan things—was the fact that his father must have known and been planning to move to Naples for some time. It was impossible to imagine it differently. This had become the focal point of his anger with his father for years, especially once he got to college. He'd finally asked his father about this directly at the graduation banquet held for his ROTC cadre. The colonel, as far as Pulowski knew, had not put on a uniform since his retirement, which was one of the reasons that Pulowski, dressed up in his ROTC greens, had felt powerful enough to ask the question on that particular day. They'd been in a hotel ballroom near the University of Pittsburgh, the cadets in white gloves, the tables covered in fancy tablecloths, napkins frilled in cups, and when Pulowski's mother had gotten up to go to the bathroom, he'd leaned over to his father and said, *You knew you were leaving us, didn't you? You knew it and you never said anything. Isn't that true?* His father, a fastidious man, gray-haired, not far from his own death (though, of course, Pulowski hadn't known that then), had rearranged his utensils around his plate and then said, *And what use would that information be to anybody?*

At the time, Pulowski had considered his father's response to be, at best, cowardly. But now, as he pushed through the crowded hallways, looking for an interpreter to read the detainee's note, all he hoped for was his father's equanimity. He could still see Beale's splotchy, glistening face peeking out from behind a metal dumpster once they'd started taking fire in the alley off the Muthana intersection. "You think it's such a stupid idea to check these buildings out now?" Beale had said, hands shaking as he tried to aim his weapon. "Fuck that, man. Fuck you and your bullshit."

"Try the radio, at least," Pulowski had said.

"It's jammed," Beale had said. "I got nothing."

"We got to sit tight," he had said. "We stick together, it'll be all right."

"We got to get on that roof," Beale had said. "That's where the shooter is. There's a door up ahead. I'm going in."

"No," he had said. "No, just hold on."

"What the fuck am I holding on to?" Beale had said. "You?"

Early on when they'd first started sleeping together at Fort Riley, he and Fowler had talked about Beale quite a bit because he'd been the one soldier in her platoon whom she had the most trouble with—and also the one they had the most pleasure arguing about. Pulowski had still felt adrift in the Army then. As a signal officer attached to Headquarters Company, he was not in charge of a platoon, like Fowler was, and thus had no soldiers under him, no relationship to their day-to-day concerns. Instead, despite the surface activity of the fort, which itself wasn't all that different from a college campus, he had spent most of his days in a classroom in the back of the battalion headquarters, working to bone up on the command-and-control programs for the computer systems that they would be using when they got to Iraq. None of the equipment actually existed there, physically, at the fort: it was all in Iraq, already installed, and so mostly they worked from manuals and on a few emulators that McKutcheon had managed to wrangle out of the supply chain. The whole thing had felt dry and dead—worse, in its way, than anything he'd done in college. Not to mention the fact that, in a way he'd not considered when in college—in a way that he'd thought he'd be protected from, since he had assumed that the war would be over by the time he graduated—he had for the first time the realization that he'd made a terrible mistake in judgment to join the Army.

He was not the only person, he figured, who was having this feeling. But it didn't filter into daily conversation that much except for McKutcheon's side comments, his tendency to repeat tidbits from the Secretary of Defense's press conferences in a flat voice, without any clear inflection one way or the other, and then to stare at Pulowski, or some of the other junior intel officers, as if he wondered what they were looking at him for.

So talking about Beale had become a way of admitting, indirectly, his fear. Or even of really, clearly defining what that fear might be. As a soldier, Beale had been everything that Pulowski wasn't and hoped never to be. He was brash, he was boastful, he was exceptionally jingoistic, he was constantly disregarding Fowler's instructions to him—or, if not disregarding them, complaining that their training was not more active, that Fowler wasn't aggressive enough, that she did things too much by the book. All of this Pulowski had taken as a joke—and Fowler had too, in at least some way, or she wouldn't have told Pulowski stories about the troubles she'd had with Beale.

Fowler, of course, had already been through something like this. He assumed that the difficulties she'd had with her brother—his running away, his stealing, his drunk-driving arrest in Texas—were at least part of what made her comparatively cheerful at the prospect of leading a platoon of soldiers into Iraq. He'd learned most of this at the La Quinta Inn in Council Grove, Kansas, about half an hour south of Fort Riley, which was where he and Fowler slept together in order to keep their relationship secret. Maybe if he had been closer to Fowler, if he had made some public commitment to her, they might have been able to find a way through this together. But in the La Quinta Inn, the thing he'd liked most about Fowler *was* her secrets. There was a darkness in her, which he recognized, and a good strong streak of anger—at her mother, for instance, whenever Pulowski brought her up. (And only if Pulowski brought her up.) She'd believed that she was a poor officer, she fretted that she would not have her platoon properly trained, worried about packing, about what Captain Hartz's opinion of her was, about her weight, and most frequently about Beale. None of this had been said self-pityingly, which was how it would've come out had Pulowski been talking. But naturally, and at intervals—usually after they had made love and were lying in bed watching Leno, naked, and she had her leg draped over his and she would yawn and reach over to pat his chest and deliver whatever concern it was that had troubled her that day in a flat, direct voice.

He could see Fowler now, through the doorway of a different schoolroom, seated on a folding chair beside Masterson, interviewing the local sheikhs: she looked mannish, not fat, but full in the shoulders, very muscular in the thighs. It had been a violation of the prime directive of being a signal officer, lying there in bed talking to a lieutenant—all of which could not have been more exciting for Pulowski. Not the sex, which was fine, or even excellent—better than you might imagine if you chose girls only from looking at a magazine. But it was the part about lying in bed with her watching Leno, naked, and listening to her worry that had truly excited him, because those worries bore her own private weight. And secondly because Beale's antics, Hartz's opinion, the concern about whether she'd measure up as an officer, were exactly the kinds of things that he'd given up worrying about a long time ago. Which meant that whatever was happening now would be worse for her than it would ever be for him.

"Hey," Pulowski said, as Masterson's interpreter stuck his head out of the schoolroom door. "I need you to talk to somebody." He hustled the 'terp down the hallway to the room where the deaf man had been. What was he expecting? Nothing, he hoped. *And what use would that information be to anybody?* But when he and Faisal Amar entered the room, the deaf man cowered, went wide-eyed and spooked, jumping up so quickly that his chair tipped over backward, and that sound, the sudden scatter of metal against linoleum, acted as the ground for a high-voltage charge that had been running secretly through the room all along, buzzing, humming, burning just beneath their skin. Pulowski grabbed his arm, shouted uselessly, "Stop!" and then the two soldiers on guard outside swept in and tackled him. The man went down as if he'd been dropped from the ceiling. Pulowski heard his head slap linoleum and in a moment he was trussed, one soldier pinioning his arms behind his back, the other shouting, "Down! Get down!" with the muzzle of his M4 pressed into the man's ear. This occurred in view of the other Iraqis lined up in the hallway, who craned their necks to see, until Pulowski kicked the door closed, rounded, and found Faisal squatting before the man's bleeding face.

"It's all right, okay, guys, no problem here," Faisal was saying.

"He just freak out a little bit, this guy. Is he crazy? Did he say something?"

"He's *deaf*," Pulowski said.

"No weapons," said the soldier kneeling on the man's back. "He make a move on you?"

"No," Pulowski said. "He just bolted when I came back in."

"He tell you what he want?" Faisal asked. He'd picked up a greasy, stained notebook that had fallen out of the man's pocket.

"He wanted me to read something," Pulowski said.

The man had ceased arching his back in an effort to get free. Instead, his brown irises seemed curiously calm, completely resigned as he gazed up at Pulowski. There was something off there, maybe. But Beale was dead by now. He'd lumbered out from behind that dumpster and run to the open door he'd identified. Once there, he'd glanced back at Pulowski and pointed up, as if to indicate where he was going. There had been nothing hidden in his face. He'd been terrified. He'd known that Pulowski would not help him. And he'd barged into the darkness anyway. The last thing Fowler needed, after all the favors Pulowski had done for her already, was to know how good Beale had been. Or to believe there was any hope of getting him back. In the schoolroom, Faisal whispered quietly and patiently in Arabic, which the deaf man gave no sign of understanding, and then, chuckling to himself, turned to a clean page in the notebook and, his face aping broad emotions of forgiveness, of generous importuning—his thin eyebrows raised, his lips folded into a clownlike moue—wrote something in Arabic and held it down beside the prisoner's eyes, turning it sideways so that he could read.

"Well, he can go now, I think," Faisal said, when the deaf man had finished reading. And when the soldiers holding the man hesitated, looking at Pulowski, who was the ranking officer in the room, he added, "I mean, if you want to let him, of course. These are not my decisions. Unless you want to let him talk to your female lieutenant. Do they allow these things? I admit he's not all that good-looking, quiet type, I don't know—but who am I to say what a woman like that would find attractive—"

"What are you talking about?" Pulowski asked.

"This guy, he loves your lady officer," Faisal said. His accent corrupted this phrase into something that sounded slurred and drunken. Pulowski noticed that Masterson's soldiers—now gently tugging the prisoner into a sitting position, checking his wound, finding a rag to mop the floor where he had bled—grinned in spite of themselves.

It was possible that even the prisoner, fresh gauze taped to his temple, looking dazed, added a bittersweet and hopeless smirk.

"No, seriously." Faisal was on a roll by now, getting laughs, and he continued with all the subtlety of a lounge singer. "He says, *'Azeezati'*—that's dear woman, okay? 'I know that you don't see me but I think that we are a couple made in heaven and I am offering to you the opportunity to be my wife, *zawja*.' Yes, well, it's flattering, I think? No? He says here he has fifteen goats and a 1984 Toyota Camry—"

"All right, okay, I get the idea," Pulowski said, flushing. He was still holding the piece of stationery, with the man's sketched pictures. The unsettling male angel. If he'd had any balls he would've thrown it away. Instead, he stuck it in his pocket, which felt like the only truly cowardly thing he'd done all day. "Get him out of here. We've had a nice ha-ha, so let's give Romeo his walking papers and move on."

"We could always ask the captain if he has a policy on this," Faisal said.

But Pulowski already had the door open, waving the deaf man—now transformed back into a civilian from a prisoner—out the door and into the crowded hallway beyond. "Yeah, yeah, yeah, very funny. Okay, who's the next case?"

Fowler collapsed against the wall of her trailer at Camp Tolerance, head tilted back, still sweating, having just returned from the schoolhouse and her last, fruitless attempt to find Beale. "It was my fault," she said.

Pulowski lay on the floor with his arms winged behind his head, like he did when he was thinking up a line. By now she was ready for one.

"If you're going to make me lie here and listen to you say stupid things like that," he said, "you could at least have the decency to clean the place up."

Not bad. Maybe she could work with that.

"You're a fucking classic, Pulowski." She grabbed an old T-shirt from the floor and smacked him in the center of his skinny chest, shaking her head. "The one person in the Army who'd try to fix a disaster like this by *cleaning*."

It was an experiment, she understood that. Some attempt to touch the world as it had been before they'd lost Beale. As it had been when they'd made love here.

"Controlling your environment," Pulowski said, doing a passable impersonation of Captain Hartz's crusty bark, "is the first step on the road to clarity of mind."

"I hope not," she said, gazing around her trailer. The place was a disaster of crap. The tops of her two lockers were cluttered with backup supplies, razors (unused now for a week), her extra soap, her iPod dock, her camera charger, her stacks of toilet paper, baby wipes, bug spray. The top of the fridge where she'd put together a tiny kitchenette, hot plate, coffeemaker, powdered Gatorade. The corner where she'd tossed USPS Priority Mail boxes that contained the rare postings from her dad—never anything from her mother—the plastic bags of trail mix, almonds, the copies of *The Kansas City Star*, already yellowing. Cleaning up her personal space had been one thing she'd let go since her commission. She'd done enough of it back home with Harris, loads of laundry, the toilets, the showers, not because she liked it, but because it was part of her imitation of what a mother did. The other option was to take about four Tylenol PM and just go dead—except she wasn't even sure, with the way her head was spinning, that meds would work. "All right, let's do it. Clarity of mind. I could go for a little bit of that."

Pulowski scrounged up a couple of plastic bags from the PX and began stuffing them with papers, the bits of food, and empty soda cans. She went to the closet for a broom and swept and then found somewhere back in her locker one of those dustless mops with the pads that came in a box—she tried looking at the box, at the instructions on it, the brightly photogenic housewife in her jeans, and somehow this terrified her in a way the broom did not. She had to set the box down quickly and walk away.

She wondered how it could be so simple for Pulowski. He wasn't like Dykstra or Waldorf, who might look a hell of a lot tougher on the surface but who'd cried like kids once they'd given up the chase. Pulowski was more like a wasp—nervous, always buzzing around about something, attacking to protect his fragility. Once, he'd told her a story about how, after his father had left, he'd come home in tears from the bus, because the kids at school had claimed he threw a ball like a girl. So he'd led his mom out in the front yard, jammed a baseball glove on her hand, and said, "Look, I'm never going to be good at this, okay? I just need you to teach me how not to suck." So it wasn't like Fowler had to worry about him treating her like she had leprosy just because she'd committed the worst sin an officer could commit. But he was also not exactly someone you'd expect to keep quiet after a firefight—even if, as he'd said, he'd been too far away from Beale to see what had happened. Still, for a good twenty minutes they strained and encouraged each other toward some objective that had nothing to do with Beale. She opened the door to let in a breeze. Pulowski was squatting on his haunches, thumbing through the back issues of *The Kansas City Star*, and when she walked back past him, she rubbed his scalp offhandedly, as if stealing something.

"So what do we do next?" he asked.

She sat on her bed, unbuttoned her blouse, and stripped apart the Velcro on her shoulder brace. "I don't know, Dix. You can tell me we're gonna find him someplace."

"You don't really think he's alive?"

She took a long, deep breath. "You can't not think that," she said.

He tucked his chin against his chest. "Look, what you've got to realize is that this is just a bad accident. It just fucking *feels* bigger than that, okay?"

"You're kidding me," she said. "That's the best you've got?"

"It's true," Pulowski said. "You think you're in the middle of some life-crushing, horrible event. Losing a soldier is the worst thing that can possibly happen to a platoon leader." When he said this, she felt an electric stab through her entire body, as if it were the first thing he'd said that was true. "Okay? I agree. But that's not the same as saying you're to blame. It was Colonel Seacourt's idea to set those cameras up. I was the one who asked your platoon to take me outside the wire. And your sergeant was the idiot who charged into that building—and got himself shot. Or whatever happened in there."

Here was his buzz, coming back. The problem was, she had asked herself all the same questions. Why hadn't she been there?

If she had been there, couldn't the same thing have happened to her? What would it be like if it *was* happening to her?

"I should've gotten in the building sooner," she said.

"We were getting shot at," Pulowski said.

She dropped her head back. "We were *all* getting shot at."

"And you told us specifically not to go into that building without a full team," Pulowski said. "Didn't you do that? Wasn't that the case? Okay, so that was ugly. That was something I never want to see, and I hope I live long enough to forget about it, but I am not going to sit here and let you destroy yourself because you didn't follow Beale into doing what was obviously a stupid thing."

"You knew that," Fowler said. "You knew that was a stupid thing."

"Sure as fuck turned out that way."

She saw the flinch, the darting way his eyes shifted to the dingy trailer window, a quick grope of his armpit. "How were you so sure?" she asked.

"What difference does it make?"

"Because the shooter"—Fowler pointed at the trailer's ceiling—"was on the roof. We missed it. I missed it. But Beale saw it. Beale was trying to protect me, and my soldiers, a twenty-eight-year-old sergeant—"

"Oh, come on. You are not going to—"

"A twenty-eight-year-old sergeant," Fowler said, rising to her feet, "who risks his life to help my team, and meanwhile I'm lying around inside my Humvee, farting around on the radio—"

To her shock and surprise, as she reached this crescendo, Pulowski laughed in her face. "Oh, man, that is some desperation, Fowler. What do you want me to do? You want me to take the blame? What do you think would've happened if I had gone in after Beale?"

She'd done the same thing with her younger brother, Harris. She could remember it perfectly, as if that moment had been permanently encoded in her memory, waiting to reflower now in this version of her worst self. Meaning she'd found out that Harris had boosted a car—it had been a Mazda, owned by the Ryersons, who'd had a daughter in her class at school. She might be a schlub lieutenant now, who was overweight, who ran a half-assed recovery team—who was fucking scared and terrified, who'd been fucking scared and terrified every second out there in that intersection—but back then she'd been tougher, lean, and she'd had plans for Harris. So she'd been terrifying in her righteousness, ambushing him in the parking lot where he'd hidden it, forcing him to admit where it had come from, rubbing his nose in it. She didn't want to use anger now—she knew better, or she ought to have known better. Not against Pulowski, especially.

"No," she said. "Hold on, hold on—let me walk that back."

"Fuck you, Fowler!" Pulowski said. He was crying then, which was the last thing that she'd intended, the last thing she wanted to see. "You think you're going to be able to walk this back? What are you, some kind of idiot? Don't you know what happened out there? What are you, fucking blind?"

The last words had been a howl. It had been the same way with Harris when she'd confronted him about the car: sarcasm, anger, contempt—goading, which she'd never been that good at handling. And then when she pushed back—which she did way too hard, she knew that—there was nothing there when you broke the shell. "Know?" she said. "Know? Fuck, yes, I know what happened. I was in command and I lost a soldier. Do you have some kind of different take on this, Pulowski? What the hell else happens when somebody disappears? You try to get them back."

"Aha!" Pulowski said, jabbing a finger at her. "We're going to start in on this. Fowler's sad story of her brother."

"Because I'll tell you what happens when you lose somebody and *don't* try to get them back. You end up lost too. That's it."

"I am not going to sit here and discuss your family."

"It's not my family," Fowler said. "It's *me*. That's me, okay? If that had been you out there, wouldn't you want me to get you back? You don't think your fucking mom would expect me to make an effort?"

Something had shifted ever so slightly in the conversation. "Yeah, well, good for you," Pulowski said, his angular face becalmed, as it usually was when he'd won an argument. "But I *was* there. I was with Beale in the alley. He wanted to go in the building and find the shooter and I wouldn't. I bailed on him and lied about it and I'm not sorry about it and I'd fucking do it again. That's it. Okay? *That's* me."

The feeling was like stepping into an air shaft that had been gaping there in the middle of the conversation from the beginning. On the way down, in the loose, falling sensation that accompanied the drop, she did the math. Not only had Pulowski failed to help Beale. But if he *had* tried to help, she'd probably be looking for him. That was all there, present in his face—and had been, probably, from the minute they'd come into the trailer. Instead, she'd fucked it up, exactly as she had with Harris. She could never back off, never shut up. "I'm an ass," she said. "I'm sorry, Pulowski. I didn't see."

There was a deliberation in his movements that she recognized, as if some decision had been made whose terms she hadn't been informed of. He gave a shaky laugh. "Yeah, well, at least his mom'll know who to blame, huh? You can write that to her: *Your son Carl is dead because Lieutenant Pulowski sat on his fucking ass.* I guess they can write that on my epitaph."

“Dixon.” She propped herself up on her elbow and gave him her best version of her father’s icy glare, wanting to contradict him in some way. “No.”

Pulowski paled and began waving his hand as if to wipe out any further sentiment. He’d reached down into his pocket and produced a folded scrap of beige paper. “I get it, okay? I am *not* saying that you’re wrong. You got to look for Beale. I understand. It’s just that I’m out. But before I get out, you’re gonna want to see this, okay? I don’t know if it means anything—”

He unfolded the paper and handed it to her. There were two sketches, one of the Iraqi, another of an unknown man with wings. The one who looked like Beale.

“An Iraqi gave this to me at the schoolhouse,” he said. “I think you should go to Masterson’s patrol base, find his interpreter, ask him about it. If you get a bite, if there’s something there, you don’t walk it back.”

5

It was nearly June when Faisal Amar stood on the roof of Ayad al-Tayyib's house and offered Ayad twenty dollars a week American for the use of his property and the fields surrounding it. The offer was not completely insane, not completely unexpected. Previous to that spring, it had been possible to switch on the Al-Iraqiya network, watch the jarring, bumpy footage of a bombing's aftermath, mangled bodies being carted off on stretchers, or the wailing crush around a casket, and then walk outside and feel none of the same tension in the surrounding air. Breathe in eucalyptus, watch a flock of crows dance in unison over the date palm trees. But since the bombing of the Al-Askari Shrine in Samarra that winter, Ayad had begun to feel a constriction reaching out from the city, tightening the air of the surrounding fields. There were rumors now. Mysterious flyers in the markets in Bini Ziad. Gunfire occasionally at night. He did not frequently agree with his mother's assessment of local politics, particularly when it came to the Shi'ites. (Seeing televised footage of the shrine's exploded golden dome, his mother, dressed in the brocaded jacket she had once worn for trips into the city, had texted his phone crisply from across the living room, *Now they'll have an excuse to do anything.*) And yet, recently, from this spot here on his roof—shielded by the spaceship that he and Faisal had built—he'd seen headlights out across the fields, winking, disappearing, with no practical explanation for their presence except that, following their visits, their old Sunni neighbors tended to move away. Even he might define those convoys as a *they*.

The money, which Faisal flourished now from his suit pocket, would've been useful. If it had come from Faisal himself, he would've been less concerned, since he viewed Faisal as a *we*. But instead, it came from Raheem al-Najafi, the Shi'ite mechanic who worked in town, whose identity, once fixed and stable, beneath Ayad's mother's notice, had been mutated and altered by the invasion, until nobody knew what, exactly, he should be named. Ayad's mother would've called him *takfiri*, or unbeliever (which really meant uppity Shi'ite). The word in Bini Ziad was that he was a member of the Grand Brotherhood of the Golden Dome, whose angry flyers papered the marketplace. But Ayad's main concern was with how the Americans defined Raheem. Insurgent being the worst case. *Explain this to me again*, Ayad wrote in his notebook, jabbing it back at Faisal. *Why would Raheem al-Najafi want to use my house? When did he get so rich?*

Raheem's objective is not an issue. You will not be involved in it.

You're involved in it.

I know you, so Raheem has asked me to make the contact.

What does he want to use the house for?

It would be better if you did not ask.

I thought you were working with the Americans? Can't they protect you?

I am working with the Americans. But I can't be with them all the time.

Why don't you tell them that you're in danger?

I am not in danger, Faisal wrote. *You are in danger.*

I am not in danger if I do not have a side. If anything, I am in favor of the Americans. None of them have bothered me.

Are you saying that you would support a group of infidels against your own countrymen? Do you have no pride in your religion?

Ayad laughed at this last note when he read it. *You are not a religious person*, he scribbled. *You don't fool me.*

Faisal considered this, stone-faced. Then responded: *You don't know what I am.*

Ayad had had long arguments with his mother about what, exactly, Faisal was back in the day. A shape-shifter. A user. That was what she called him. According to her, the only reason a Shi'ite like Faisal played with him was that the other Sunni kids ignored him. That and the fact that what Faisal *really* wanted was to marry Ayad's cousin Hanan, who'd been living at Ayad's house then. Admittedly, there had been afternoons when Ayad could remember his friend sitting out at the wooden picnic table just below him, in his mother's rose garden, doing voices to make Hanan laugh. On the other hand, the other Sunni kids ignored Ayad too. So maybe there had been some using, but it had gone both ways. Normal using, if there was such a thing. So Ayad had worked out a compromise: Faisal could still play up on the roof, in the spaceship, which he'd helped build. And which Ayad considered to be the best avatar of his friend, a physical manifestation of his desire to escape who he was consigned to be.

The spaceship as a whole had always been a frivolous project. Its blueprints had been drawn up loosey-goosey—the word Faisal had preferred was *mu'wajj*, or literally "crooked"—on bits of paper; then it was constructed from scraps. And yet despite its absurdity, its impracticality, there had never been a moment during its conception and assembly, executed on this very same gravel-covered rooftop more than a decade ago, when Faisal had dropped the extraordinarily grave and deadpan seriousness that he adopted when consulting his friend over aspects of design.

Unlike you, I am on all sides, Faisal wrote. *Especially the side that wins.*

Which side is that?

I don't know yet.

As the two men crouched beside the rusting remains of their old toy, Ayad could still remember Faisal's expression, his exact method of nodding and running a thumbnail through his eyebrow, as he pored over one of Ayad's drawings, or picked up a pen and responded to one of his notes on their pad. He mentally cleared the present from the rooftop and relit the roof with the daylight of the past, revealing the palomino speckles of its pebbles interseeded with doomed eucalyptus shoots (he could summon these familiar things as casually as a photo in a book), and then—though this took a bit more concentration—he disassembled the spaceship into its constituent pieces, hoisted the great geared wheel that served as its floor back out into the open air, and balanced it atop two sawhorses.

Faisal's father had retrieved the wheel from a grain works in Ramadi and hauled it onto the roof. A quiet, sepulchral man, he'd rented a house from Ayad's family, done odd jobs for Raheem al-Najafi, for whom Ayad had worked too. But it was Faisal who'd imagined the spaceship. Faisal who'd bartered for the American comics that they'd read, secretly, inside its shadowed cockpit. Faisal who'd brought his old telescope out, charting the stars, and convinced Ayad to draw the worlds they would see. Ayad's mother had disliked the spaceship, largely because she had disliked Faisal. But in Ayad's opinion, the shape-shifting quality that allowed Faisal to recast the two of them as astronauts had been Faisal's strength, the very thing that allowed them to be friends. In that sense, it had seemed natural when

Faisal applied to work with the Americans. Translating paid one hundred dollars a day—a gigantic sum. In almost no time, Faisal had a better cash flow than Ayad's family, especially after their government pension payments dropped away. And so it unnerved Ayad that Faisal was standing here on the same roof where they'd played as children, asking for help. But not exactly asking either—more like telling Ayad what he should do, as if he didn't have a choice, while at the same time pacing about so nervously that it seemed clear that maybe it was Faisal himself who didn't have a choice.

Ayad wasn't going to rent him his property. That was for sure. On the other hand, he had no power to enforce his refusal, so he was going to have to find some other appeal. Downstairs, Ayad made chai in the kitchen, offered it. They sat alone in the living room, Faisal casting his gaze about the environs, as if trying to match it up with the past.

They had once watched movies here, before Faisal had gotten himself banned. Faisal had always been the better actor, but in the silence that was between them—a silence that Faisal had always accepted better than anybody else—Ayad tottered over to him, imagining a pantomime. What should he act out? A hug? An embrace? Fall to his knees and beg? He paused and squatted before his old friend. Nothing so dramatic; Faisal had never been a fan of sentimentality. Over the past two weeks he'd watched the headlights gradually work their way in, stopping sometimes in a field all night, other times a steady crisscrossing to the south until, two nights ago, a small patrol, two vehicles, had cruised the road outside their gate. They'd stopped, the twinned white lights of reverse blinking on, and jolted up the driveway for a sniff. Then he'd seen Faisal's blue sedan come speeding up, heard an angry shout, and their brights had flared, whitening the walls of his father's house, as the patrol pulled away.

I am afraid I cannot sell the spaceship, Ayad wrote. He reached across and held Faisal's hand, his expression (he hoped) as grave and deadpan as his friend's had been when he'd built the spaceship. *The world is not prepared for such advanced technology.*

Stay here was what he meant. Hide with me.

Pulowski tucked his hands beneath his nuts. He was in the back of Fowler's Humvee; Fowler and her driver, Carl Beale, occupied the front. The thing that he was processing was how much smarter he'd felt in Tennessee. Leafy streets? Regis and Kathy in the morning? A coffee shop called the Ethical Bean? The whole town had seemed a kind of cartoon invitation to irony: Hey, guess what, these people don't care about your soldiering. It crossed his mind that maybe the exact thing that had comforted him about being home was that America seemed *designed* for the easy take: Regis Philbin, clown. New England Patriots, arrogant. Even Bill Moyers, his mother's favorite, didn't do much more than hit gassed-up Republican piñatas off a tee. While Iraq, rolling past Fowler's Humvee window, left him slack-jawed and empty. Looted rows of strip malls. A lot filled with pureed bricks. A string of trash-roofed garages. Then the blocky quad of the University of Baghdad Agricultural College, identified by a neat roadside sign in English. "First time I came out," Fowler said, pointing to the college, "the thing that surprised me the most was the architecture. For an Arab country, it seems pretty sixties."

It was the fourth or fifth cheerful thing she'd said to him since they'd left the gate, a fact that made no sense, given how he'd treated her recently. But his nuts tingled anyway, appreciatively. "What were you expecting, minarets?" he asked.

"I don't know," Fowler said. "I guess, when we were back at Riley, I used to imagine I'd be dead in sixty seconds if I ever came out here at all. Like it'd be the surface of the moon or some real bleak thing—"

"Who says it ain't?" Beale asked.

Fowler punched her driver in the shoulder, then swiveled around, a plastic bottle of Mountain Dew clutched in her right fist. "Don't listen to Beale, he doesn't know shit. And forget McKutcheon's doubts about your camera system—I appreciate you asking us along, okay? It took some balls to do that. Not a crazy amount of balls, 'cause we're gonna be fine. But some balls, a *decent* amount of balls. Pulowski on patrol. That's high speed. High speed." She reached back and hit his knee with her fist. "Trust me—McKutcheon's wrong on this one. You did the grown-up thing."

This was less a take than a Disney fantasy. Doubt was the core principle of the camera system, whose batteries, encoder boxes, and D-link switches were stowed beside him on the Humvee's backseat. Doubt had been the point—that and staying the hell away from places like the Muthanna intersection, where they were headed currently.

"You know where I saw a lot of grown-ups while I was on leave?" He dug his hands out from his crotch and laid them tentatively atop his thighs. "Malls."

"Funny, that's not where I would have gone."

"You wanna know specifically what I thought about? I thought about all those women—or not just women, all those people, sucking up designer ice cream. Back there walking around Nordstrom's where their biggest concern is, I don't know, buying panties, and you're"—he gestured out the window—"here. Doing this."

Fowler blew air out past her lower lip and turned to him with a wrinkled grin. "Beale can get you all the panties you want at the PX."

"Thongs," Beale grumbled. "I like thongs."

"He's very adult," Fowler said.

"Yeah," Pulowski said. "Well, you know, hey, I'm just saying I shouldn't have blamed you for this mission. I'm sorry. It's taking me a while to get back in the groove."

Speaking of easy takes. This, he understood, was where he was having problems adjusting, where he felt out of step and quavery, like some newborn colt, in the face of Fowler's perkiness. Hadn't he dumped this woman four weeks ago, right before he'd gone on leave? And now, five days after he'd come back, he'd asked her to help him install his cameras at the Muthanna intersection. The old Fowler would've had a take on that kind of hypocrisy. And if that wasn't enough, what had he called her? A "cow-eyed innocent." Because here's the thing he hadn't said about the women at the mall: fucking beautiful creatures. Coeds, with nails done and dainty flip-flops on their feet. Legs as trim and taut as an airplane fuselage. *Are you single?* If you're asking, I am. Oh, yes, I am free. And also not stupid, not chained down to a war that you could already tell was about as popular as a canceled Lifetime series—and so his honesty with Fowler had been a form of fairness, as he'd seen it. If he was totally direct and honest that he still wouldn't be getting back with her *even if* she helped him bring the cameras out to Muthanna, well, then it was on her if she was stupid enough to take the mission anyway.

But this Fowler, the Fowler whom he'd expected to be angry and bitter with him, instead turned in her seat and chortled. "There it is! You hear that, Beale? You two are the worst! The worst motherfucking malcontents I've ever seen!"

"Malcontent?" Beale said. "Is that show still on TV?"

"Fox, I think," Pulowski said.

"Malcontent in the Middle pretty much describes every

soldier in all of Iraq, if you're talking about how people think this place ain't worth a shit."

"Aw, fuck!" Fowler said, beating the roof of the Humvee with her fist. "Here we go. I can see it now: one compliment to these guys, and they shit the bed immediately. Come on, Beale, bring it on!"

"Maybe this McKutcheon's the first *reasonable* dude we met," Beale said.

"Oh, shit! Yes! That's right!" Fowler shouted. Though it seemed as if Beale was directly contradicting her, she took a surprising pleasure in this. "I'm sorry, Pulowski, I am completely wrong about this thing. We *are* fucked. We are undeniably fucked. We got no chance. We're losing. All the dead people are dead now for no reason at all and every fucking lick of work we've done in this place is total crap. Let's all be McKutcheon. Let's all sit on our ass and complain about how shit is broken. Life sucks, war is bad—what a genius concept! What an incredible insight!"

It was, maybe, possibly the closest thing he'd ever heard from her in the way of a semi-decent speech, a rallying cry—surprising only in that it was delivered in the negative, a mockery of what not to be, rather than a statement of belief. Even so, as he listened to Fowler's voice, he felt a burbling in his throat, a buzzing clot of emotion that stuck there uncomfortably. "What about the Iraqi you took down?" Pulowski said, trying to resist this. "In the war-is-bad category?"

Fowler checked her mirror in silence. This too was different.

"You know what the colonel did to the Muthanna intersection after it got hit?" Fowler said, pivoting around again in her seat. "Nothing. Totally abandoned. Go on, Beale, take us through Muthanna. Let's go in the front door like we own the place."

He'd seen the bombed Muthanna intersection twice: once on a flat-screen television beside the Camp Tolerance chow line, which normally showed poker tournaments, and once back in Tennessee sitting in his mother's living room on leave—the grainy column of black smoke, the evacuated soldiers, half dressed, some down to their underwear. But it had mutated over time—after the details about the deaths of the two soldiers had come out—into something more organic. The bombing at Muthanna was the thing that skittered and scratched inside his brain when a warm gust of breeze touched his cheek, or he picked the paper up off his mom's lawn, or he drove past his high school—anytime that he relaxed back into the ease that was normal life, there it would be, even if what had happened to those soldiers had nothing to do with him. Even if the only thing more ridiculous than getting killed at a traffic control point, at a completely unimportant intersection, was Fowler's pigheaded insistence that this kind of ridiculousness needed to be stamped out or solved in some way. He'd said as much to Fowler—hell, he'd dumped her for that, basically—and, despite her compliments, he worried that she had brought him here to shame him, so he made an effort to keep a hard expression on his face and especially not to show fear. "I mean, okay, so the barracks don't look too good," he said, peering out the window at the crumpled slabs of concrete where the soldiers had stayed. "But it's not . . . well, it's not completely insane. I mean, look, what's that?" He craned his head so that he could see through the windshield. "There's people out, lots of traffic. That's a good sign, isn't it?"

The worst part had been the feeling he'd had *before* he'd separated from Fowler, the premonition that he was going to do something cowardly and that he was powerless to stop it or make it change. And this was it. Forgetting his resolution, believing that maybe, in Fowler, there was something very, very serious he'd missed. "So tell me, where are the bad guys?" he asked. "What is it I don't see?"

"Same thing we don't see," Fowler said. He noticed that her tone had turned grave, respectful—though not frightened—and that she and Beale were upright in their seats, scanning both sides of the street that they'd now entered, while patting the . . . what was it? a broken shackle? . . . that Beale had welded to the roof, one, two, three, some ritualized version of a handshake between themselves and the Humvee.

"Touch it," Fowler said.

"Touch what?"

"Touch me, touch Beale, give us a little love, Pulowski."

He reached up, awkwardly, not wanting to undo his shoulder belt, and brushed the backs of their hands with his fingertips.

"That's good," Fowler said. "That's for Fredrickson and Arthur, who fucking bit it right fucking here. And now, in their honor, we're going to fix this place."

"Hooah," Beale said.

The traffic *was* a problem. Fowler could handle the bomb crater, the pile of slag left from the building that had collapsed, but what she hadn't accounted for were the cabs, mini Nissan pickups loaded with melons, overladen buses, hatchbacks with angry-looking men that zoomed around her platoon's vehicles as they pulled into the intersection outside Muthanna. So she pretended that she had. She called the battalion and requested four additional Humvees. She established a security perimeter, her Humvee's .50-cal warning traffic away, then she ordered her platoon to fill the blast hole with gravel and tow away the chassis of the truck that had blown up Fredrickson and Arthur. And what did Pulowski do during these two hours of steady work? Nothing. He slouched around her truck. He unpacked his cameras, fiddled with some wires, and generally acted terrified—which, you know, fine, but so was everybody. It had always been her one weakness, trying to take care of a man who couldn't take care of himself. You told yourself you were going to change things, then you just kept making the same dumb mistake over and over again. It wasn't exactly what she'd imagined when the ROTC recruiting officer, Captain Granger, had shown up at her high school wearing dress greens that had been cut so tight that everyone—including, Fowler had noticed, Miss Simmons, her homeroom teacher—could clearly see his biceps through the fabric. *That* was the kind of officer she'd expected to teach her about life in the Army—energetic, confident, and hard as fucking nails. Instead, she'd gone for the complicated option, the sensitive model, the one that had seemed more interesting, which was how you ended up in a tactical situation that was far more fucked-up than anyone had realized it would be.

More than anything, she resented the way Pulowski had accused *her* of being responsible for this mission the night before. The whole lecture on how she had the free will to say no, as if the connection between them had never existed. Which was a lie. But then again, so were the arguments she'd used to keep her platoon together, functioning, and in the field. It didn't help that she got a call from the TOC, informing her that the reinforcements she'd requested had been diverted to provide security for a tour that Colonel Seacourt was giving that day. Or that, hearing this news, her platoon sergeant, Carl Beale, became increasingly nervous, pacing back and forth, scanning the windows of the nearby buildings incessantly. "Why don't you give me a couple guys, LT," he said finally, "and let me walk this west perimeter, go in these storefronts? I don't like them."

Beale had freckles so thick that in places they blended to solid patterns on his cheeks, and a body that resembled, in its doughiness and the flat-footed way his boots creased at the instep, an old-fashioned power hitter gone to seed. They were standing at the fender of Fowler's Humvee, which she'd parked in the center of their work site. Pulowski had stopped for a water break a few meters away. "Stick with the plan, Beale," she said. "We secure this area, we get the T-walls for the new checkpoint up, then we wait for the extra manpower to go in the buildings and get those cameras installed."

"You knew you were bringing the cameras out. So why didn't you bring the extra trucks in the first place?"

She knew Beale knew the answer to that. The answer was that neither Pulowski nor McKutcheon had given them an accurate report on how congested and unruly the intersection was going to be. "It's an unforeseen circumstance, Beale. Okay? But I'm not going to abandon protocol just because you're nervous, okay?"

"Yeah, well, imagine how you'd feel if you lost somebody just because Pulowski was too much of a pussy to go do his job."

"It's not about Pulowski," she said. "I don't want to send you in either. Or Waldorf. Or Crawford. Or anybody."

"You deserve better than that."

"What?"

Beale was an awkward soldier; he'd never touched her except out in the bean field, when she'd saved him from a fight. But now he grabbed the collar of her body armor and pulled her down into a squat, holding tight. "You laid out for me with Seacourt, didn't you? Huh? You lay out for me, I lay out for you. How would you feel if we got hit because you spent two hours waiting for backup, just because you wanted to protect Pulowski? He doesn't have your back, ma'am. Not like we do, anyway."

She should have let it pass—ignored Beale, made the proper call. Instead what she saw, like the tiny picture she used to get when she turned her father's binoculars around and looked through them the wrong way, was the image of herself sitting in the recruiter's car, out front of her father's house in Junction City, Kansas, signing the papers. All she could see was that image and, along with it, a tight, high pressure in her chest, as if someone were stabbing her in the center of her breastbone with a piece of glass. It had been there ever since they'd left the gate that morning and it frightened her because she almost never felt this way outside the wire. She also had this feeling associated with it that felt like guilt, as if she had committed some grave sin—which was impossible, since she'd been waiting for eight months for her platoon sergeant to speak to her in this way. Maybe she felt guilty because the eighteen-year-old Fowler would've agreed with Beale. That Fowler had sat in that recruiter's car and signed those papers as a declaration of freedom from Harris, her life, that house. She had never intended to allow anybody to make her as vulnerable as she'd been then.

"You got a specific plan in mind, Sergeant?" she said, standing up and addressing him in a more formal voice, so the soldiers nearby could hear. "I got guys posting security, we need people setting the T-walls up—so if you want to do a sweep, you're gonna need people who aren't already doing something."

"I'm not busy," Beale said. He had a sly look on his face.

"Yeah, but you need a team. Can't go in solo."

"What about camera boy here?" Beale said. "It's his shit, his equipment, his fucking project. We're good with these T-walls, ma'am. The only thing we're waiting on is for Pulowski to get off his ass and *do* something."

She glanced up at Pulowski. If it had been anyone other than Pulowski, she would have shut Beale down immediately, played it safe. But then again, if it had been anybody other than Pulowski, she wouldn't have been put in the position of being humiliated in front of her entire team. All she wanted from Pulowski was a little backup: nothing fancy, no apology, no sympathy, just a decisive opinion, a suggestion, some admission that they were together in the mission, that they shared responsibility. It was no excuse, of course—if you were a good lieutenant, you weren't supposed to care about these things. But today she did.

Instead, Pulowski punched his hands down in his pockets and bit his upper lip, grinning at her and Beale as if they were the biggest idiots he'd ever seen. "Well, it seems like you guys ought to make the best tactical decision you can, don't you think?"

It wasn't even something he actually believed.

She pushed between the two of them, grabbed a water bottle off the Humvee's seat. It was a bad idea to make decisions out of anger, but now she did. "Beale's right," she said. "Pack up your gear and get moving, Pulowski. I got a fucking platoon to take care of. You should've manned up an hour ago. Stop making us wait."

"Roger," Beale said.

"Grab Crawford to go with you," she said. "But don't go inside. You can look, but we're not rushing any buildings with anything short of a full team, and I can't spare that many men. You got it? You understand me? That's a direct order."

"Oh, yeah—I copy," said Beale. He jerked his Kevlar down tight over his ears, fastening his chin strap. "That's a direct order. Nobody gets to hurt Pulowski. Come on, camera boy, let's beat it, please."

The first shots were muffled and therefore hard to locate. They could have been far away. She dove in through her Humvee's door and scrambled for the portable radio that she kept under her seat. Once she got it and looked up, her platoon had begun firing at the market on the right-hand side of the intersection. It was empty, the bare metal pipes that defined the abandoned stalls knitting and unknitting like lace. And yet, once a single soldier aimed there, the entire platoon "unleashed" and these shadowy frames skidded and upended under the steady hose of rounds, sparks flaring and receding like lit match heads, a constant gloriole of sound and motion that was just confusing enough to be satisfying to shoot at. Just enough to give the illusion that a target was there.

Fowler saw all of this. But what she also saw was that every single one of her sentries—the Humvee crews that she'd posted at all four corners of the compass—had abandoned their appointed sectors and faced the firing. She tried to correct this, but when she flipped the portable radio on, the channel was overloaded, emitting only blips and burps, *Wrrock, SCREEJAARGH, Go! Go!* And then *Enemy at three o'clock*, and then *Fucking something moving, down in that market right there, see that hut, and then the fucker dropped into the canal, somebody shoot his ass* . . . until the feed dissolved into a high-pitched whine.

Okay, you've got to move. Where's the danger? she thought, and slid out in a crouch from her Humvee with her sidearm in her hand. *Who's hit? Is anybody hit?* She didn't think so. She was already in a hurry then, telling herself to slow down and think, and fighting against that hurry. The medical building was up ahead and to the left—the opposite side of the street from the market. They'd set up T-walls across the road, so she could only see its upper story and the roof. *Nice thinking, Beale. Good place for shooters, Beale.*

"The roof!" she shouted to her own gunner, McWilliams, whose .50-cal machine gun, pumping out rounds above her head, made it almost impossible to think.

"What?" McWilliams said.

Fowler stepped up onto the door frame of the Humvee, grabbed him by the shoulder, and pointed at the roof of the medical building. Then she dropped down onto the dirt and began running hard, tucking her chin, that way.

"All right, all right," she was saying a few seconds later, as she crouched behind a newly installed T-wall, halfway to the medical building. The intersection was quiet. McWilliams had silenced the shooter on the roof and the horseshoe of Humvees circled around the intersection had quit firing at the marketplace. That was progress, at least. She peeked up over the T-wall and checked the roofline again: nothing. *Okay, what next?*

"Okay, I need my perimeter security to do their jobs. Just stick to your own quadrants. Keep your eyes open. I'm going to call out sectors. South is toward the highway. Okay? South."

"Clear," Waldorf said.

"West."

"Clear," Dykstra said.

"North," Fowler said. This was Jimenez, whose Humvee was on the other side of the T-wall, nearest to the alley where Beale and Pulowski had gone in.

"Are you clear?"

"Almost, Lieutenant," Jimenez replied.

"What's that supposed to mean?" She tried to keep her voice steady during this, trying hard not to ask directly about Pulowski. She was supposed to be the platoon leader for all these people, not just him. But still, she felt a wave of relief when, after some rustling of the microphone, Pulowski's voice came on the air.

"Crawford and I are here. We were in this alley, and the team leader"—this meant Beale—"said we were under fire and he, uh, we got separated from him." There was muffled whispering here, a mic covered with a hand.

"You say you last saw Beale in the alley."

"Yes, ma'am."

How the fuck did three guys get separated in an alley? Here's how three guys get separated in an alley: their lieutenant gets pissed off and sends them in.

She pushed out from behind the T-wall and ran hard to the medical building, got herself under the second floor walkway, pressed her back against the louvered steel door that covered the front window. She peeked around the corner. No Beale. A car with its windshield shot out. A big steel box that looked like a dumpster someone had made from scratch. Okay, what would be the most dangerous place for Beale to be? The answer was inside. By then a cancerous black tentacle of fear began to curl itself, glistening, around Fowler's wrist, sneaking up the cool wincing skin of her inner bicep, nesting inside her armpit: Beale had a headset radio with him too. Why wouldn't he be answering?

"All right, Eggleston," she said. "Button up the Hercules and drive it right over to me. Punch a hole in this wall, then back up and head down the alley. They're not going to be able to hurt you, okay?"

It was a risk. Risky to send an armored vehicle into such a restricted space. But only if the alley had been mined, and she doubted that. Everybody knew that alleys were places where U.S. forces didn't drive. The AKs wouldn't touch the Hercules. An RPG might, but fuck it, if they had RPGs, they would've shot them already. By then the big vehicle had already crossed the open street, its treads clanking, chewing up the asphalt, Eggleston dropping the boom that he'd been using to lift the T-walls on the fly. "Do it soft," she said. "Do it soft or you'll take the building down." And Eggleston slowed and put the nose of the Hercules against the louvered steel door and she heard the diesel engine gun and the frame of the whole vehicle began to shake and the anchor for the metal screen tore away from the concrete overhead, and the whole sheet bowed, and there was an opening just big enough along one side that she put a boot up on the Hercules' fender and dove in.

It was dark inside. Glass on the ground. Shelves. A counter, the space behind it empty but in disarray, papers spilled out on the floor. Cardboard boxes of Band-Aids. Cotton balls. Q-tips. Amber glass bottles of medicine. Other supplies that she recognized by the colors of their brand, though the name itself had been transcribed into Arabic: the brown and gold of Bayer aspirin. Less stuff than you would've seen in an American store, the shelves flimsy and in places empty. The shooting had started only after Beale and Pulowski had gone off to inspect this same building. First the guy up on the roof, taking aim at her platoon—and maybe even someone firing from the empty market on the other side of the street. Then, after that had ended, a final, muffled series of shots. Something she heard without maybe even recognizing that she heard it. Probably from inside the building. What did that mean? It meant there had been people waiting for them in here. Not a random shooting. An organized attack. And the muffled shots at the end probably meant that, despite her orders, Beale had gone in.

By her judgment, the door she'd seen halfway down the alley had to be farther back in the building, past the wall behind the counter, probably into a stockroom, or an apartment in the building's back half. She was hurrying by then. Why hadn't she hurried sooner? Fowler had already been worried before she heard the shooting, as if it had been prefigured in her mind—or at least as if she'd already recognized her mistake, which was that she'd been right to be afraid and shouldn't have resisted the feeling. The only thing she'd been wrong about had been imagining that anything between her and Pulowski could be clean or hard or quick. The part of her that had imagined that it would be easy for her to cut someone off that way, send Pulowski in and forget him. Or Beale, *even if* it had been his idea. That was her flaw, to pull back, to get offended, to assume that the hurt would be coming, and so then push someone away. Claim that order called for it. Claim the rules told you that it had to be that way. There was a door at the far end of the counter, and she pressed her cheek against the floor and tried to see underneath it—nothing. The space wasn't wide enough. *You are slow. Imagine somebody dying because you took too long to get through a door. No one would know. But you'd know.* Her hands were shaking and she felt like a fool, walking into a firefight with nothing but her Beretta sidearm, and she reached out and swung the door in and then pivoted quickly around the door frame in a crouch.

The hallway was a wreck, torn and bunched-up carpet, pictures on the wall, a light at the far end. Rooms on the right and left. "Beale! Hey, it's me. You here?" It was a bad place, she could feel it. Nowhere to hide if someone took a shot at you in here, so she ducked into the first room that she passed. It was some kind of stockroom. Blood spatter and cardboard boxes in disarray, but no people—and the door out to the alley, she saw that. Beale could have come in there. She went back to the hallway, passed a staircase going up, sighted it, but nothing, and then she shouldered through a door, and she was in a bedroom and there were a man and girl sitting on the bed, shot, lifeless, small sprays of blood on the wall behind them and soaking into the bedspread, the girl's feet bare. In front of them, a woman knelt on a prayer mat, prostrate, with blood glistening in her black hair like oil. That was when she saw the kid, hiding underneath the bed. He was wearing a Spider-Man shirt and cutoff sweats and looked to be about fifteen. They stared at each other. Fowler had flattened her sidearm on the floor and she could hear her own breath coursing through her chest. The rest of the apartment—if that's what it was—was silent, uncomfortably so, as if whatever was happening to her had reached some new stage of development, which she had yet to comprehend. "I don't want to shoot you," she said. "I don't want to fucking kill you, okay?" As soon as she said it, she knew that this was not the case. The kid must have figured that out too. They waited there together in that awful space until the kid's eyes flickered briefly to the dead woman on the prayer mat and he bolted from beneath the bed and Fowler jumped on him. She shouldn't shoot. "Stop!" she was shouting. "Stop! Get down!" She shouldn't shoot him, not up close. She'd never shot anybody, and she didn't know for sure what he had done, didn't know for sure that he was guilty. There was just his face, dark-eyed, frightened—or maybe just confused. And then Waldorf's voice in her ear, full-blast, like she'd become something dangerous, *Get off, LT! Get off, LT! He didn't fucking do it*, and when he pulled her off, she heard a wet rattling as the muzzle of her Beretta chipped the kid's teeth.

Later, the Hercules had bulldozed its way far enough down the alley that dismounts from her platoon could get in the doorway. They charged down the hall, going room to room, tearing up the place. Fowler herself swept clear through to the end of the hall and out the back of the apartment to the alley there. No Beale.

Waldorf came out, sweating, looking bleak. "We got nothing in here, ma'am," he said. "I don't know. Maybe this isn't even the right place."

"It's possible," she said. "Except where the hell else would he be?"

And then, a few minutes later, Beale's voice whispered over her earpiece, cutting in and continuing on until all the other traffic died away:

"Okay, I got this turned down, the audio part, so I can't hear you. So don't call back. But this should be . . . it should be really easy. I am in—I didn't see it, okay?—but I am in a trunk, definitely, so we're talking about a passenger vehicle. Three guys, Western dress—I think. I don't really. I really only saw flip-flops, pants cuffs. A pair of blue flip-flops was what . . ."

A long, long pause followed. Everyone was listening: the platoon's other members at the intersection, Operations Sergeant Simpson and Captain Hartz, who were manning the radio back at Camp Tolerance. All of them could hear that the pathetic and utterly useless detail of the flip-flops had done something bad to Beale.

"I'm in a blue sedan.

"The car has been driving just a couple minutes. I'm lucky I got my hands free.

"They aren't pros. They were frightened and in a hurry. If they'd been pros they would've taken my radio away.

"I have a dislocated shoulder."

There was other traffic by now, of course. There were people shouting orders in other rooms, over other radio frequencies; there was Fowler out in the dust, trying to mount her team up in their Humvees. But wherever Beale lay, it was quiet. And he was whispering into his microphone, in a way that seemed meant for her ears only:

"I'm good. It's all good. You guys come and get me. Please."

The night after Faisal Amar had left, refusing Ayad's offer of shelter, a convoy arrived at Ayad's house: two pickups and a familiar blue sedan. From the roof, Ayad watched as the front truck turned violently up his driveway and extinguished its lights. And then—Ayad was already moving then, hustling breathlessly along the roofline—a bright rooster tail of sparks danced from the chain on the front gate. On the ladder, coming down, he fumbled the boxlike trapdoor lid and its corner smashed his fingers. At the same time he felt a strange warmth boring into his heel. He jerked his right knee into the air, swatting at the cuff of his jogging pants. And then, peeking between his legs, down the canted steps of the ladder, he saw his mother in her veil. If there had been a moment when he'd contemplated doing something heroic, it ended there, in this hollow glimpse, down between his thighs, of his mother so absurdly pulling herself up that ladder, concentrating on her feet so that she didn't see him, a snuffed candle in her upraised hand.

Now downstairs, past—he noticed this only in fragments—the shadowed pictures of his brother in his military dress, on leave from his brigade, on vacation, during his first promotion, the illustrious record of his family's past which he'd long ago insisted be packed away. And which his mother, in her pridefulness, had refused to move. Next in this dumb parade was the actual physical body of his brother's son, Ahmed, stationed in the front hall, every bit as proud as his grandmother, brandishing a paring knife. All of them would have to go, the living and the dead. All of them should have been sent away or hidden the minute that he'd rejected Faisal's offer, the minute he'd made the mistake of believing in his friend. For now, in a single, furious swoop, Ayad wrenched the knife from Ahmed's fingers, twisted up his shirtfront in his fist, and dragged him back, away from the front door (there were lights playing and flickering around its edges by then), and shoved him down the back passage that led to the kitchen, the women's side of the house. He ran back to the door and stashed the knife in the frail top drawer of the hall credenza, which was still crammed, as it had been since Ayad's youth, with the scraps of his father's correspondence, cards, birthday invitations, stamps. From these he grabbed a writing tablet—a gift from some fertilizer store—and first a gold pen, then, throwing that down, a Bic. And armed with these, Ayad opened the door, pen and pad in hand. He held up a single word—*Welcome*—as if it were a shield.

Hands thrust him into the back of Faisal's sedan. Cigarette butts littered the floor carpet, along with a dried-out slice of tomato, bread crumbs, the golden balls of foil from the upper wrapper of a cigarette pack, the pull tops of Mirinda cans. This must have been where his friend had been living when he wasn't on the American base. The front door jolted open, hard enough to sway the chassis, and then Faisal himself was thrust into the passenger seat hard enough that his elbows struck the parking brake. Ayad thought he'd been shot: that must have explained why, as he was humped over the glove compartment, he kept his arms curled up tight and pressed against his chest, moving only in a series of tiny upper-body jerks, as if clasping a wound. Only now, as Faisal squirmed around to face his friend, his forearms pressed together against the seat back, as if begging, did Ayad notice that his wrists were bound in clear plastic.

A fat man in a head scarf piled in behind the wheel and they drove, at Faisal's direction, through the side yard of his house, the sedan in the lead this time and the pickups—one of which had a mounted gun—trailing. Their tires had bungled through his mother's orchids and rose garden, which occupied a delicately terraced and espaliered space just to the north of the driveway. They clipped a bleached lawn chair that Ayad's mother had modified, cutting off the legs, so that she could sit in it to do her weeding. They tore through the sandy badminton court, where Ayad had scheduled many an intense match with Faisal, the sagging net looming up in their headlights, then vanishing, as if no more substantial than a cobweb. At the back gate, the fat man cut Faisal's bonds and, eyes glinting in the dash lights, Faisal reached back to tug on Ayad's sleeve. Ayad assumed he'd turned to say goodbye. What else was there to say? Both of them had failed. Neither of their strategies had worked. And yet, as they examined each other, closely and intimately, in a way that Faisal had refused to do the previous day, his friend blew a jet of air out between his lips, buffeting his overhang of rakish black hair. Then his tongue poked into one cheek, distending it, and he tilted his head as if to say: Minor setback here. No worries! And Ayad found himself staring at a familiar picture in his hand.

He recognized it immediately as the dry well. Or what he and Faisal always called the dry well, anyway, since nobody knew for sure what it had been.

Clearly Faisal had told the men about it. As they waded out into the grain, the hooded fat man who was tramping along with them, gun strapped across his back, kept flapping the picture of the well in front of Ayad's face, then gesturing to Faisal, as if asking whether his friend was lying. Ayad ignored him. He could have also ignored the search, played dumb, led them wrong. He was furious with his friend for bringing the *takfiri* to his property, for violating his neutrality. Furious with him for being stupid enough to try to work with them in the first place. On the other hand, there had been his friend's expression in the sedan: not carelessness, exactly, but defiance, cunning; his old assurance, the thing that he had taught Ayad, that in the end, together, they would always imagine a way to escape. That was the technology of the spaceship. So he did look. He stopped;

he folded up the darkness as if it were a hinged panel that he could, with his mind, like a magician, push away. And there was the daylight of his father's wheat field in midsummer. And there was Faisal in the straw hat that he'd affected back then, both of them in shorts, knees whitened from dust, walking out to play at the well. They were not supposed to. The well's depth was unknown; for years a board had been placed over it to keep fieldworkers from falling in, but it was otherwise unmarked, protected only by the maze created by the thigh-high wheat. Still Ayad had always been able to find it. He had not known how, specifically, back then. He'd done it by some navigational device that he didn't fully understand, lining things up according to the ragged pattern of the field's distant tree line, the single big palm to the west, wandering along while Faisal did imitations, bugging out his eyes or sucking his cheeks like Rambo and pretending to shoot himself in the foot. The imitations were pantomime-only. Then Ayad would drop to his knees and shift the board away, the crickets sounding around them, the grasshoppers whirring up with the sound of bicycle clackers, and the well's mouth would be revealed . . . and now, in the darkness of the wheat field, the lightless sedan following, here they were again. Could Faisal remember the same things? It was impossible to tell. Faisal's magically pliable features were all blank, shut down, as if he wore a clear plastic shell over his face. When Ayad thought that they'd reached the well, he plucked Faisal's elbow and his friend turned and gave him one last bug-eyed grimace: I am afraid, but also, I am aware, quite frightening.

The opening was found fifteen yards away. It appeared surprisingly small when Ayad was dragged to look at it, a tiny black crease, hay-strewn, barely large enough to stick a hand in, but a circle of machine gun butts enlarged it. What now? Ayad waited, flinching, for a bullet. Instead, the men gathered at the trunk of the sedan, and then returned with the white glow of headlights worming about their knees. The body drooped between the man who held its feet and the man who'd hooked his forearms through its armpits. A third handed Faisal his flashlight and obscenely tried to support the corpse's ass. They pivoted, shuffling through the dust. He saw camouflage. A blond American boot sole. And then they squatted and laid the body out, like a limp roll of sod, and tossed an M4 rifle atop the corpse's chest and freckled face. Ayad grabbed the flashlight from Faisal: a boy, perhaps, really a child, too young to have such a long, heavy body. By then, Faisal had caught him and snatched the light away. With no further ceremony, answering to commands that Ayad could not hear, the three men lifted the body and, holding it upside down, headfirst—that part, when he would be forced to review it later, seemed the most obscene—shoved him down, face first, into the earth. Pounding around the edges of the hole, they forced his shoulders through, his body armor, his belt. One man grabbed his legs around the knees and furiously leaned down, like a plunger, and then all at once the body disappeared entirely.

They all stood for a moment, watching the dust rise from the opening. Then Faisal tucked the flashlight under his arm and scribbled something on a pad, tore off the sheet, and handed it to Ayad as if presenting him with a receipt.

This is my gift, it read. *Keep it hidden and your family will be safe.*

PART TWO

CAMP TOLERANCE

6

"We gonna fuck before or after I kick your ass?" Fowler said, her thighs wrapped around Pulowski's sparrow-thin ribs, her breasts brushing the back of his stubbly head as they finished a round of *GoldenEye* while spooning in her bed. Fowler had never been a gamer back at Fort Riley, or even before. Maybe a little *Madden* at parties as an excuse to drink. But here in Iraq, with no parties in sight, it was calming to spend an hour as James Bond, swiveling and swooping her Aston Martin through a pine forest with a decisiveness that had escaped her in reality—particularly after a twelve-hour shift emplacing concrete T-walls in the northern section of their camp.

Or at least it had been calming until Pulowski had started hassling her about the Muthanna bombing, two weeks back. And had informed her, just this morning, that he was going on leave in a couple weeks. "I thought we just covered before," he said.

"No," she said. "Right now is before."

"Okay, then what was it that we just did?"

She peeked over his shoulder and down the dry pale curve of his hip, to the thatch of black hair, and his prick, which flopped out against the bedsheet.

"That was so long ago," she said, evaluating it. "I'm not sure I remember."

Pulowski tossed his controller to the floor and rolled over and tilted his head back and touched his lips to the bottom of her chin. "I seem to remember it okay."

"Maybe I'm just not big on living in the past."

"Really?" Pulowski raised his head. "Who taught you that?"

"I thought it was Professor Pulowski."

"I think you've misinterpreted the lesson," Pulowski said. "The professor, as I remember, suggested that you try not to plan everything. Go with the flow."

"You sound like Beale," she said.

"So?"

"So *somebody* needs a plan, don't they?" she said. She rolled Pulowski over and slid her tongue down his flank. "What do you think would've happened if you'd wandered by to get laid and I wasn't here?"

This was only the second time since the bombing that they'd had sex.

"I'm not really the right guy for the family values happy talk, Em," he said.

"Do I look like I'm interested in family values?" Fowler asked. She picked his prick up and held it at eye level. "I am a corrupt and morally deviant officer. Beale's vulnerable. That's what *you* told me, anyway. I don't expect him to know how to screw me properly. But you—well, I think you've got some skills there." She put him in her mouth gently, held him, then released. "I just like to plan for it."

What Pulowski didn't understand was that when he said "Go with the flow," what she heard was "Give in," which happened to be her specialty, not his. It was exactly what she was doing when, an hour later, she crunched her way up to the E Company TOC and manned her desk in the plywood-floored front room of a double-wide trailer, starting a twelve-hour shift. The Army was all about giving in. Every decision, every order, every mission, every battalion update, every PT session. If your colonel ordered you to set up concrete T-walls inside the wire, you gave in—even if you thought that the walls could have been better used outside the wire. The flip side was you belonged to a structure you could trust, with rules that you didn't have to just make up. So that the giving went both ways, and there was nothing to distinguish one person from the next, nothing too embarrassing or too horrible to share. So far, despite everything, it had pretty much worked this way. The one exception had been her relationship with Pulowski, and she wouldn't have had to keep that a secret if she'd been a guy. Then she could've told people that she fucked Pulowski. Boasted about it. She could've said, Goddamn, I banged the living hell out of this lieutenant an hour ago, which was true.

But the body parts, the chunks of bone that they had bagged and iced at the Muthanna intersection (the cleaned and emptied coolers were stacked by the back door, red chunky Gotts, which nobody touched anymore), were a different kind of secret. It was like the Muthanna bombing contained within itself everything that was both great and ugly about who she was and what she did. Her platoon had been drawn closer to each other by it, had given in and cleaned it up—even Beale. And yet she was unwilling to talk about the details with Pulowski in part because she couldn't find even a scrap of language to explain what had happened at the Muthanna intersection. Instead, the story of what might have caused it lurked above her shoulder, like a Warthog jet she knew was there but couldn't see. She had her laptop on her desk. She had her paperwork spread out in front of her, fuel requisition slips, leave requests. She had her email open and blinking, and she could see Halt and Crawford bullshitting around over by the coffee machine. But her head was filled with things that were true and could never be admitted into this space.

The TOC, where she spent the next two days, was not designed for this. It was a cross between a nest and a clubhouse: plywood-floored, with a swaybacked velour couch along one wall, a scale, a map of their AO, and a whiteboard on which Fowler wrote the instructions and maxims for the day. Her desk was front and center in the main room, which was how she liked it—and there were side offices for Captain Hartz and for Operations Sergeant Simpson, who manned the radio. But where she worked there were no doors, no partitions, and she could see everybody who came in or out—an open shop, in its way. Professional, organized, and clean: that was how she liked to keep the TOC, but not so clean that it drove her soldiers away.

Which meant she allowed herself certain personal touches. On the whiteboard, next to the maintenance duties her platoon had on tap that day, she kept a list of movies available for checkout. In her desk drawer, antibiotics she'd wrangled for bronchitis. Traffic in the TOC was always heavy. You could easily forget, just by the sheer stream of incident, anything bad that you might have to worry about. Here was Waldorf, pretending to read the *Stars and Stripes*, but really just waiting until the room was clear to ask her, sternly, if she'd heard any news about his wife, who was a supply sergeant up at Camp Speicher, near Tikrit.

Here was Corporal Halt, unlacing his boot and showing her, shyly, a blister on his girlish, rosy heel. Here was Eggleston, the Hercules operator, who had spent too much time alone down in the motor pool and wanted to talk about the Jets. Did she know that the dumbshits over in Alpha Company had recovered an actual flintlock musket during a cordon-and-search? She did not, but she speculated on the meaning of this development with Jimenez and Dykstra, who had become, over the past six months, a pair just as tightly matched as her and Pulowski. If they'd invaded Philadelphia, Dykstra believed, they would've found sawed-off shotguns, nunchuks, and throwing stars—whereas from Jimenez's point of view, among his people, all they'd want was papers.

Three straight days like that. Then five. She plowed through paper in the office, with side trips to the motor pool, where Beale, Dykstra, and Waldorf ran the show, changing oil, checking transmissions, and caring for the battalion's vehicles generally. You could get lost in it and, to a certain extent, she had. Every evening before chow, she led a run for PT. Crawford, she had discovered, spent a fair number of his off-hours *walking* around Camp Tolerance, which itself was so large and cumbersome that it had an actual bus service. He knew all the special trails and so she allowed him to set their route, which he executed with a child's innate artistic flair: long tours along the beaten outer ring, under the silver-fluttering leaves of eucalyptus trees. Afterward, she touched their sweaty backs, emphasized hydration, broke open stacks of shrink-wrapped water bottles, and handed them out to drink. No one spoke to her crossly. The nickname that Beale had saddled her with, Family Values, was more a faded watermark than a brand.

At night, she settled down in a yard chair inside her trailer, her workout clothes drying on the doorknob, a notepad in her lap, intending to write down a list of activities for the next day. But instead she dozed off and saw Beale and then Pulowski, oddly paired, on the far side of a long, dark canal, waving to her furiously. It was strange that the two of them should be joined together in agreement, but that's what the dream implied, their movements coordinated, their semaphore the same. Come to us. Wake up. Get out of there.

Opening her eyes, she had the feeling that the trailer itself, and everything around it, had a purpose, which she couldn't define but nevertheless was specific, threatening, and directed her way. It was similar to how she'd felt the last time she'd made love to Pulowski, shoving her ass up in the air, as he had stood above her—and later when she'd straddled him, her bare feet planted firmly on the floor and her hands kneading the muscles of his chest—and they were quiet except for their breathing, and they could feel the heat of the day pressing the walls of the trailer, and they could hear other soldiers walking by and talking, separated from them only by the thin skin of the aluminum, by a metal door, by a window with a construction-paper shade—and she would occasionally see a part of Pulowski's body—an elbow, foreshortened like a wrinkled peach, a foot with its toes flexing, the skin callused at the heel, his belly button, his translucent ear whorling out—and she would be aware of the body parts at the intersection, and the baggies, and the ice, and the GPS. The difference was that with Pulowski she hadn't been afraid, because his body and her body were the same, whole but penetrated, jumbled but not destroyed, one and the same. But on this night, when she woke up, she was alone, and this time, in the grainy darkness, her aluminum walls and iron-framed bed and plywood floor seemed as impersonal as a prison—hard, bare, and temporary in every way.

"Remember those shackles I lost back at Fort Riley?" Her platoon sergeant, Carl Beale—whose bad temper she generally tried to avoid while on base—stepped up beside her at the refrigerated drink case in the center of the Dining Facility and they both peered in through frosted glass. "Why'd you bust my ass for giving those away?"

"I trusted you," she said.

"Bullshit. You didn't trust me to pick my nose back then."

"True," she admitted.

"So how about now?" he said. "You trust me any better? Would you say that I have or have not become significantly less of a dick?"

She evaluated this question. The answer was that Beale *had been* much less of a dick lately. His reliable combination of bravery and stupidity was something she'd begun to, if not value, then dismiss less completely after he'd helped her save Lieutenant Weazer out at the Muthanna intersection. On the other hand, it would have been real progress if he hadn't felt the need to bring this up so quickly.

"Since when do you fish for compliments from me, Beale? Are you still upset that the guys dimed you out for playing Kid Rock when we're on convoy?" She cracked the door of her case—the line of refrigerators was a block long, running down the center of the five-thousand-seat dining facility—and grabbed a Gatorade.

"Aw, fuck, come on with that. What the hell else am I going to play?"

"I'd go more Tom Petty," Fowler said.

"He su-ucks," Beale said in a singsong voice.

"Not as much as Kid Rock. But it doesn't matter what you or I think. It matters what the guys think. You play *their* music, you aren't going to have people upset about you playing tunes when we're outside the wire. Think about that."

"Okay," Beale said. He didn't protest, which was itself a surprise. Instead, he followed her grimly, past a half acre of crowded tables, the flat-screens showing highlights of early season baseball games back in the States. "But I don't think that's the real problem here," he said. "I think the real problem is Muthanna."

She dumped her tray on the dish conveyor and pushed out through frowzy plastic strips into the blacktop of the DFAC parking lot, the blistering noon air.

"I know you saw what I saw," he said, following her. "Seacourt shouldn't have had soldiers at the intersection. That place had no defenses. At worst, we should've been setting up T-walls out there, instead of working inside the wire last couple weeks."

"I thought we were talking about music."

"And I listened to you, didn't I?" Beale said. He pointed back into the DFAC as if there would be a statue there, erected to the memorial of his listening. "Maybe our guys legitimately don't like my taste. But I'm telling you that they're unhappy about what went down at that intersection. Lots of bitching. Lots of grief. You told me that we do the right thing even when other people aren't doing it. That's the Family Values rule, okay? Okay, well, I'm telling you that they all know something isn't right."

Two days later, she left her desk at dusk. The center of Camp Tolerance was a broad, open concrete square bordered by the PX, its lifeless Stars-and-Stripes bunting, the wilted tents of a small hadji rug seller, the barber, the dry cleaner's. She veered off onto a dirt road that wound its way through truck yards, chain-link fences coiled with vine, the back entrance to the 66th Armor Regiment's motor pool, where Pulowski was waiting with a thistle blossom pinched between his teeth. Questions like the ones Beale had asked her in the DFAC were usually the kind of thing that she discussed with Pulowski. But she was still afraid to get too graphic about what had happened at the intersection—afraid somehow that she would be tainted by it. "You know what Beale asked the other day?" she said instead, glancing over her shoulder. "He wanted to know if he was 'still a dick.' "

"What'd you tell him?"

Fowler shrugged, as if the jury was still out. "Depends on the context."

"Yeah?" He dropped back half a step as two sergeants passed, then pulled her by the elbow through a gap in the fence. It was a small bower: broken fountain, a couple of crumbling benches left over from Saddam days. They kissed and then started walking up a small dirt path that led up a rutted and bushy dirt hill that housed the communications antennas for the camp. "Rough day?" he said. She nodded, took his hand. "Personally, I think if Beale was running the war, he'd start by shooting every adult male over the age of eighteen. So if he's sucking up to you, he's probably got a motive. What is it? Muthanna? He pushing to get outside the wire?"

Here it was again, the rotting stink of the intersection. She swung his hand up, sniffed, but smelled only live Pulowski. "Muthanna was a disaster waiting to happen," she said. "That position was undefended. We're moving people in and out too regularly. If you think it's a bad idea to shoot people, maybe the T-walls would've helped things."

"Don't be naïve."

"That's not naïve. It's just a fact."

They had climbed far enough up the hill that they had a view over the camp, the dingy Mylar dome of the DFAC, the main highway. They sat down on the edge of the track. Pulowski tucked his forehead against her cheek. "Facts are naïve," he said.

"So what—I just go along with Seacourt. I just let things suck."

"I would." He was still nuzzling her, touching her, playing.

"Isn't that what you always wanted? You want to be pals with Captain Happy? You want to get invited to Seacourt's house for fucking cocktails and *SportsCenter*? Then tuck your head down, suck it up, and stay quiet while they clean up their mistake."

She should have left it. When they made love, they didn't play. It felt awkward now for both of them, like they were imitating another couple. But she went along with it, slipping her leg over his, pressing her pelvis down on his lap, kissing him, then like a tease pulling back. "So when we were at Riley," she said, "it was good for me to think for myself. Good for me not to take any shit from Masterson. Pathetic that I was even marginally interested in impressing Seacourt and Hartz—"

"I think pathetic is a little strong."

"But now I'm supposed to love them up and forget about anything I saw out there at the intersection. Just be a good soldier and roll on."

Pulowski stiffened. Now she'd ruined it. "I gotta get going," he said. "McKutcheon managed to get me on an early flight."

"Are you punishing me?" she whispered in his ear. He had once told her that when he looked at the sky over Camp Tolerance, he saw ones and zeros. Signals, orders, satellite tracking, Wi-Fi, cellular communications, encrypted channels, tethered zephyrs that videoed the world beyond the wall, then beamed it back to someone's desk. The point was to receive and interpret the signals clearly, not to fool yourself into imagining that you could affect them in any way. "Because if you really want to punish me, you ought to take me back to the trailer. Wouldn't it be more interesting to do it there?"

"I said I've got a flight to catch."

"Today?" They were tangled up, Pulowski trying to slide his legs out from under her. She held him with her thighs. "You didn't tell me that. That's not even fair."

"You think it's fair to ask me to be connected to this?"

Fowler glanced down at herself, rumpled ACU blouse, scuffed and faded knees on either side of Pulowski's clean fabric. "I showered," she said.

"Aw, Jesus fucking Christ." Pulowski gave her his rat smile, upper teeth biting down on his lip. She sat beside him. The base spread out below them like an industrial resort, ranks of trailers like grubs, motor pools, junkyards. "Not you. This," he said.

"You're an Army officer, you dumbshit. You're already fucking connected to this. What are you going to do, fly to Canada?"

"Canada's in the coalition, you mope."

There was a brief flash of humor there that she liked: Pulowski still had a little game. He turned to her and straightened out the collar of her blouse, so that the backs of his fingers touched her collarbone. It was more a fussy gesture than a loving one. Patronizing. She was frightened by how in control he seemed to be, by his lack of uncertainty. "You tell me what it was really like out there at Muthanna, picking up those pieces. It's not just remains. Or that's not the right word. There were dicks, right? I mean, there were actual physical dicks out there, right?"

"Come on, Pulowski. That's wrong."

"No, no, no—it's *exactly* right. It is *exactly* accurate. You remember all the ladies running around kissing Mel Gibson's ass in that movie Hartz showed us? Waiting around to get their death letters? I am not going to do that. I want to do things differently." He paused as if he had something more to say, staring at her cockeyed, then stood up wearily and beat the dust off his pants. "I want to be alone when I come back."

"All right," she said. It was the opposite of what she meant.

"Fuck, yeah, it's all right," Pulowski said. "It's perfectly fine. It's *me*."

The RG-31 was a specialized mine-clearing vehicle that the U.S. government had purchased from the South Africans for more than half a million a pop. There was a .50-cal on the roof, with a flared steel cowling around it, but its most important features, according to Colonel Seacourt's PowerPoints, were the extra-wide, specially armored windows that would allow their soldiers to search for the culprits in the Muthanna bombing without having to dismount. To Fowler, it seemed the kind of strategy Pulowski would've liked. Separation. Distance. *I'm not going to get involved.* She was also curious how, given all those windows, this RG's grille had become embedded in the mud wall of a canal off Route Serenade, a hundred meters from the main road. "Nice," said Jimenez. "Man, shit, you'd think for the money they'd have some airbags in these things."

"Or TV," said Dykstra. "Huh? Nice fucking flat-screen."

"Fuck the TV, man," Beale said. "They need to get about four fifty-cals on this baby. Show the hadjis how we party." The RG's rear bumper was propped up on the near side of the canal and Beale dropped beneath the chassis, checked for wires, then chinned himself up into the RG's cab, pants V'd with sweat, burrs cockling his pockets.

"Shut the fuck up, Beale," Dykstra said.

"What, Jimenez gets to do jokes on airbags but I can't say anything?" Beale said. "What's that, a cultural thing?"

"It's a shut-the-fuck-up thing," Dykstra said.

"Guys," Fowler said. And that ended it.

What she paid attention to instead—what she sensed, flowing alongside her anger and her impotence, calming it, easing it, compensating for it—were the motions of her platoon as they dispersed. She kept track of them like a melody, Waldorf across the canal to the northeast, Dykstra opposite him to the northwest, Jimenez behind them to the south, Crawford guarding the road, each of them concentrating his focus on the trees and grass and bean fields that stretched out from the RG on all sides. Even Beale, who—dick or not—she kept as close to her as possible, seemed to have things under control inside the RG. It was her first recovery mission since Pulowski had left, and she was happy to be away from the maintenance bay and her desk. Her platoon moved exactly as they'd practiced, just exactly according to the basic, simple rules for foot patrols that she herself had learned back in the woods around Fort Hays State: post security in all four ordinal directions, follow your team leader, do not speak. Not as good as sex, but definitely better than *GoldenEye*, or answering emails all goddamn day. So she noticed and secretly approved—and reminded herself to congratulate—the small hiss that Waldorf made across the ditch, and the response from Dykstra, which was to slowly, as if he'd sprung a leak, deflate himself into a prone position amid the thick bushy grass, each and every considered movement a redemption for the emptiness and confusion that had shamed and overtaken all of them, Fowler included, since they'd packed Fredrickson's and Arthur's body parts up at the intersection. To be involved in a battle in the proper way.

"I got something." She could hear Beale banging around excitedly inside the RG. "There's somebody down along the canal, north," he said.

Canals were bad places for people to be, generally. Canals, especially dry ones, were where people hid to detonate IEDs. "How far away is he?"

"Hundred meters—he's coming our direction, Lieutenant."

Fowler was trying to imagine why an Iraqi would walk toward a patrol of U.S. soldiers down an empty canal, not hidden enough for an ambush, but not in the open enough to show he came in peace. It did not fit into any known categories of behavior. Or at least no category she'd been introduced to yet.

"Want me to take him?" Beale said.

"No, I want this motherfucker alive," she said.

"He's gonna be here soon," Beale said after some delay.

"Don't shoot," Fowler hissed, climbing up on the roof of the truck.

There was something wrong with the whole setup. From the height of the RG's roof, she could see the guy down in the ditch. A male, maybe twenty-five. He wore gray dress slacks with an elastic waistband and he was thin and his tan leather shoes were delicately pointed. She got her binoculars out and scanned the far side of the canal. There was a tree line about a hundred meters out. A house behind it.

"Everybody down in the canal," she said. She got the glasses up. This time she saw movement, a filtering sensation behind the trees. She called to Beale through the opening in the RG's roof, where the gunner would've stood. "Get around the bend," she said. "All of you, go down the canal and get around the bend."

Beale swung out the door and dropped, running.

The first shot was an RPG. Fowler saw a white puff of smoke, and then heard the bad sizzling sound, and she ducked her head behind the turret flanging. It hit the bank beside the RG. Dirt rained over her head. She sat up, got the binoculars out again.

"Three guys," she said. "One's in a blue shirt, two of them are in dishdashas."

A second puff of smoke. This RPG flared high and right, way off course, into the bean field behind them. She didn't even duck for that weak shit.

"All right, that's it for the fucking rockets," she said. "They're gonna run, they're gonna fucking run. Shoot 'em, Wally. You can engage. Use the canal for cover."

The RG was slowly tilting underneath her. She had to keep leaning to the right to keep the glasses straight. Beale was yelling at her but she deleted this. "I got a pickup," she shouted. "They're in a white pickup, heading south, call that in. Right now, call that in." And she dropped the glasses and the canal came back and the roof of the RG was tilting, the thing was rolling over, and she thought, *This is fucking easy*, and she ran up the sloping roof in a crouch and jumped off the back. Or it would have been easy except for the big antenna that she bumped going off, and it rotated her a little in the air and slowed her down just enough that she hit the edge of the canal, left shoulder first. "Whoof," she said, as she rolled down the dirt incline. "Okay, that fucking hurt."

"Hey, hey, hey!" She heard Beale shouting around the bend. "Don't move! Don't move. Shit! LT, you okay?"

The RG's cab had impacted only a few yards away. She tried to sit up, but her left arm was pinned, so she rolled over and pushed up with her right and said, "I'm fine, Beale. I'll be right there," and checked her sidearm, and patted herself all over, and then tested out the shoulder where she'd hit. It wasn't dislocated, and seemed at first okay. But when she lifted the arm above her waist, it felt like two electric wires had sparked and she dropped the arm quickly and said, "Oh, yeah, definitely kicking ass," and started running.

When she got around the bend in the canal, Beale, Waldorf, and Dykstra were all waiting for her there. Beale had his weapon aimed at the Iraqi's chest.

"He was a fucking decoy, is what I say," Beale said. "Supposed to get our attention while those other dudes slipped up for a shot through the trees."

"Is that right?" Fowler said.

The Iraqi made a noise that was something between a laugh

and a reaction to being hit in the balls. She raveled up the collar of his shirt tight against his neck and turned just for a moment, checking for her zip cuffs, and that was when Beale drove the butt of his M4 into the center of his face.

The Iraqi was a mess. Beale's rifle butt had squashed his nose and levered a cut above his eye, his collar lined with blood. Fowler checked his airway and his pupils, then wiped the blood on her pants. He wasn't dead. As a recovery platoon, it was their responsibility to tow the RG back to their base, so she had brought the heaviest equipment that she had, the Hercules and a flatbed, and ordered their crews to start hitching towlines to the RG and left Crawford with the Iraqi and ordered Waldorf to assemble the platoon on the far side of her Humvee. Then she walked back to the ditch.

It was quiet there. A few yards away in the weeds, she could see a scatter of brass where someone had fired on the pickup. No weapon on the Iraqi.

When she turned, Beale blocked her way.

"Ma'am," he said. "I'm asking a favor here."

She stiff-armed him. The back of her hand was rusty and dark against Beale's armor, as if she'd been playing in clay.

"I think I might know a way to fix this." Beale sidled in close and spoke in a whisper, as if they were old buddies. "Why don't we take this guy out to my friends at the patrol base? I'm just thinking maybe they'd give us a hand with the Iraqi."

"Masterson's platoon? You mean the guys who ripped off our gear and then spent three days smoking you? Those friends? Why the hell would he give us a hand?"

A long silence. Beale's face looked like a hot water bottle from an old cartoon, swollen, red, and steaming. "I fucked up, ma'am," he said finally. "Okay? You happy with that? *You* want to bail on me, that's fine. But at least give me a fucking chance, huh? I didn't *kill* this guy. I broke his nose. Take me out to Masterson. He can cover for me."

"We're in recovery," Fowler said. "That's what we do. And it's our job to recover this vehicle and take it back to camp. If we violate the rules of engagement, we report it. The minute I put you outside the rules, that's when I bail on you."

"Masterson," Beale said, "will let us off on this."

"Us? What the fuck did *we* do here, Beale?"

"Is there a problem, ma'am?" Dykstra said.

"No, we're fine," Fowler said.

"Good," Dykstra said. He grabbed Beale's wrist. "Come on, let's go over here, Sergeant. Let's be fine in a different place."

"No, no, no, man," Jimenez said. He untied a sweat-soaked bandanna from around his neck and held it out. "Don't do that. The sergeant is a sensitive guy. You gotta talk nice. Here, sir, you need a hankie?"

"Fuck you both," Beale said.

"Let's go sit down first," Dykstra said.

"I am not sitting down, Dykstra, you fucking moron. You were fucking there. She hit that guy first. So I don't want to get busted down a rank just because you and Jimenez are all up in the LT's ass—"

"Hankie time." Jimenez came forward, dandling the bandanna at arm's length, as if he were going to wipe the tears from Beale's face. "Come on, let it out, buddy."

"Shut up!" Beale said. And he swung at Jimenez, a flailing, awkward punch, impeded by his weapon, but enough to knock Jimenez sideways into Dykstra, who in turn dropped to a knee and then came up, growling and burly, and went after Beale. It was inevitable. She'd been pushing Beale further and further outside the circle, criticizing him, isolating him, doing exactly what Masterson had suggested, until it had been natural for Dykstra and Jimenez to go after him, to come to her defense. She dropped down and wedged her way into the scrum with her elbow, prying and worming her way in, then pushing them apart with her outstretched hands.

"All right," she said when she got them separated. The wires had touched again, but she kept her bad arm up anyway. "All right? Gonna be okay?"

"I'm good," Dykstra said, wiping dust away.

The pain from her shoulder was a furious force moving inside Fowler's head, like a wheel that kept spinning faster and faster. Beale was right. The position he was in now, beaten, humiliated, isolated from the rest of the platoon, was on her as much as anybody. "You? Are good?" she said to Dykstra, getting very close to his face. "Well, I'm not good. The detainee is my responsibility. That's on me. So if you and Jimenez want to fuck with somebody, fuck with me. Is that clear? As for you, Beale, no matter how much of a shithead you are, you still ought to be smart enough to know I wouldn't send you down for this. So . . . so—" She scanned their faces, trying to figure out what to say next, something to replace the silence that had overtaken her at Muthanna. "So we're all fucked, okay? Beale"—she grabbed the sergeant by his body armor and dragged him into the group—"is fucked because nobody likes him. Dykstra is fucked because he's forty pounds overweight. Jimenez is fucked with his hankie. Fredrickson and Arthur are more fucked than anybody. But I'll promise you one thing, okay? It's not going to feel any better if we start fucking each other, too. In fact, the only thing that might make it feel slightly better is actually doing our job *right* despite getting fucked. Okay?"

It was a bad speech, she could see that, but maybe its badness helped; she could see Jimenez cover a smile with his bandanna. "Are we clear?" she said.

"Yes, ma'am," Jimenez said. "We all equal in the fuck."

She crossed the field. The detainee was conscious, cuffed, and moaning a little bit. He had thick black unwashed hair and a long, delicate nose, and a mole high up on his cheekbone, like a beauty mark. "He have any papers?" Crawford handed her a heavily worn wallet. She opened it and thumbed through the cards in the plastic sheaths—an identity card. Other printed cards on stock paper. All in Arabic. In his jacket pocket, a folded piece of paper with a pencil drawing of a *U* in the center, nothing else there . . . "So this wouldn't give me any information on why you were out there during an attack on my men?"

The man averted his gaze. "This is stupid," he said.

"Okay, that's progress," Fowler said. Then, tucked inside an interior flap of the wallet, a plastic military ID card—Faisal Amar was the man's name—a worker number, and an interpreter pass signed by Bert Masterson of Delta Company.

"Jesus Christ, Beale," she said. "Why not get lucky, for a change?"

Beale's and Pulowski's voices argued inside her head as she sat at her desk, staring numbly at the sworn statement form, on which she was supposed to describe what had happened during the attack on the RG, the commands she'd given, the order of events. What were the choices? It was one thing to tell her platoon that the detainee was her responsibility, it was another to write it down in a sworn statement whose facts could be checked. The right thing was to tell the truth. The other right thing was to accept responsibility. But when she tried to put the two together, the report seemed more doormat than brave: *As Dogpound*

Platoon leader, the injury of the detained Iraqi was my responsibility. I did not have zip cuffs with me and thus was unable to secure the detainee quickly enough in the immediate aftermath of the attack. If I had done this properly, Sergeant Beale would never have struck the Iraqi . . . She stopped there, unable to close the sentence. Maybe the mistake was sitting around whining to herself about wrong and right at all. Whining never helped—it made as much sense as telling someone that you were so concerned about their safety that you couldn't be around them anymore. And then disappearing to fucking Tennessee.

And yet, if there was one thing that Pulowski *had* taught her, it was how to formulate a thesis and then back it up objectively. That, and facts were naïve.

She erased the last line and wrote, *I caused the injuries to the Iraqi's head and face.* And then she pulled out a second piece of paper and added this:

On April 9, 20–, two specialists from the 1st Battalion, 27th Infantry's Delta Company were killed by a truck bomb at the intersection outside Muthanna, she wrote. *At the subsequent battalion briefing, Lieutenant Colonel Seacourt said that two soldiers had died in the explosion, in large part because they had been occupying an unreinforced checkpoint. And yet, I had been installing concrete T-walls* inside *Camp Tolerance for three months prior to the bombing at the Muthanna intersection. I had also frequently volunteered to use my platoon's equipment to haul a load of T-walls out to the entrance of Muthanna and build a reinforced checkpoint. Colonel Seacourt did not follow through on the idea. Instead, he insisted that the Muthanna intersection was "the one place in Iraq that I'd take my grandmother."*

She filed the report by slipping it into the wire basket that had been nailed to the trailer wall beside Hartz's office, openly in view of her desk. Its disappearance that afternoon was followed by a period of silence that her imagination feverishly tried to make permanent, imagining that her comments on the T-walls might not even be noticed. They had no business being in the report anyway, since the intersection bombing happened four weeks in the past. That evening Captain Hartz informed her—emphasizing that this was only a "bureaucratic requirement"—that she was now officially "relieved of duty" pending an investigation into her conduct. In addition, she was under orders to avoid contact with her platoon, and so, for the next two days, she lived primarily in the fifty yards between her trailer and the head. It was awful. Pulowski's absence, his lack of emails, and her own stubborn refusal to ask for a response had been bad enough when she was at work. Now Crawford silently delivered her meals in Styrofoam boxes from the DFAC, their tops dusty from his quarter-mile walk along the ravines and footbridges that stood in for sidewalks along their battalion's main street. She no longer attended morning briefings at the battalion headquarters, but she was cc'd on the email that Colonel Seacourt sent to every member of Echo Company, assuring them that "every soldier in the division" was currently engaged in looking for bombers at the intersection, and that he would know more when the official investigation of the incident was complete. Finally, on the morning of her third day of isolation, Captain Hartz knocked on her trailer and invited her for a ride in his Humvee.

"You understand that they're going to come after you, don't you?" Hartz said as they left the parking area, Hartz and his driver in front, Fowler in back.

She glanced up. Hartz was a fireplug of a man, five foot four, a solid 175. Despite his florid sunburned face and rocklike gut, his small tapered hands were curiously delicate, uniformly clean: the kind of guy you might imagine coaching women's basketball at Junction City High, decent, fair, soft-spoken, and, as Pulowski had phrased it, "aggressively naïve." "What difference does it make?" she asked. "Fredrickson and Arthur are gone anyway."

"No, no, no. We are *finding* whoever did this. You've got to believe that, if there's any chance of it coming true at all. Now take my hand and we'll say it together."

"I don't pray," Fowler said. She'd respected, and even courted, Hartz's advice back at Fort Riley, his nostrums about teams and taking it one day at a time being a comfortable kind of truth. Familiar. Not exactly groundbreaking. But spoken in good faith. Today it all seemed aggressively naïve.

"Look, I'm just saying—what's wrong with a positive thought?"

"Positive thought? What positives are there? You saw my statement. It's the truth. I screwed up. I should've had the zip cuffs on me. I should've checked the detainee's ID immediately. I should've been more skeptical of the intel. If I'm going to get my ass in a sling for fucking up an Iraqi, the least I can do—"

"Zip," Captain Hartz said, holding a finger to his lips.

"—is do something to improve the situation," Fowler said.

"I said stop." Hartz lunged over the backseat to grab her shoulder, but the shoulder strap of his seat belt caught the bridge of his nose, giving him the appearance of a man mysteriously caught and held motionless by a finish-line tape. "You've got to stop overthinking," he said as he finally, in anger, unclipped the seat belt and threw it to the side. "The way you're acting, this worrying about stuff, this questioning everything—let me ask you this, do you like it?"

"I don't have questions," Fowler said. "I have bad facts."

"If *I* was in a situation where I had my own and *other people's* careers at stake, I might start asking some questions," Hartz said.

"Oh, yeah? Like what?"

"Like, 'Should I piss and moan about where colonels put their T-walls? Which I *can't* control. Or—' "

"Now we're getting somewhere."

"What's that supposed to mean?"

"Well, jeez, I don't know, sir. I thought we were talking about what happened to that Iraqi out by the RG. I thought we were talking about me."

"The second thing I'd do is ask myself, 'How do I help my team?' All of us, every single soldier on this entire base, practically, is sick to death about what happened at the intersection. We're *all* trying to fix it, and I think you need to consider whether this report of yours is contributing to that. Have you done that?" Fowler shook her head. Mostly she felt a strange, rising excitement at the thought of having sunk so low that she didn't have to care about these kinds of things.

"Oh, come on, Sherman," she said, trying out this new Pulowski-freedom by using her superior officer's first name. "Even if they clear me on this—which would be a total crock, but possible, I admit—there's no way I'm getting my platoon back."

For the first time, Hartz's glance flickered back at her and, in his reflection in the windshield, she saw him give a covert grin. "I don't think your hand is as bad as all that."

"We're playing poker now?"

"My advice to you," Hartz said, "is that you listen when the colonel talks to you and if he makes you an offer, you take it. He won't offer again."

She was feeling fairly cocky the next day as a guard escorted her out back of headquarters to the latticed gazebo that had been constructed as a congratulatory present for Colonel Seacourt's assumption of command. If there was one thing she'd learned from Pulowski, it was the power you could gain by *not* caring. By stepping away. She also figured the colonel—who was waiting for her in the gazebo's dappled shade—had more to care about than she did. He was about five foot nine, wore a Swatch, a lieutenant colonel's brass star, and a gold wedding band, and to go along with his extremely normal stature he had an extremely normal, clean-shaven face with a proportionate nose that maintained a permanent pink sunburn but never tanned. He pulled out a metal office chair and patted its back, inviting Fowler to be seated, as if she were somebody's wife at a battalion party. False confidence was how she read that. Nerves. She stayed in place. "This is Major Henry Harmon," he said, introducing a lanky, dark-haired major on the opposite side of a folding table, a manila folder in his hand. "Henry and I were lieutenants together back in Saudi," Seacourt said. "How long ago was that?"

"Forward Operating Base Bastogne," said the major. His voice carried a faint southern melody that set her teeth on edge. "In the good ol' days of 1991."

"Hard to imagine what we were like back then," Colonel Seacourt said. He'd attended West Point and had a graduate degree in political science from Florida State, but in presentation he emphasized his midwestern roots, his lack of adornment, his faith. Having abandoned his attempt at chivalry, he'd circled back around to his seat. "A young lieutenant, first time in combat, terrified of making a mistake—and then sick to death when, as is inevitably going to happen, things don't go according to plan. These are . . . well, they're the mental habits of a responsible officer, wouldn't you say, Henry?"

"If they weren't, we'd have to court-martial half the generals in the Army," Major Harmon said. "Not to mention pissant majors like me."

"Does that apply to lieutenants, sir?" Fowler said.

The two friends exchanged glances again, a very brief communication in which, if Fowler had to interpret it, the colonel asked, How much should I tell her? And the major had raised his eyebrows to say, Whatever you think is right.

Maybe Pulowski was wrong. She felt something at least mildly human there.

"I brought Henry in to investigate your report, because I think the major is capable of lending a friendly ear," Seacourt said. "How do I know this? Because, back in Saudi, I was once involved in an incident that was as ugly as yours. I felt as bad about it as I possibly could—worse, actually. And I believed that the only honest thing that I could do as an officer and a man . . . or woman, in your case"—the transition here was abrupt and professional, no hint of embarrassment—"would be to write a report like this one you've written, in which I basically forced the Army to court-martial me."

"If I could ask, sir," Fowler said. "How'd the major help with that?"

"He convinced me that self-destruction is not necessarily an honorable choice," Seacourt said. "Particularly when it isn't warranted by the facts."

"So you're saying I shouldn't take responsibility for the Iraqi, sir?"

She asked this question by design, to shock—borrowing one of Pulowski's techniques. To her surprise, Seacourt reacted to this in stride. "Not at all. Did I say that, Henry? No, obviously, your testimony has to be the truth as you see it. It's only that Henry here—because he's an old friend—has alerted me to certain discrepancies that are indicative, to him, of an officer who is—how did you put it, Henry?"

"*In extremis*," the major said, shrugging and yawning, as if he were discussing a subject as innocuous as a baseball game. "Possibly experiencing battle fatigue."

"I'm not sick, sir," Fowler said.

"I'm not *saying* you are," Colonel Seacourt said. He spoke with the same offhanded and ingratiating tone that he'd used when she'd first entered, but the words contained a bit more heat. "I'm saying you're in a difficult situation. You've got a soldier who has done something wrong. You're interested in protecting him. You feel responsible for him. But I am trying to tell you that, in certain situations, there are individuals that you can't save. You've got to let them go, or you'll go with them."

For the first time, Fowler felt her confidence waver. The one thing she hadn't expected was for Seacourt to speak as if he was on her side.

"Let me just fold in a couple of questions here," said the major, like the host of a dinner party gently guiding the conversation back on track. He slid Fowler's testimony across the table. "*Before* you allegedly injured the Iraqi, did Sergeant Beale follow basic tactics, techniques, and procedures established for detaining a civilian in the field?"

"In my opinion, sir, Sergeant Beale acted with extreme bravery and courage in leading my men out of a fire zone, in an attempt to—"

"Did you *see* him do all of this?"

"As the report indicates, I saw movement in the tree line on the far side of the canal. So I remained at the RG in an attempt to identify the unfriendlies."

"Who shot at you."

"Sort of," she said.

"So your testimony is that you identified their vehicle, moved your soldiers to safety, drew enemy fire, got an ID on the shooter's vehicle, radioed this information in—all of this entirely clear-headed. All good things. And once your men were safe and you'd handled every single threat, you proceeded down the canal, found an Iraqi who'd been properly detained by your sergeant, and *then* you decided to ruin your career?"

"Yes."

"Yes, you *did* hit the Iraqi, or yes, you did not?"

Fowler sat back in her chair, feeling almost mesmerized. It was a good story. Had she really done all that? It was exactly the story she would've liked to tell about herself. Why couldn't she just accept it and let it be?

"So wait, I just want to be clear," she said. "'Cause this means a lot to me, sir. Your concern, trying to keep me out of trouble. I only have to change the stuff I wrote about Beale and *not* the intersection?" She was surprised by the bitterness beneath these words—she would never have allowed herself to speak this way in front of her platoon. But here, with Seacourt, the bitterness felt good. "It really would be easier if I could just take this stuff about this being *my* fault out. And nail Beale for the whole thing."

Harmon leaned in. "What the colonel means"—he glanced over at Seacourt for affirmation, and the colonel, making a grand effort, managed to nod, though without making eye contact—"is that he's willing to look the other way when it comes to your faults, especially in the realm of personal relationships. But if you force me to do a full investigation here, every line you've ever crossed, every mistake you've made—it all comes out. It's bad news for everybody. Especially for people you care about."

Aggressively naïve, her ass. Too bad for them Pulowski had dumped her two weeks back. "So you *do* want me to change the part about the T-walls," Fowler said.

"I want you to write a report that's accurate and fair."

This must have been the offer Hartz had talked about. Time to cut a deal. "Well, that's not the same thing anymore, is it?"

she said, turning to Seacourt, holding his gaze steadily. "So if you want *that*, then I want something back."

"I'm going to grab a Coke," Major Harmon said.

"No, no, you can stay," Fowler said. "We're not doing anything criminal. Or if we are, we should do it as a team." Harmon gave a wilted grin. Seacourt's expression was distant, not exactly defeated, but something more equivocal, as if reluctantly impressed.

"We can't just ignore what Beale did," Seacourt said. "The Iraqi's injury is in the system now. If you'd wanted that, you shouldn't have written a report in the first place."

"Then no investigation. Reprimand only. Beale stays in the field."

"No," Seacourt said. "Court-martial. Honorable discharge."

She sat down in the chair that Seacourt had offered her. Crossed her legs.

"Fine," Seacourt said, tossing Beale's file aside. "I'll give him office hours. A week in detention. He drops rank, E-6 to E-5. But you'll go on the record. You'll rewrite your report, and you'll be grateful to have walked away."

She turned back to the major. "If Sergeant Beale did hit that Iraqi, he would have been disobeying my order, my direct order. Intentionally."

The first email that Pulowski managed to send her in four weeks was an invitation to a meeting with his CO, Major McKutcheon, at the 16th Engineer Brigade in Camp Victory. *Sorry I've been out of touch*, he wrote. *But I do think you'll be interested in this.* You're an idiot, she told herself, deleting it. Then later, *Well, in that case, showing up won't change anything*. And so in the end she went. Camp Victory was a forty-five-minute drive, clear across

Camp Tolerance, through the stop-and-start madness of fuel and water convoys, and around so many orange-coned roadwork areas she felt as if she'd been teleported back to Kansas in summer when the potholes on I-70 got patched. A stone bridge marked the entrance, its carved balustrade arching over a cattailed canal that divided the fighting soldiers and the brass. She and Pulowski had driven over it the first week that they'd arrived in-country, gazing out like tourists at what Pulowski had termed McSheikh palaces strung gaudily along a vast lagoon. They'd asked a passing private to snap a picture of them outside the white walls of the Al-Faw Palace, which housed the entire brains of the Multi-National Force–Iraq. For Pulowski the background had been ironic—"Say WMD!" he'd prompted, as the private framed the shot—but the foreground had been something else, something personal, the two of them together, arm in arm, with nobody they knew watching. She'd had the same feeling at the party he'd organized for her at the Cracker Barrel outside Fort Riley, when she'd glanced down from the national broadcast of a K-State basketball game and caught him staring at her, concentrating. Not *I agree* (though she didn't necessarily disagree) so much as *I am with you*, and she'd agreed to see him now because of that. The offices for the 16th Engineer Brigade were salmon-colored, the plain concrete walls roughed up with adobe-style spackle, in which the imprints of some lucky Iraqi contractor's blades could still be seen. On the other side of the flimsy varnished door with its fake brass handle, she found Pulowski waiting on a bench. As she entered, she caught an unguarded glimpse of him, nervous and pale as a fifth-grader, a spiral notebook jogging compulsively on his knee. "You're here!" he said, leaping up, his voice lifting in awkwardly high-pitched relief.

"I'm only five minutes late," she said, pointing to her

watch. "Oh-nine-hundred, right? It's not like I'm on vacation, Lieutenant." Before his leave, she'd always liked calling Pulowski "Lieutenant" formally, out in public, as if they were barely acquainted, when of course they each knew every hair on the other's body. This "Lieutenant," though, was just the formal one, and saying it that way made her knees feel weak. "The traffic sucked," she added, to soften things.

"No shit," he said. "McKutcheon was telling me that the guys who actually laid out this whole camp—and I shit you not—like two-thirds of them were from Kansas. No sidewalks *anyplace.* Can you believe that?"

"No," Fowler said.

"McKutcheon's got another meeting upstairs. So I was freaking out because *this* guy"—he nodded to a bulky sergeant at a metal desk—"wouldn't let me call up to tell McKutcheon that I was here. So I didn't want to leave in case you actually showed up, but then I started to worry that McKutcheon was gonna think I'd bailed—"

"Yeah, well, I found you," Fowler said. Pulowski's chatter, its faint edge of panic, both irritated her and felt familiar in its irritation. An abrasion she had missed.

They were standing there in the entryway of the 16th Engineer Brigade. Past the sergeant, there were rows of desks, maps pinned to the wall, glowing computer screens, and the little wooden stands that you could buy at the PX, where you could hang your body armor once you got to the office, as if it were Mr. Rogers's sweater. This was the moment when, if she was going to stand on ceremony, she was going to need to do it. She could've asked him what the hell he was thinking even asking her here, what the hell he had been doing when she'd needed him during the past four weeks. On the other hand, that would've meant she had to be prepared to turn around and walk out that door permanently and accept never being irritated by a Pulowski story ever again.

"You know I'm not real comfortable in places like this," she said.

"Well, thank fucking God for that," Pulowski said. "Because if you were, I would have had to ask somebody else."

They climbed three flights of concrete stairs and pushed out through a red-painted fire-exit door onto a flat, industrial rooftop. There were five or six white shipping containers on the rooftop, shaded by blue tarps, their sides marked with the red logo PODS. Major McKutcheon waved to them from the doorway of the third, bareheaded, with a sunburned, thinning scalp, each follicle strangely stout, so that his skull appeared to be sprouting mechanical pencil leads. He grabbed Fowler's hand with his stubby, baby-soft fingers (Pulowski was a few steps back, out in the heat) and said, "My God, Lieutenant, I am so appreciative of you being able to come here, in the middle of—well, I mean, look at us—you have my—I am so sorry about—"

"Sorry for what, sir?" Fowler asked, before he could mention anything about Pulowski. It was the last thing she needed, the idea that their separation had been broadcast out over the network, so remarkable as to find its way here.

"Yeah, sorry for what?" This voice, to her dismay, belonged to Beale. They'd steered clear of each other ever since, in Beale's view, Fowler had sold him out to Seacourt and gotten him demoted. Or saved his ass, in hers. But there he was on a rolling chair beside a wooden shelf that ringed the inside of the pod, staring up at a television bolted to the ceiling. "That's one thing we don't do around here is apologize."

Turning, she gave Pulowski the stink-eye. He reacted like a

Broadway singer, eyes bugged, hands flapping as if he'd thought that inviting Beale would be a good thing. Which, four weeks ago, would've been the case.

"Why would I apologize?" McKutcheon said. "I have no idea. Maybe I just figure we'll screw something up here eventually."

"Like Frenchy here?" Beale asked, staring at the TV. On it, Lance Armstrong pedaled through a mountain meadow in France, his shadow racing out in front of him.

"He's an American," McKutcheon said.

"Really?" Beale said, squinting. "Well, there's your answer. I'd damn sure apologize if I got caught riding around France in a yellow shirt."

"I don't think he intends to get caught," the major continued smoothly. "Speaking of which, I understand you've been having some trouble with the colonel."

"Who told you that?" Fowler asked warily.

"*My* understanding," Beale said, "is that the lieutenant and the colonel have a hell of a good relationship when it comes to covering each other's ass."

"Did I *say* that this has anything to do with covering the colonel's ass?" asked McKutcheon, who was either entirely oblivious to the tension or experienced enough to ignore it. He picked up a stack of xeroxes and waved them in the air. "As the chief information officer for the First Battalion, Twenty-seventh Infantry, I would neither confirm nor deny such a thing."

The *A'am al-Bina'a* newsletter, which McKutcheon handed out, was a battalion publication, printed in Arabic and English, publicizing the improvements that Colonel Seacourt had brought to their AO. Fowler was relieved for the break. They were on the verge of what felt to her like almost total anarchy. The three of them—Beale, herself, and Pulowski—all at odds, all resentful, all bitter. The only person who knew why they all felt that way was her. As for the newsletter, it described exactly the kind of reconstruction work that Colonel Seacourt had promised the battalion would do when Fowler's platoon had been training at Fort Riley: COALITION REBUILDS SALMAN PAK ELEMENTARY, WATER PLANT REPAIRS PLANNED FOR MUSAYYIB, BAGHDAD IS BEAUTIFUL PROGRAM A SUCCESS. Beale laughed, a stringy, surprisingly cynical yip. "Jesus Christ," he said. "Who writes this? Captain Kangaroo?"

"The question is, is this better than what you've been doing?" Pulowski asked. He'd hunched into the crate by now, leaning in the doorway, lanky and poorly shaved.

This was dangerous territory around Pulowski, the closest they'd come to the subject they'd argued about before he left. "Look, I'm for rebuilding some kid's school," she said. "I just don't see what that has to do with me and Beale."

"The main problem with the Salman Pak school," McKutcheon said, "is that it has since been blown to smithereens."

"All right, then, what about the Musayyib Water Treatment Plant?"

"Also blown up," Pulowski said. Then in the scalloped profile of his face, lit by the slate blue of the Mac screen, she saw a twinge of uncertainty, as if he'd answered too quickly. "Wasn't it?" he said to McKutcheon.

"Read that one, Lieutenant," McKutcheon said to her, dropping his earlier politeness. There was a bit of the geek tyrant in his demand, generous to sycophants, but vain as Napoleon with his equals or better, Fowler would've bet. Women especially.

She could also tell by McKutcheon's tone how this was going to go. Disaster following disaster. Not one word accurate on its face. What surprised her was that Pulowski and McKutcheon still saw her as the kind of officer who would be shocked that Colonel Seacourt would put his name on this kind of transparent crap. "'The Musayyib Water Treatment Plant in Babil Province is currently pumping water directly from the Euphrates River into the city's drinking water system with little or no filtration,'" she read aloud. "'This type of treatment was insufficient for fully treating raw river water.'"

"Ya think?" Pulowski said. There was a forced pleasure in his voice.

"'The coalition recognizes that operations and maintenance of public infrastructure is one of Iraq's biggest challenges,'" Fowler continued.

"Translation," McKutcheon said, still sounding like Thurston Howell III. "The last two foremen on this project had their heads cut off and their bodies dumped into the main . . . thingy, whatever it is. The place where the water would be going. Reservoir?"

Pulowski sat on the floor with his legs stretched out in front of him, looking about as cynical and blank as McKutcheon. Except for the brief burst of nerves that she'd seen flash across his face when she'd first shown up for their meeting, she hadn't been able to get a read on his intentions. Was he trying to humiliate her? Or did she just feel that way? "I don't know about you guys," she said, "but this sure cheers me up."

"I wanted you to know the risks," Pulowski said.

Beale made a fart sound. Which Fowler appreciated, mightily.

"The risks of what?" she asked.

"The cameras I've been working on are designed to prevent stuff like this. Give us a chance to monitor sensitive areas and projects outside the wire," Pulowski said. "The colonel wants them deployed ASAP. I'm asking you for an escort. But I wanted to make sure you had good reasons to say no if you felt that way."

A tapas restaurant had opened in the small cluster of Iraqi-owned shops known as Hadji Town that had been established in a eucalyptus grove outside the airport. Fowler found Pulowski at a table near the door. He'd framed the dinner as "official business" to discuss the camera mission. By itself that shouldn't have been too threatening, since "official business" was the thing that she'd improved the most on since he'd left. A crash course starting with Beale's rifle-butt incident, ending with Seacourt's final exam. As far as she could tell, she'd passed. Hadn't been overly idealistic, hadn't been naïve, had gotten the best deal she could from Seacourt, hadn't folded or gone negative. Had remained detached—all strategies that she'd learned *from* Pulowski. A learning curve that, as she lowered herself cross-legged on a pillow, tucking her unwashed socks protectively beneath her thighs, she felt pleasantly ready to diagram.

It was a long curve. And Pulowski was the only person who'd appreciate it.

"Sorry McKutcheon's being pissy," Pulowski said, after they'd stared at their menus for a while. "His wife's filing for divorce."

"Your CO?" she said. "How the hell did he get married in the first place?"

"Apparently by mistake," Pulowski said. "On the other hand, a friendly legal divorce is a hell of a lot more civilized than fucking people over behind their back. Which I didn't think was *your* style, but hey."

It was the first time that she'd ever been on the receiving end of Pulowski's contempt and she felt its directness like a sting, as if she'd been elbowed in the nose. She picked up her water glass in an attempt to cover her emotion, but she tipped it too far back, the water pouring out in a glob and wetting her shirt and chin. She wiped it off with her hand, before remembering that she should've used her napkin.

"I don't do a lot of fucking *over*," she said. "Up, definitely. Or maybe even in a cluster. But over isn't really me."

"Yeah? So who filed the complaint about the colonel forgetting to put the T-walls up at the Muthanna intersection?"

"I don't know," she said.

"That's funny, because the Muthanna intersection is the *first place* I'm setting up these cameras. Right where the bombing was. And McKutcheon says the reason I drew this assignment is that somebody filed a report blaming Seacourt for the whole thing."

Pulowski hadn't mentioned this in McKutcheon's office. In fact, when he'd asked for her help, she'd had an old-fashioned Fowler vision that everything would work out—Pulowski was coming back to her. Her platoon would escort him outside the wire, fix what needed fixing, and life would return to normal—which meant that all the other shit had been worth it. Worth it to hold Beale to account. Worth it to fight Seacourt over the intersection. Instead, Seacourt had made good on his promise and come after him. Which meant that Pulowski was right: she had gotten him into this. "Maybe I made a mistake," she said. "I thought you were asking me to *help* you with this mission."

"You're going to help *me*?" Pulowski said. "Why do you think I got assigned this mission, huh? You got any ideas? And don't play dumb about it either. Don't give me that cow-eyed, 'Oh jeez, I didn't mean anything. I'm just trying to do the right thing, sir' bullshit, because you are fucking smarter than that—I know that for a fact."

As much as she'd disliked what Colonel Seacourt had done when she'd confronted him about the intersection, she had to admit that his refusal to even deny her charges had been a tactical success. A strategy that Pulowski didn't have. "I'm sorry you drew the mission, Dix, since it's clearly pissing you off something fierce. But that doesn't mean I know why it happened."

“Nothing at all you might want to share?”

“We almost got the shit blown out of us doing the recovery on an RG,” she said. “Sweet little ambush—so that was amusing.”

She could see, despite Pulowski’s attempt to answer this nonchalantly, that this admission had affected him more than he was willing to let on. But he also didn’t ask for details. “I’m sorry to hear that,” he admitted, “but I don’t think that’s the whole story.”

“Well, you weren’t here, were you?” she said. “And I don’t remember getting any emails from you asking what the story was.”

“Yeah, well, it’s about time.” The voice came from over her shoulder and, while Pulowski glanced up in surprise, Fowler did so only slowly. It was Beale.

“Aw, shit, man,” Pulowski said, throwing down his fork as if he’d lost his appetite. “Once a day is enough with this guy, don’t you think?”

She’d invited Beale as a hedge, in case Pulowski’s invitation turned out to really be *only* about official business. After she paid the bill, the three of them strolled across the leaf-strewn paving stones, past the small hadji stores hawking bootleg DVDs and T-shirts. The Morale, Welfare and Recreation Center inhabited a fanciful, marble-floored building at the end of the strip, with a fountain out in front and a green neon sign mounted over the door that read CLUB COBRA—the kind of place that gave her the creeps, due to the intense effort that was being made to distract its patrons from reality. But tonight, as they sat down on a trio of barstools in the back, she’d decided that intense distractions might be necessary to get Pulowski and Beale where they needed to be. If the good they’d had together was going to turn into something other than just ash.

"Beale is still my platoon sergeant," Fowler said, starting out with the easiest lie. "You may think this particular mission is stupid, but if we help, it's going to be our stupid. So before we decide anything, I'm going to need him to agree."

"Yeah, well, good luck with that," Beale said.

"Why am I not shocked?" Pulowski said.

"I don't know," Beale said. "Why am I not shocked that you'd spend the last four months piddling around with some camera system? Then, the minute you figure out that you've actually got to set these things up"—Beale made a horrified, effeminate face, touching the flat of his fingers to his open mouth—"you fucking come running straight to me. Or to your girlfriend here, which is about the most pathetic thing I've ever seen."

"You talk to Seacourt about that?" Fowler asked.

She'd worked this one out over dinner. Beale was the only person who had the motive to tell Seacourt about her relationship with Pulowski. A glance in the sergeant's direction, met with a smirking grin that wilted to a cough, told her that this was the case. So the camera mission *was* Seacourt's payback, just as Pulowski claimed.

Which meant that they had all bent each other over in some way. Beale had screwed *her* by telling Seacourt about her affair. Pulowski had screwed her by leaving. She had also screwed both of them: Beale, by turning in the detainee; and Pulowski, by filing the complaint. But she had a competitive advantage; neither Pulowski nor Beale believed she was capable of doing anything other than shooting straight. If they were going to pull together for this mission, it was the only play. "What I told you, Fowler," Pulowski said, "was not to be naïve. I told you to go along with Seacourt. Be yourself. Don't get caught up in macho bullshit when it came to Beale."

"Be myself? You want to talk about something that's naïve."

"No, naïve is this guy, okay? Naïve is anyone who tries to stand out, or do anything more than the absolute bare minimum that your job requires you to do."

Beale lightly hunched his shoulders, as if he took this as a compliment.

"That's funny that you should be so pissed at Beale," she said. "Since you're the guy who kept telling me to lay off his ass at Riley."

Pulowski swallowed uncomfortably, flattening his lips. Beale tore open a packet of sugar—the club served only tea and coffee—and began shyly grinding the white powder into the tabletop with his huge thumb. "Come on," she said. "You guys don't remember that party you threw down at the Cracker Barrel? What the hell was that? You never worked together? You never cared for each other? And now we're going to sit here and argue about a mission that we all know needs to take place?"

"You tell me what happened, then," Pulowski said. "You tell me why I drew this assignment. Because from what I hear, the reason I'm fucking sitting here is Beale lost his shit and smacked some Iraqi, and you went after Seacourt to cover for his ass."

"It wasn't him," she said.

"What are you talking about?" Pulowski said.

"I'm saying it wasn't Beale," she said. "Beale took the rap for it, sure. But he didn't do it. He was just looking out for the team."

It was her first truly *professional* lie. As soon as she said it, Beale tucked his head and ran a palm over his bristly orange crown of crew cut, which looked silky in the stage lights. No more mention of her relationship with Pulowski. No more complaints. He'd stick with her after that. "It's true," Beale said.

"Oh, fuck. Who did it, then?" Pulowski asked.

"I did," she said. She could feel her lie working, even better than Colonel Seacourt's had. It had everything going for it.

Beale wanted his innocence. Pulowski wanted her to take the mission. "I busted the guy up. If you want some paranoid reason that Seacourt's coming after you—which I don't think there is—it's for that."

"You happy now, Pulowski?" Beale said. "Because if you're not, *I'd* be happy as hell to just chuck this camera mission and walk away."

"No." Pulowski smiled weakly. He scanned Fowler's face, trying, she guessed, to find a weakness, see a break. She gave him nothing. "But it's my idea. I'm in."

She watched them carefully, fondly. She'd been wrong about the dream she'd had of Pulowski and Beale standing along a canal and flapping their arms. They hadn't been calling her closer; they'd been waving her away. "So," she said, "are you guys going to sit there and flirt with each other all night? Or can we shake?"

PART THREE

MUTHANNA

7

There was no traffic. Beale balled the convoy in at sixty miles an hour and peeled off the highway and cruised straight across the open dirt shoulder to the Muthanna intersection, where the traffic control point had once been. The convoy stopped facing the exploded, smoking front of the nearby building that had been the home to the thirty soldiers billeted there. It was as if, staring at the toy snow globe of a disaster, they'd been sucked inside its distorting glass. Bits and pieces of vehicles decorated this area, axles, tires, hoods; the rattletrap, clanking flagpole that had been mounted in the center of the checkpoint (topped, on her prior visit, by American and Iraqi flags) had fallen and lay like the arm of a sundial across the turrets of several Humvees. Fowler dismounted. Her second step caused a windshield wiper to lever from a yellow-green puddle of antifreeze. Larger hunks of metal were strewn across what had once been pavement, their wiring still cooking off. Tires collapsed and boiled in upon themselves and the bombed soldiers, some in nothing more than boxers, shoeless, jostled and sprinted around the open street with aimless and stunned expressions, emptied fire extinguishers in their hands. The report said that a truck bomb had detonated at the Muthanna intersection, but a different report—*This is what it looks like to be losing*—was what ran through her head.

She pushed through the crowd until she found herself at the edge of what must have been the blast crater itself. An ossuary down there, soft white smoke, made worse by the fact that the checkpoint hadn't been fortified—no T-walls, no machine gun towers, not enough personnel. Nobody had wanted to station troops there except Colonel Seacourt, who'd volunteered. Short on manpower, he'd tapped a battery of artillerymen who'd been stationed in Dusseldorf sampling the local beer gardens, procured them a handful of Humvees, and ordered a platoon from Masterson's Delta Company to show them the ropes. Those soldiers, Masterson's soldiers, were what worried Fowler as she began to climb the pile of rebar and concrete where the front of the barracks once had been. She did not want to show her platoon another dead soldier from their own battalion, did not want to demoralize them any more than necessary. And so when an unfamiliar sergeant flagged her down on top of the pile and said, "I think one of your guys is trapped," and pointed to a long, flattened slab of concrete, the first reaction she felt was despair.

"Is he alive?" she asked.

"Hell, I don't know," the sergeant said. "Peters, you hear anything?"

The soldier he'd called Peters was lying flat down in the rubble and had his arm thrust in up to the shoulder under the slab.

"I'm touching him, sir," he said. "I can feel him. He squeezed my hand. He's right down there, just right down there." He shouted down into the hole, "We got some equipment. We're coming down. We're gonna lift this baby up and you're out. You're getting out, okay?"

They had practiced and practiced this, both at Fort Riley and in the first five or so recovery missions they'd so far made outside the wire. But these situations had involved vehicles that had broken down or been hit with an IED, and thus no actual human life had been at stake. Usually by the time they arrived on scene everyone had been evacuated, the area cleared by an Explosive Ordnance Disposal Team. "Eggleston," she shouted, banging on the Hercules. "We got to go up this hill. Come on. There's a guy pinned in the rubble up top. Get the winch fired up, get the painter cable out."

Eggleston popped his head through the hatch on top of the Hercules and gazed at the pile of rubble doubtfully. "This is a flat-ground vehicle, ma'am. Even if I did get up there, there's no way that I could brace her enough to lift anything."

"Waldorf!" she shouted, turning away. She could see the rest of her platoon, some dismounted, some still in their vehicles, standing around in shock. Thinking the same thing she had thought when she came in. "Take the painter and a bunch of chains and go up the pile." There was silence, stubborn gloom, horror, probably.

"There's nobody fucking alive up there," Waldorf said.

"Where'd you go to school, Waldorf? Plano High, right?" She was unloading gear from the hatch on the side of the Hercules. "And I *know* you played ball there."

"Yes, ma'am. Middle linebacker."

"Good. Texas football. That's a real sport." She tossed him a bundle of cable. "Give your weapon to Jimenez. You're leading us up."

"Why do I got to hold his weapon?" Jimenez said.

"You volunteer to go up?"

"No."

"That's reason one. Reason two is that you're Mexican. And

reason three is that you played, what, beach volleyball? Come on, man, don't front me."

"That's discriminatory, ma'am."

"Good," she said. "Give those weapons to Crawford. You're next on the pile." She banged the side of the Hercules. "You hear that, Eggleston? Let the painter out. You got the pride of beach volleyball at San Bernardino High leading you up."

"I played soccer," Jimenez said over his shoulder.

"What, at recess?" Fowler asked. Humor. That was what she'd learned from Pulowski. Disarm them. Push the fear away. It wasn't exactly Leno, but still, Eggleston dropped down inside the hatch. She could hear the painter cable playing out. Humor and momentum. Motivate each guy individually. Don't be afraid to look like a fool. That's the other thing Pulowski would've said. Don't just tell them it's the right thing to do, tell them why. She hopped up on the fender above the Hercules' tracks and began to unshackle the boom for the main winch and nodded to Dykstra and Halt and they climbed up to raise it. She was still working on how to calm Eggleston down when Beale stormed around the back of the Hercules, weapon at the ready (for no good reason), trying to pinch his face into what she assumed was his version of tenacity and authority, but which to her looked like he had a stomachache.

"Sergeant," she shouted. "Do you fucking trust me?"

Beale glanced around as if confused, as if maybe someone else in the platoon would share his sense of how ridiculous Fowler was being.

"Just be honest," Fowler said. "I'm in a hurry."

"No, ma'am, I don't fucking trust you?"

"Why not?" From up on top of the Hercules, some ten feet above the ground, she could see why Eggleston was worried about the huge vehicle tipping. "It's because you think I'm too fucking cautious, isn't it? I don't push the envelope. I got no balls. Literally." She stood and pointed at her crotch. "No fucking balls! I'm too safety-conscious. I got all these stupid family values rules—"

"Uh," Beale said.

"Tell him." She pointed at Eggleston, who'd poked his head back up through the Hercules hatch. "Tell him I went to Pussydale High School in Vaginaville, Kansas, and I fucking don't know shit about how to take a risk."

"Why?" Beale asked.

"Because we are going to drive the Hercules up that pile and Eggleston thinks it's too dangerous and I want you to explain to Eggleston that if Family Values Fowler is in on this thing, then there's no fucking *way* it could be dangerous."

"She's got a point there, Eggy," Beale said.

Fowler walked backward up the pile, waving hand signals to Beale, who stuck his head down into the turret to talk to Eggleston. Whenever the Hercules paused or seemed to teeter, Beale shouted, "Pussydale High!" down into the hatch, and Eggleston would gun the diesel engine and the Hercules would rise farther up the pile like some undersea beast. Fowler hand-signaled Eggleston to stop right at the edge of the fallen wall, like they'd practiced when towing junked cars out of a mud pit at Fort Riley. Beale laid the steel painter cable just along the slab's edge and Fowler flattened herself beside it and peered into the darkness underneath and tried to shove the cable through, but it bent and wiggled in her hand. She scrabbled at the rubble and got her arm in underneath and wrapped the cable around her wrist and she nodded to Beale and said, "Tell Eggy to drop the blade," and Eggleston dropped the blade that descended from the front of the Hercules and braced it against the bottom edge of the slab. Fowler wriggled her shoulder in until she could feel cold stone against her cheek. "Pry it up," she said. Her team jammed pry bars under the top edge of the slab and with every little cautious hand's-breadth or so that they achieved in lift, Fowler kept edging underneath, careful, careful, careful, with Beale digging under her shoulder until she was beneath the slab entirely and she could feel the weight of it smooth against her chest and her arm was extended beneath the concrete. Something plucked her sleeve. She tried to ignore it, imagining a rat, until she felt the trapped soldier's fingers silently circle the soft skin of her wrist. Her head was turned in the wrong direction, though, so that instead of being able to see him, she was looking back at Beale's sweating face.

"Aw, fuck-all, Jesus Christ, what were we thinking?" Beale was saying. "Get the hell out of there, ma'am. Even if we get this cable through, we're at the wrong angle to lift this thing." He was unhappy about the uphill slant of the Hercules.

"Tell him how we can't do this," she said to Beale.

"What the fuck you talking about? I'm telling *you*."

She couldn't move anything else so she tried to roll her eyes to indicate the fingers she felt around her wrist, in the dark. "Tell this guy we're never getting him out," she said. "Tell him what a lame-ass job we're going to do, you and me."

Beale had his hands cupped around his eyes in order to see into the shadow beneath the slab, so his dawning comprehension played out entirely in the tiny expansion of his pupils, the slackening of muscles about his eyes. "We got this!" he shouted abruptly into Fowler's face. "You're going to be drinking iced tea in about two seconds, buddy. We're moving this rock ASAP."

Her entire platoon had climbed the pile by then and they

pried and strained at the top edge of the slab and she pushed the painter cable as far as she could into the darkness until she heard Waldorf shout on the far side of the slab and there was tension on the cable and Waldorf pulled it through, the braided metal slithering between her belly and the slab. The painter cable was too thin to lift the slab itself, so Waldorf hooked it to a chain and then they had to pull that back through, the links grabbing and bumping over her ACU and tearing out her hair, which she tried to deal with quietly, gritting her teeth and letting it pull away. They got five chains beneath the slab this way and she could hear Beale and Waldorf hooking their ends onto the main cable from the Hercules' winch and Eggleston gunned the Continental diesel in the Hercules' guts and everything shook, her flashlight rattled in her pocket, the gravel beside her eyes popped like jumping beans. And then she felt the weight lift, and for the first time she was afraid, because if Eggleston dropped it now, she would be dead, but he did not drop it and the slab rose and she scrambled out from under it and the men swung it away on a tether and there was Delta Company's Lieutenant Weazer, blinking, pale with dust, and Eggleston dropped the slab to one side with a crash.

That night, Fowler climbed a metal ladder to the roof of the nearest intact building overlooking the intersection, and stopped when she heard voices. Crawford squatted twenty yards away, face illuminated by the radio he'd set up atop a crate; Beale was nearby in the shadow of the roof's edge. "Any calls?" she asked Beale, as she crawled across the roof to him.

"Usual traffic," Beale said.

"You ring up Hartz?"

"Yes, ma'am."

"No new orders?"

"Captain Happy advises us to stay safe."

Fowler waited for her eyes to get used to the darkness. They'd spent the entire day making sure the living members of the Artillery Battery got on convoys back to Camp Tolerance, dousing fires, and then searching every single one of the spooky, dust-splashed bunks in the back of the blown-up barracks, checking for other bodies. It ought to have been a depressing detail, but once they'd seen the artillerymen haul Weazer from the rubble, his slender thumb poking up in the air, every empty pocket of rubble felt like a present, a victory, a prize. Her project now was convincing Beale to enjoy this. "So what's it feel like, being a big war hero?" she said. "Saving a life."

Bad start. Beale snorted, looked down at his boots.

"Just doing my job."

"Oh, shit. Oh, no." She punched Beale in the shoulder. It was like hitting a HESCO barrier that had gotten wet. "Listen to this guy, Crawford. Beale was just doing his job. Saving people. Which is funny, because what I remember from back at Riley was that he never *liked* this job in the first place."

"Family Values, man," Crawford said.

"I'm more worried about his emotional state," she said to Crawford. "I think he might be depressed. I think he was genuinely fucking worried when Eggleston was listing that slab off of me. Is that true, Beale? Do we need to get you some meds?"

Beale took this in, absorbing something into his lumbering frame—hopefully the good vibe she directed at him beneath the talking. His face *had* been there, peering in at her, as the darkness closed down on her. She'd known he would've stuck his arm in and lost it, just to hold on to her. A fact both stupid and in some ways great.

"You might want to talk to the assholes who set off that

bomb," Beale said, "about what their emotional state happened to be."

"Probably real disappointed," Fowler said.

"*Werd*," Crawford said.

Everything she'd been trying to communicate to Beale, every positive thought about what her platoon could do, might be—not all the bullshit stuff, not the benefits, not the personal glory, not the assholes (like, for instance, Captain Masterson) who told him he was somehow lesser and weaker for being in support rather than infantry, lesser and weaker for having a lieutenant who was a chick, but the good stuff, which she admittedly sucked at defining but *knew* was there—all of that had appeared in physical form, in the teamwork that had gotten the Hercules atop that pile, lifted that concrete slab off Weazer, and saved his life. A refutation of losing. That was what it felt like.

Three months ago, she might've just *told* Beale, Look, dumbass, *this* is what I've been trying to accomplish. *This* is what happens if you pull your head out of your ass and follow my advice. But Pulowski had taught her that the direct approach didn't always work. That it was a poor idea to be so certain about being right.

Instead, she sat with him for a while, waiting it out, leaving silence and some space. He squatted on his heels, his hands flattened on the roof in a strange position, wrist to wrist, as if preparing to climb into the starting blocks for a race.

"Remember those shackles Masterson stole from us?" she asked.

Beale shrugged, as if she were referring to a distant, murky past.

She dug into the flap pocket of her fatigues, pulled out the heavy metal clip. It was solid steel, forged in the shape of a G, thick as her index and middle finger put together, but the hook of the shackle's lower jaw had been bent, distended.

"That one came off the Hercules," she said. "That was the one we used to lift the slab. Thought you might want it for a trophy."

"A bent shackle?" Beale asked. "Oh, that's nice, LT. Jeez, that's sweet. Just what I always wanted." He held it between two fingers, examining the lower part of the shackle, which had bent so much that it was clear they'd been two centimeters away from dropping the slab.

"I thought you might want to give that to somebody. A trophy."

"Who?"

"I didn't fucking get one," Crawford said.

"I don't know," Fowler said, in a light tone that she hoped suggested that she knew exactly to whom he might give it. "Somebody who's hard to impress. Somebody back home who doesn't understand what you've been doing."

"How about somebody I might want to piss off?"

"Maybe," she said. "You could go that way."

With no lights on at all and the moon still low, the darkness seemed to pulse and crest beyond the edges of the rooftop as if it were a liquid. Beale had gone to bed. She thought it had gone well with him—not perfect, not Eisenhower-worthy. But better. An improvement. They weren't lacking for food out at the bomb site. Plenty had been brought in during the day and she sat with a pile of chips on a paper plate, staring out over the empty entrance to Muthanna, and thinking oddly of Beale's father—the one who'd run away, the one who, according to Beale's mother, he'd been trying to impress by joining the Army. What Fowler had wanted to do, what she'd considered doing, was telling Beale to take that shackle and mail it to his dad, show him what he'd done. Make up his own story, rather than look to somebody else for what his story ought to be.

Crawford sidled up to her, his gold glasses floating like a strange, delicate cage on his face. "The colonel sent a message."

"What's that?" she said.

"You ain't gonna like it."

"Try me."

"Fredrickson and Arthur. Remember when we stole their shit?"

"Yeah."

"Okay, so, the word is that those two dudes didn't show up on the convoys back to Camp Tolerance. No account of them."

"Where'd they go?"

Crawford swung his boots over the roof's edge. The pile of rubble that had once constituted the checkpoint's barracks slumped to his left, while between his arches she could see the focused darkness of the blast zone, like a rotted molar, then some three hundred yards of emptied street and blasted cars. Nothing moved down there except rats.

"Maybe they just walked off, quit, dropped their weapons," Crawford said, hopefully. "You know, went native on the thing."

"Native what?" Fowler asked. "Native fuckheads?"

"Shit, man, I ain't native."

"They're Delta Company. Masterson's guys. They're not dropping weapons anyplace." She stared out for a while longer. "We looked pretty hard."

"If I ever go native at a shitty checkpoint, you write my moms something different, you know. This boy died heroically."

"Don't sweat it, Crawford," Fowler said. "If anyone's writing their mom, it'll be you writing mine. And when you do, ask her why she never came to visit."

Crawford chuckled at this. Fowler handed him her plate of chips. He ate a few in somber silence, then said in a more serious voice, "Damn. That is the case."

The day before, there had been grumblings about the checkpoint's conditions, even after Weazer had been saved. As they'd hunted through the wreckage, Beale had pointed out that everyone had known the intersection's checkpoint didn't have any T-walls and soldiers would die if they were posted there. Which meant, as Waldorf noted, that the soldiers there had died to prove something that most everyone knew already. And finally, Dykstra had heard that the Iraqi bomber had been contracted to haul gravel to the checkpoint because it was Army policy to hire locals, even for jobs they could have done themselves. Which meant that Weazer had been killed (except, of course, they'd saved him) by someone that the U.S. Army was *paying*. So as Fowler prepared to address her platoon the next morning, she felt less like a lieutenant and more like a sex-ed teacher, hoping against hope that there were certain questions her students wouldn't ask.

"Okay," she said, standing behind a rust-scabbed folding table that she'd salvaged from the wreckage, "we have a couple more soldiers unaccounted for. Fredrickson and Arthur from Delta Company. I've drawn up a grid. You will be assigned to work an area in pairs. Whenever you find anything that might be significant, the first thing you do is that you take a picture of it. So don't move it."

Beale raised his arm for a question. She noticed that he was holding the bent shackle she'd given him the night before in his hand and, flushing, she ignored him.

"What I want you to do is flag it, come back here, get the camera"—she picked this up and showed it to everyone, as if she were the hostess on a game show—"and a Garmin"—she showed this too—"take a picture, write the coordinates of your object down on a note card, write down the photo number, and then bag it, okay?"

Beale wiggled the shackle. "Is it true that we were paying the guy who did this?" he asked. "The bomber? Do you have any intel on that?"

"We're in recovery," Fowler said, trying to pretend nothing was out of the ordinary. "That's what we do. It doesn't matter how this happened. Our job is to recover these missing men, if they are here, or be absolutely sure that they aren't."

"No, no, no, I get that," Beale said. Beale always "got" the first explanation of any order, which made Fowler wonder why he was also always the first person to ask a question. "What I'm saying is, why do we have to do the GPS thing? We already spent a whole fucking day searching this place. If they *are* here, they're not worth finding."

"The fuck!" Dykstra said. "You wouldn't want us to find you?"

"Find me, yeah," Beale said. "But what are you gonna do, call up and give my mom the coordinates of my ass?"

"That's not the part she'd want," Dykstra said.

"I mean this seriously," Beale said. "This is not fucking *CSI.* What, you think they're gonna fly Grissom out, put a bunch of these pictures up on the wall in the TOC, shine a blue light on 'em, and tell us how Fredrickson got whacked? I don't see that—"

"No, no, no, man," Jimenez said. "That's cum stains, man. For a blast they check the fibers. They do a spectrograph—"

"Jesus, you two are a piece of work," Dykstra said. He stood, balled up a kerchief he'd been using to cover his bald head, and threw it at Beale.

"What's that for?" Beale persisted.

"Show some respect. This might be a grave site."

Beale, however, shrugged off Dykstra's distress—as well as Jimenez's attempt at humor. He seemed more determined than usual. More confident, really, than he'd been when they'd saved Weazer, as if that had been merely an unexpected exception to what he had always believed, even back at Riley, was the truth of this place. "I'm saying we risked our lives to get Weazer out of that pile. You did it too. Look at this shackle. You and Weazer were about a couple centimeters short of biting it." He held up the drooping shackle for the rest of the platoon to see. "I was thinking about what you said last night, ma'am. I say we shove this puppy right up Colonel Seacourt's ass and ask him who the hell's accountable for this shit."

Okay, Beale, Fowler thought. *Thank you for misinterpreting everything I said.*

"Do you have any actual tactical suggestions for me to give the colonel?" she asked. "After I shove the shackle up his ass? Like how to better provide battalion-wide security? Maybe a new interpretation on all the intel you've been reading?"

"We don't need any fucking intel, ma'am," Beale said. "What I'm saying is that we deserve a story that makes sense."

It was true. Everything they'd done right, wordlessly, with no speeches, when saving Weazer was trumped by the very bad story of Fredrickson and Arthur.

"All right, Beale. What's your story?"

"There's no mystery to solve here. They got their asses kidnapped by Osama bin Laden's boys, so unless you think that Osama himself was riding in that truck, my suggestion would be that we ought to be using these little gizmos to find out who did it. That's the only justice there can be."

He'd been good up until then, so she was surprised to find herself relieved to hear Beale's story—as well-intentioned as it may have been—devolve into something as half-assed as chasing Osama bin Laden with their GPS. After all, the Shi'ites were fighting in this area, not Sunnis. And yet, for the first time in her command, staring out at the faces of her platoon whitened with dust, she had nothing better to offer. The how and why of the bombing were blanks, or worse. All she had left was the where. Maybe Pulowski had been preparing her for this. Leno versus Letterman. The argument they'd had about tradition in her dad's backyard. Listening to Pulowski grouse that the war made no sense—in part because there wasn't any OBL to find—and still believing that her platoon would be exceptional. But they weren't, and neither was she. It was almost a relief, therefore, when Corporal Halt, who'd been off pissing along their security perimeter, wandered shyly up to the edge of her table and interrupted her, holding a small object away from his body with his right hand. "I found something," he said.

Compared with the Hammermill paper on the table, Halt's object had a surprisingly sharp color, a yellowish, phlegmy gray. Its exterior—the whole gobbet was the size of a fingertip—seemed rumpled, like a bit of coral, something that had grown in on itself, accreted, and then there were the horrifying white strings, feelers, Fowler wanted to call them, extending from a charred, frowzy skirt at the base of the main piece. Standing on her tiptoes, she scanned the intersection, the dark maw of the blast hole, the Humvees scorched to the color of tinfoil, the field of rubble beside the barracks, trying to imagine two human bodies separated into pieces as small as the one Halt had brought back. She glanced down at the insufficient white roll of Hefty trash bags in her hand.

Then Shoemaker started to cry. She was a burly, cornrowed sergeant, normally assigned to Delta Company, and she bolted, her boots crunching over the gravel that Halt had just crossed, her pie-tin ass wobbling beneath her body armor.

PART FOUR

FORT RILEY

8

Colonel Seacourt and the tight, sunglasses-wearing phalanx of his personal security detail marched to the far end of the Fort Riley gym, where a stage had been hastily constructed—bare risers, three flags, a podium whose front had been covered with an office-paper printout of the 1st Battalion, 27th Infantry's seal. A television on a metal gurney played a DVD of still photos taken during the last six weeks of the battalion's preparations to go overseas. Shots of soldiers shackling Humvees to railcars. Shots of volleyball games. Shots of PT—all of it too far away for Pulowski to see from the back row of the bleachers, but this didn't matter. In his opinion, the DVD was static, designed to mask the fact that he and the entire battalion were in this gym under armed guard. And they would not be allowed to leave until 1800 hours, when they departed for Iraq.

"He looks a little smug, don't you think?" Pulowski's mother said. "I wonder why they haven't kept him in the gym with everybody else."

This was exactly what Pulowski himself was thinking. "Don't worry about him, Mom," he said. "He's just the battalion commander. I barely see him."

"I guess that makes it easier to be smug, then, doesn't it?"

said his mother, yet another point with which he found it difficult to disagree.

When his boss, Major McKutcheon, talked about Colonel Seacourt in private or out at the bar in Aggieville where Pulowski and a few of the other Headquarters Company officers met after work, he referred to him as "Bucky." Normally, this would've been exactly the kind of information he would've been happy to share with his mother, make her guess how he got the name—or at least get her opinion on whether Bucky fit as well as Pulowski thought it did, because, in a certain sense, Bucky somehow seemed to exactly capture the essence of Colonel Seacourt's spurious and cheerful blandness. Maybe it had to do with his teeth: Bucky, as in buckteeth. That too would've been amusing to share with his mother, except for the fact that it was not any more reassuring than the armed MPs at the gym's exits. As if even Bucky understood the purity of Pulowski's desire, at this last moment, to never see Iraq. And so, as the colonel bowed his head to begin his speech with a prayer, Pulowksi shifted his eyes nervously to the rafters of the Fort Riley gym. Not much comforting up there, save some old satin banners that looked to be from the fifties and the wiring for a PA system that he could see was equally out-of-date.

Then he found Fowler on the crowded floor below him. She was on the opposite end of the gym from Seacourt's stage, kneeling beside a pile of packed rucks that he presumed belonged to her platoon. Her head was bowed and he could see the sash of brown hair across her forehead, and then the curve of her haunch underneath her fatigues, which was about the only actually, personally reassuring thing that he saw in that entire gym. She'd been more positive on the subject of Colonel Seacourt than he'd ever been, a defender of his organizational abilities, not to mention his fairness—able to overlook what Pulowski felt to be his cloying optimism by pointing out that at least he wasn't a screamer, or a bully, or a crook. "What are *you* looking at?" his mother asked.

Startled, he glanced up at his mother's face. Their coloring was much the same, pale and paler—but the winter air of central Kansas had dried her skin, causing new wrinkles to appear at the edges of her lips. Now, for the first time, he saw a flush to her cheeks, some twinkle of amusement in her green eyes.

"Sorry?" he said. "What are you talking about?"

"That girl you're looking at, Mr. Dixon Pulowski. Who is she?"

"I wasn't aware that I was looking at anyone in particular," he said. "Just spacing out." He spun his finger beside his head to indicate mental confusion.

"Yeah, well, that's about the most intense spacing out that I've ever seen."

"I've been practicing," he said.

"I'm talking about that woman, right there," his mother said, loudly enough that the family in front of them responded with a windy, movie-theater shush.

"Mom—come on," he whispered, thrusting a chin toward the colonel at the podium, who by then had begun his speech.

Pulowski and McKutcheon had adapted the colonel's speech from four or five other public speeches that McKutcheon had stored on his hard drive. It had seemed standard enough work, sitting up in McKutcheon's office, banging out transitions, trying to find language that would, according to the memo that Seacourt had sent them, *cause us to appear both resolute and certain in our purpose. It is VERY IMPORTANT that these people believe their sons and daughters are heading out on a clearly defined mission that is important to protecting the security of the United States and is beneficial to the Iraqis.*

Unfortunately, they'd had to take out the sections in the speech—still good only six months earlier—about protecting the country from WMDs, since the Iraq Survey Group had now delivered their finding that there hadn't been any WMDs. They'd had to remove, by executive order from the DoD, any references connecting the invasion of Iraq to the 9/11 attacks and, given the so-called facts on the ground—including casualty reports that said the coalition forces had so far lost more than two thousand men—they'd had to strike any references to their victory in Iraq, or nation-building, or peacekeeping.

After that, there hadn't been much left, except to focus on reconstruction projects, school-building, and the colonel's intention to return electricity to every family in his area of operations—none of which was likely to happen, given the security intel that Pulowski had seen. Still, a bullshit speech was a bullshit speech. You wrote it and got it done. And if you knew where the bullshit was buried, as he believed he did, you could protect yourself, as he believed he had. Or at least that was how he'd felt until he listened to this speech with his mother and felt her fear and disbelief. And he realized that he had nothing better to tell her, no words that wouldn't make her more afraid.

"We have made a commitment to freedom," Seacourt was saying. "As a nation and as a people. The men and women that you see in this room, your sons and daughters, are a living, breathing example of that commitment."

"Good Lord," his mother muttered. "Who *writes* this dreck?"

The prayer would be coming next. Quickly, before Seacourt could say more, Pulowski bent down and unzipped the tightly packed ruck at his feet. He had bought a present for Fowler just the night before. It was . . . well, he wasn't exactly sure what to call it. A token of appreciation? For what? For screwing his brains out?

"What would you think of this?" he said to his mother, handing her the cardboard-and-plastic package, in hopes of distracting her from Seacourt's speech. "Like if somebody gave it to you? I mean, presuming you were athletic."

A double crease appeared in the soft skin of his mother's forehead—a mark that he was always pleased to elicit, though the specific actions that led to its appearance often surprised him. She withdrew her reading glasses from her purse, slipped them on, and squinted first at the pedometer—the brand name, he was now a little embarrassed to realize, was Pedassure—then at Fowler, barely visible over the heads of the family who'd hushed her earlier, a mountainous man and woman dressed in Harley-Davidson T-shirts, surrounding an equally mountainous son with a huge bald skull, whom Pulowski recognized as Lieutenant Anderson, from Delta Company.

"How's your sex life?" his mother asked.

"What?" Pulowski coughed. "Hey, ease up, there, hoss."

"You mean you didn't buy this for that woman you were staring at?"

"I mean I'm not really up for discussing this with my mother," he said. "Or anybody around here, for that matter."

His mother checked her watch. "I'm not sure when you think a better time might be," she said, and she reached out and held his hand in hers, slipped the pedometer back.

"All right," Pulowski said. "Okay." He was grinning in spite of himself, first at the pedometer in his hand and then, to his surprise, at the pleasure of imagining himself in bed with Fowler, of having *been* in bed with Fowler.

"So it *is* good," his mother said, watching him coyly.

"Yup," he said happily. "Yup."

"Well, then I guess you don't have to worry about getting her trust," his mother said, with a certain amount of asperity. "That's a good first step, you know!" She was grinning now. Both of them were.

"Yeah? Really? And what would you know about it?"

"Not very much, these days," his mother said.

This last remark by his mother stuck out into an unexpected silence and, gazing out over the crowd, Pulowski saw that the other parents and soldiers in the audience had bowed their heads. "All right," he said, whispering only a little, and standing long before the colonel's address had come to an end. "I got someone I want you to meet."

There were many things that Pulowski proudly rebelled against. He'd enumerated them to Fowler frequently. One was arena rock—not the most brilliant pet peeve, but still. Another was football commentators, singers, or celebrities of any kind who spoke highly of the great valor and bravery of American soldiers while at the same time selling something. Mostly he did not like the underlying implication that they were all supposed to be brave, that it was somehow the soldiers' duty to be brave—and that there was something grand and significant in taking leave of their families in a shitty gym in central Kansas, which was one of the reasons he'd loaded up the colonel's speech so completely with clichés. There was a kind of coercion there, don't you think, something going on subliminally, he had more than once said to Fowler, who had more than once said to him, *Well, you can always not listen to it.* Or later, when he'd gone on enough to make her impatient, *When the fuck is something not going on with you subliminally, anyway?*

He had to admit, as he led his mother down the ranked stairs of the bleachers and onto the familiar flat varnish of the basketball floor, that he definitely felt something subliminal going on. It certainly wasn't rational. He'd seen Fowler a thousand times, dressed and undressed, seen her in her jog bra, her black and yellow Fort Hays sweats, but he'd never seen her *with his mother*, which, apparently, was an entirely different way of seeing things—because otherwise Fowler looked the same as usual. Still kneeling, she was now sorting through an open ruck (while at the same time, if he had to guess, ignoring the colonel's speech, so she didn't have to feel disappointed by it), her hair pinned back, cheeks lightly flushed—nothing out of the ordinary, unless you counted the Beretta strapped to her thigh. Certainly nothing that could rationally explain the thickness in his throat and the charge that electrified his scalp when he swung his mother around to greet this woman, his mother with her public radio tote bag and her chapped face. "Hey, LT," he said. "You looking forward to this historic opportunity?"

"You got a bag?" Fowler asked, without glancing up.

"Sorry?"

"You got a baggie or something, Pulowski?" she said. "Come on. Beale's wasted, and he packed all fucking wrong. Look at this!" She held up a pair of Hawaiian swim trunks. "He's got so much crap, I'm going to have to cram some of it in with my gear."

"Did your brother show up?" he said.

"Does it look like he did?"

"He might have liked the speech," Pulowski said, squatting beside her.

This would have normally been a comment that Fowler would've enjoyed, but instead she tucked her chin and kept rummaging through Beale's ruck, more and more contraband spilling out. "Is that your mother?" she asked.

"Yes, that's my mother."

"You want me to meet your mother."

"I'm standing right here," Pulowski's mother said.

They stood up. Fowler approached stiffly, arms behind her back, and her chin out stubbornly, as if his mother—in her crew-neck sweater—might at any minute punch her in the face. "Yes, ma'am," Fowler said. "I'm sorry I'm a little busy here, ma'am. I hope you are enjoying the colonel's speech."

"Not really," Pulowski's mother said. "I've heard better."

Fowler flashed him a look of panic and uncertainty. A regular person might have interpreted this as a look of hostility, but Pulowski felt confident that it only meant that Fowler was afraid—not of going to Iraq but of his mother. Fearful that she might not measure up, which was the usual thing that made Fowler afraid.

"I'm not sure what you would've wanted him to say instead."

"Oh, I don't know. A little bit of honesty might have been reassuring. Fewer clichés wouldn't have been bad. Have you ever read any Orwell, Lieutenant?"

He could tell by the wrinkled pucker of Fowler's chin that she was working hard to remember her Orwell. And that she'd begun to get nervous about them standing together in the open like this, particularly in view of her platoon. "Emma was a history major," Pulowski said, breaking in. He put his hand on her elbow, shielding this gesture so no one could see. Then to Fowler he said, "Mom teaches English. And public speaking. So she's got some strong opinions on this."

"Yeah, well, I'm not sure what kind of honesty she exactly means. We're going to win and we're going to come back. That's what we're doing. That's how it's going to be. I'd assume you don't want to hear anything different."

"I don't think Mom's opposed to that," Pulowski said. "Are you, Mom? I mean, if Pop was going, that might be different—I just think she felt like the speech was a little too rah-rah, a little too cheerleady for her. So I thought I would bring her down and talk to somebody who actually knew what she was doing."

Fowler flushed, glanced back at her platoon. "I'm not sure that we're all exactly ready for inspection," she said. "I'd sure as hell like to meet that person."

"Wouldn't we all?" said Pulowski's mother.

"Don't let the lieutenant fool you," Pulowski said. Because it had gotten awkward holding on to Fowler's elbow, he squeezed it once and then backed off and gave her a chuck on the shoulder, harder than he normally would—hard enough that she would know that he was fucking with her. Which, judging by her brief, suppressed smile, and the flash of anger in her eyes, she did. "She and her platoon have just spent the past three weeks standing around in the snow, loading about fifty thousand tons of equipment onto railcars, while the rest of these lazy fucks"—here he gestured at the auditorium as a whole, and particularly the soldiers from Masterson's infantry company, who'd camped out in the visitors' bleachers, under a sign that read DELTA ME TO DEATH—"sat around and polished their boots. Three weeks of preparing for the DRIF is no small thing."

"What's the DRIF?" Pulowski's mother asked. "I was married to an Army surgeon, so I'm used to the acronyms, but that's a new one for me."

"The acronym is really DRRF," Fowler said, with the first real confidence she'd displayed in the conversation—much to Pulowski's satisfaction. "What *that* means depends on who you're talking to. The colonel translates it as Deployment Ready Reaction Field. That's where we get our stuff ready to be loaded onto railcars. But it's also a state of mind. So we leave an *R* out and call the whole thing the DRIF."

"Sounds even worse than OIF," Pulowski's mother said. She

squatted down with her tote and began to examine the ruck that Fowler had unpacked.

"One or two?" Fowler asked.

"I don't know. Any number."

"Or DFAC," Pulowski said.

"My ex-husband used to talk about the NBFC zone," Pulowski's mother said.

"No bullshit from civilians," Pulowski clarified.

"He was a surgeon at Fort Campbell," Pulowski's mother said. "We used to call him the Dr. Ratched of the OR. Very schedule-driven person. Rule-oriented, big fan of the acronym. One of the things he liked best about the Army was that its rules kept everything from being messy. But of course things are messy, and the *best* things are *always* messy—or at least that's what I've always believed."

"So I've heard," Fowler said.

"Have you?" Pulowski's mother said. "From where?" A coy smile there, his mother's best.

"Not from me," Pulowski assured her. "Excellence, strictness, and clarity are my buzzwords. Superb soldiering. Honor your country. Organization before oneself. Fowler knows all this. You've seen my dominant scores at the rifle range?"

But they were already working, dragging over and unzipping Fowler's ruck, which he knew from experience would be at least as poorly organized and overstuffed as Beale's, and had already forgotten him. Of course, *he* could have helped Fowler repack her gear more efficiently. And he would've recommended that she just throw away Beale's extra stuff. He'd told Fowler a thousand times that she needed to think about herself more. She might have been excellent at strapping tanks onto railcars, but her skills at personal organization—her skills at personal life in general—had always been suspect. Naturally, she'd refused his aid.

But if there was going to be somebody who helped Fowler repack her ruck other than himself, it was his mother, who after all had taught him all of his tricks. Tuck your socks inside your shoes. Fold everything, even your underwear. Don't forget your floss and toothpaste. Keep all your liquids in a plastic bag. They were talking together, the two women, crouched in the center of the basketball court, Fowler's watch cap and his mother's short black bob nearly touching, pyramided over the two rucks. His mother was unpacking all the zip-locks and bags of baby wipes that she had longed to give to him, and gently, with Fowler's serious and mute attention, explaining how to best fold a pair of panties. He would go off and get some coffee. Then he would climb up in the stands and get his own ruck and bring it down and put it in the pile that Fowler had assembled for her platoon, so they could ride together on the flight to Kuwait. And then, when he came back, after his mother had had about twenty minutes alone with Fowler—in his estimation that was all she'd need to repack her entirely—he'd stick with the jokes, whatever it took. He felt as confident as he'd felt in months, maybe ever in his lifetime. He'd made good choices; he'd done the right thing. His mother's worry was gone; Fowler was getting a little mothering. And he couldn't imagine a situation that he couldn't get out of, not if he used his head, kept Fowler out of trouble, and refused at every moment to take even one fucking second of this entire mission seriously.

9

Nothing is embarrassing unless you *decide* it's embarrassing. That was the Pulowski-ism that Fowler recited as she pushed past the Christmas tree that guarded the Echo Company offices. If she had been Pulowski instead of herself, she wouldn't have been here at all: there was too much work to do, and she herself wasn't even packed yet, and she had paperwork piling up all over her apartment, leave requests, uniform requisitions, billeting forms, travel documents that were going to be needed to get her soldiers on the plane. And yet, here she was, ever the good girl, ever the eager beaver, unstacking the boxes that she'd bought on Captain Hartz's desk and opening the first with a flourish, as if it contained nothing less important than the holy grail.

"We're under budget," she said.

"Well, that's, I guess, good?" Captain Hartz leaned over the large bright pink container and slipped on his reading glasses and squinted, as if reading the fine print of a diesel order. Then he pinched the shoulders of the dress inside, slowly drew it out of the box, and, as if he were imitating something he'd seen in a movie, pinned the pleated blue slip of fabric against his torso, gazing with concern at the bump his belly made. "What size did I say she was again?" he asked.

"Fourteen," Fowler said, from memory. "She's going to love it, sir. Blue is supposed to be a fairly conservative color. Warm. And Lilly Pulitzer is an extremely traditional brand. Classic cut. Linen. Nice enough to wear to a dinner party but not so showy that she'll never put it on again."

All of these were terms that she'd cribbed from an email that Pulowski's mother had sent, answering her son's very vague and somewhat inscrutable request: What kind of dress looks good on a fat woman?

"Nice but not too showy," Hartz said with a bemused smile, depositing the dress gently on top of its ribboned box, as one might a phosphorus grenade. "Whatever in the hell that means. I mean, obviously it means something to you—but Sarah acts like I'm supposed to know it too. Like this is somehow common knowledge, the difference between nice and showy. Is that some sort of code in the language you all speak?"

The dresses were for the annual Christmas dinner at Seacourt's house on post. The year before, Fowler had drawn staff duty and missed the party, but she'd been new, fresh out of college, and so it hadn't seemed unfair—until the same thing happened during Seacourt's golf tournament on the Fourth of July. There were rules against this sort of thing. Very specific rules about not having battalion functions that, say, female officers were mysteriously not invited to. She'd made her awareness of these rules known—not loudly, not angrily, but clearly—by congratulating Hartz on how much *fun* he and his two male lieutenants must have had. That August she'd received an invitation to the Christmas party, then nothing since. Until this morning, after Hartz had asked her to pick up the dress. "She probably just wanted you to think of it for yourself," Fowler said. She was folding up the dress and replacing it in the box, trying not to re-create the supposedly female behavior that Hartz was now questioning her about.

Hartz barked a laugh and sat back down on his desk chair, tossing a pen on the table as if it were a token of surrender. "But why? That's what I don't get, Emma—what's with the guessing? If she wants a dress for the party, why doesn't she go *get* a dress for the party, instead of waiting until the morning of the party and telling me she doesn't have anything to wear and so won't be going? Give me some insight into this. I don't get it. I never get it. Why do you do that? Why don't you just come out and say what you want?"

"Personally, I think you're making it a little more complicated than it needs to be, sir," Fowler said, as neutrally as possible.

"Really? How's that?"

"Everybody wants recognition," Fowler said.

It hadn't been completely unreasonable for Fowler not to pester Hartz about the party. After all, it *seemed* like she'd been invited. No one had said otherwise. And up until a month ago, Hartz had seemed like he'd started to pay a bit better attention to her. Nothing magic. Just a few of the old saws that Fowler had already heard in ROTC: "Don't ask your men to do anything you wouldn't do." And, "Be the first one out of the foxhole and the last one in." But they were, at least, a *form* of recognition, a *suggestion* that she might be someone worth giving advice to. Weighing against this was the incident with Masterson and the shackles, a disaster on every front, after which—paranoid coincidence or not—Hartz had restricted his communication down to a few bemused and possibly pitying glances cast her way. And then this morning had signed her up for staff duty again. Which she had been planning to discuss with him . . . well, right now seemed like a good fucking time. Hartz circled his desk and pulled on his coat.

"That's what this party *is*," Hartz said. He was back at ease now and their talk had fallen into its usual comfortable banter—more intimate, Fowler liked to think, than he was with his other lieutenants. As if she were an equal or even possibly a friend. "Recognition for the wives. And the random townie girlfriends. You think the colonel wants to spend seventy dollars a head on dinner? Plus footing the bill for a bunch of junior officers who don't know the difference between Old Style and champagne? And having tomorrow be a total wreck, with everybody hung over and not worth spit?"

"Sounds awful," Fowler said.

Hartz was quick enough to catch her sarcasm—though not quite quick enough to determine its source. That realization formed more slowly, a speck of distant dark clouds that worried the ruddy plains of his forehead: Fowler has a beef. He tucked his wife's dress box under his arm and waved the second package, which contained a shoulder wrap for Colonel Seacourt's wife. "Steve's gonna appreciate this," he said. "I told him about your Eisenhower comment too. We both liked it."

"Really? I thought you were kind of pissed."

She could see, from a slight tightening in his smile, that he still was. "Maybe a little bit. In the moment. I don't exactly like being corrected by one of my own soldiers in the middle of a lecture. So I'd say that while the content was fine, what you really need to work on, Lieutenant, is *delivery*."

"Fair enough," Fowler said. Given the mildly positive tone of the conversation, she made a quick judgment—risk of unpreparedness versus risk of embarrassment—and grabbed her dry-cleaned formal uniform as they headed down the hall.

"But I do agree with this idea of yours that a good officer

doesn't need to make a big stink about doing the right thing. You don't *need* to be recognized. That's why the colonel and I value the way you've handled this party."

"How did I do that?"

"Well, for one, Wilson and Jaffrey"—these were the two other male lieutenants in Echo Company—"have been siccing their wives on Sarah for the past three months. Suggestive comments. Notes. 'Do you want to go to lunch, Mrs. Hartz?' 'Anything I can pick up for you at Costco, Mrs. Hartz?' 'The one thing I'd really, really like, before Tom goes away, is to have one really nice evening out, Mrs. Hartz.'"

He dealt Fowler a shifty, sideways glance, inviting her to share his disbelief at these kinds of tactics. But all Fowler felt was a sinking feeling in the pit of her stomach. "Wives can do that?"

"Certain wives *only* do that," Hartz assured her. "But not a word from you. Which, again, is something that I've communicated to the colonel and which he does appreciate. And I do too. You recognize that a party like this isn't important. It's not what we're about. And you know, after this *incident* you had with Captain Masterson—"

So that was it, then: the missing shackles. The conflict she'd initiated with Masterson. Meaning if she'd just shut up then, she'd be going to the party. Or she could make a huge stink now and also go. But there were no reasonable options in between.

"A party like this is a social occasion," Hartz continued. "It's not a military maneuver. It's a family event. We may not like what our brothers are doing at every possible moment. But brothers also don't *turn* on brothers."

"I think you mean 'fraternity event,'" Fowler said.

"You been to many fraternity parties, Lieutenant?" Hartz asked.

"No," Fowler admitted.

"Imagine Lieutenant Anderson, five bourbons into the night, trying to hump a farm girl from La Cygne. Or, if the farm girl's already passed out, trying to hump you."

"I've seen worse," Fowler said.

"Like *he* cares," Hartz said. "Besides, who would you bring?"

They were in the parking lot out back of the battalion headquarters now. This was the moment, right now, when she could've argued back. When she could've demanded that Hartz take her off staff duty and give one of his other lieutenants the assignment, no matter what their dumb wives said. Hartz had led her to this moment deliberately so that afterward she could have no complaint. It was six o'clock, already dark, the snow piled up in lonely humps in front of the parked cars, the blacktop glistening with the day's melt, which would itself soon freeze. And she allowed the moment to pass.

"We can all reinvent ourselves, Lieutenant," Hartz assured her as they reached his car and he handed her a package so he had a free hand to search his pockets for his keys.

After Hartz left, she sat in her pickup, dry-cleaned uniform on her knees, and then, as if she'd been shot with adrenaline, began hammering the steering wheel with her fist. What the fuck was that supposed to mean! Reinvent herself how? She'd done what Hartz wanted but the line sounded disappointed, as if she should've argued. Except he didn't want her to argue, right? And why did she care what he wanted? She had a vision of herself standing at reveille wearing the dress that Hartz had purchased for his wife, a pair of pumps, and waving a kerchief and batting her eyes as the colonel walked by.

That lasted until she saw a small package on her dash, a little white square tied up with what looked like red insulated electrical wire. Inside was a blank CD with the words *Listen to me* written on it in red Sharpie.

“This better be good,” she said, and put it in, engendering a burst of heavy metal so loud that she pawed the volume, and then, to her surprise, Beale’s dopey voice came on over her speakers. “Lieutenant Fowler, this is your mission, should you choose to accept it. Please back up, exit the parking lot, and go right on McCormic Road. *Beep!*”

“Oh, no,” she said, staring at herself in the rearview mirror. “No, no, no! You do *not* do what he says.” Then, to her CD player, she said, “Fuck off, Beale. I’m busy!”

But she was not busy. And there had been some obvious effort made to have the recording work like a real GPS, the words timed out as if someone had actually driven the route. So after she sat alone for a few minutes, listening to the trickling dregs of the parking-lot snow, she heard another beep. *Right on Huebner Road*, Beale said.

“All right, screw it,” she said, and jammed her truck in reverse.

Fifteen minutes later, after some rewardingly aggressive driving—*Beep! Left on East Chestnut Street. Beep!*—the phrase *Turn right into the Cracker Barrel parking lot* ended the CD. She parked and climbed out, feeling skeptical as hell. A light dusting of flakes blazed in headlight glare as other cars swung through the lot. Crawford and Waldorf and Dykstra—she’d felt like they’d pretty much been on board with her from the beginning. (Though who could tell, really, especially since her little war with Masterson had earned them an extra twenty-four-hour shift on the DRIF?) But Beale? Beale was a wild card. Beale was exactly the sort of person who might sit around laughing the next day about how Family Values Fowler wound up eating at the Cracker Barrel by herself.

Still, she went in. Of course, the Cracker Barrel didn’t have a bar, which sucked. And they didn’t generally have TVs for watching the game. Instead, it was filled with old farming signs, rakes nailed up to the wall—none of which she would've noticed or felt embarrassed about had Beale not started in with the Family Values thing. The waitress who came up in her brown apron and white blouse was familiar, though: Susie Wrightman, a girl she'd known back in high school, a couple of years behind her.

"Emma," she said. "You guys getting ready to deploy yet?"

"Few more weeks," she said. "How'd you guess?"

They reached a table, Fowler seating herself while Susie Wrightman laid out silverware for her, then politely slipped a menu into her hands.

Fowler glanced up at Susie Wrightman, a face that she'd once seen every day for years, pretty, bottle-blond, ex-cheerleader, now getting heavy in the cheeks. On her good days, she still felt a small flare of pride (coupled, in certain ways, with disbelief) that she had listened to their high school recruiter, Captain Morris, rather than ending up carrying around plates for $6.50 an hour plus tips. But on a night like tonight, the uniform felt like a disguise. She wasn't any more qualified to command a platoon in Iraq than Susie Wrightman was. The difference was that Susie Wrightman wasn't arrogant enough to pretend she could. "People talk," Susie said, shrugging, with a funny expression on her face. "You hear things in a job like this. Plus you look a little stressed."

"Do I?" Fowler said. She smiled uneasily, stripped her cap off, set it on the table, and ran her fingers over her hair. There was still something odd about Susie's expression, a secret she was holding back. "Yeah, well, I got some personal problems I got to deal with."

"Like him?" Wrightman nodded toward the back of the restaurant.

Fowler leaned around the corner of her booth and saw Carl Beale grinning at her from an empty table, then swiveled around and laid her head back against the booth's backrest, slumping. "You don't serve beer, do you?" she asked.

"That bad, huh?" Susie Wrightman said, laughing.

"Shit, I don't know."

"Yeah, well, I'll tell you one thing," Wrightman said. She knelt down briefly, still with that odd expression on her face. "He's been tipping extra-heavy," she whispered. "So don't bust his ass too badly, okay?"

Fowler nodded, overcome by the certainty that Beale was, in fact, the absolute last person she wanted to see. And she had no one but herself to blame. He tottered over, grinning, eased his heavy belly in behind the table across from her.

"You mind if I sit?"

"Nope," she said.

"You expecting anybody?" he asked.

Fowler tried to remember the advice that Pulowski had given her on Beale. Be personal. Don't stand on ceremony. Let him see that you're a human being. Let him know that you can get hurt. Start with posture, Pulowski had said, and don't think about your brother. Beale isn't your brother. She tried to smile, but it felt off-key.

"Look, Beale," she said. "Let's not sit here and rehash this whole thing with Masterson, okay? You think he's a great commander, that's fine by me. I just don't like being put in a situation where I have to steal federal property. From members of the military. Which I am *in*."

"I don't know. Seems kind of Old Testament to me."

"We're not in the Old Testament, Beale. We're in the Army. I don't know about you, but I like the Army."

"You do?" Beale made a shocked face, his pliable features hunching together in an impression of deep incomprehension. He was leaning forward now across the table. Sloppy. Pushing in on her. She made an effort not to back away. "What're you doing here, anyway?" he asked slyly. "I would've thought that you'd be up there at the colonel's tonight, smoking cigars with Captain Happy." He nodded at her cell phone, which she'd set on the table. "You still waiting on a call?"

She pocketed the phone. Stared back at Beale openly but without the smile. "There's not going to be a call," she said. "Captain seems to think I'm not party material. Or maybe officer material at all."

Beale nodded. "Yeah, well, you're better off with family."

"You're not my family, Beale."

"Really?"

"No," she said. "The Army *isn't* family, okay, Beale? It's a job. And this platoon is not going to work if you keep treating it differently. Just because I'm a woman doesn't mean I'm going to clean up your messes for you. Or show up the next time you leave me a lame mix CD."

"No?"

"No. And if I can't rely on you to follow my orders when I give them, if I can't rely on you to stay inside the rules once we get out there"—she waved her hand at the front window of the Cracker Barrel, the snow swirling in the parking lot lights, as if that were Iraq—"then I can't have you on my team!"

Beale, however, appeared undeterred. To her surprise, he didn't stiffen up or flush, as he usually did when she corrected him.

"So you're saying you're not my family," he said.

"Do I stutter?"

"Does that mean Dykstra's not family?"

"Oh, come on, Beale."

This was the moment, she figured, that Pulowski had been warning her about. The mad moment. The moment when you had that very bad feeling that everything you've been trying to escape by joining the Army is exactly the fucking thing that's waiting for you there. "Beale, I'm going to order," she said. "I had a shitty day."

"Does that mean Waldorf's not family?"

"I'm going to have the chicken-fried steak. You want anything?"

"Crawford? I mean, he's going to be very, very sad when he hears that."

"You know what those guys are?" Fowler said. "You know why Crawford's never going to hear a thing like that, Beale? Because he's got his shit together. Because he's not the kind of soldier who comes down to the Cracker Barrel to ride his lieutenant's ass."

"You're going to have to admit it eventually," Beale said. He took the menu from her and pretended to examine it, while gazing at her over its top edge.

"Admit what?"

Beale smiled, tossed the menu back down on the table, stared at a spot just beside her ear, broad and childish, with his secretive-kid's face.

"That you saved our fucking asses. Took the hit for us. I wouldn't have thought that Family Values had it in her—"

"I hate that name, Beale. It's not family values that I'm talking about here. Half the guys in the Army are here because their daddy disappeared. Did your family have good rules, Beale? 'Cause mine didn't. You think I want to run my platoon like that? You think I enjoy lying to my CO? We stole Army property, Beale. We busted into trunks stenciled with another company's call letters. I want something better than that."

"He stole our shit."

"Who, Masterson? You mean the guy that you've been following around for the past six months, telling me he's the biggest fucking genius in the Army?"

"I might have been wrong about that."

"Wrong!" she sputtered. And then she could feel that it was on her, the mad moment. "Wrong?"

"Whoa, whoa, whoa," Beale said with his hands out, splayed flat. "Fellas, need a little help here."

"You pissed her off enough yet, Beale?"

"What?" she said, standing up. When she turned, she could see a door behind their booth, its edge cracked, shadowed faces peering out. "No, you didn't," she said.

"Oh, no, he didn't!" Beale said, repeating her phrase with a bucktoothed grin. He started waving the dark faces in and the door behind their booth opened and the rest of her platoon came out of it: Dykstra first, in his Philadelphia Flyers jersey, worn over the top of a blue flannel shirt. Crawford in his skinny jeans and sweater. Jimenez in a black hoodie decorated in gold lamé, Waldorf hulking out of the darkness in a starched blue oxford and, of all things, a suit vest buttoned tight around his stomach, and last of all, Pulowski in his Dockers and what she was surprised and pleased to recognize as his version of a "nice shirt": A long-sleeve, rugby-type jersey in maroon and navy, probably purchased for him by his mother, and the black turtleneck that he tended to refer to as his "geek tie." Briefly—she was corkscrewed in her seat, her thighs jammed between the table edge and the banquet—he caught her eye, and Pulowski made a twisted, goofy face, wobbling his head on his shoulders, as if to suggest that he was just following along with the crowd and had no idea why he was here.

Then there were hands on her shoulders, forcing her back down into her seat, voices, a press of bodies, everybody shouting simultaneously.

"To the queen of the DRIF, motherfuckers!" Beale said.

"Queen," Jimenez said. "Who you calling queen, man? We don't need no fucking gender-specific shit like that."

"What, I got to be politically correct when I hand out compliments?" Beale said.

"Holy shit, did Beale say he was giving somebody a compliment?"

"I didn't hear no compliment."

"Queen is a compliment, motherfucker."

"Not in this country, it ain't."

Mugs were passed. A pitcher of soda came. Everybody was jostling, chanting, giving Beale shit about something indistinct, and in order not to betray her emotion, or to look at Pulowski again, she started examining the Cracker Barrel menu, trying not to look up at any of them, or lose control of herself in an embarrassing way. "We got to have a speech," Waldorf said from the far end of the table. "Speech! Speech!"

"Get your own speaker, Waldorf," she said. "I got to eat."

"I'll say something," Beale said, standing up.

It was not exactly the kind of place where she'd imagined having her first-ever military success. If at any point during the dinner someone had stood up and accused her of knowing nothing about what they were about to do, what dangers they were about to face, she would've confessed to this immediately. In part she feared this, and in part she wished that it would occur, so that she could get it over with, climb up out of the booth, strip off her ACUs and her lieutenant's bars and go put on a brown apron and get back to waitressing with Susie Wrightman—doing something in which the worst-case scenario was that you got tipped badly, or had to work an extra shift, and nobody ended up dead. In the end, she was rescued from having to say anything further by the advent of the K-State basketball game. One of the servers had set up a portable TV on a table in the corner of the restaurant, below a two-man wood saw that had been nailed to the wall, and the players flickered soundlessly on its screen. Gradually, because she'd started watching it, they all turned that way. She let her eyes linger on the set, the glowing, orderly court, the cheerleaders waving their pom-poms, all of it more magical and electric and satisfyingly vivid compared with the long concrete vistas of the DRIF, the steady brown and tan colors of the base. After a while, she dropped her gaze, in order to pay attention to the food that she'd ordered, and she saw Pulowski watching her instead of the game. He had a sly expression on his face, his eyebrows raised, one that seemed to say that this moment, at this table, proved everything he'd been telling her about her ability to command. Suggesting that she'd made exactly the right call to break the rules and get Beale off. "What're you looking at, Pulowski?" she said. "When did I get so interesting?"

She reached out and palmed the black padded book that Susie Wrightman had brought over, containing their table's tab, brushing his fingers as she did it, briefly but firmly, giving no sign to the rest of the platoon that she had done such a thing.

10

"Pulowski." A winter Sunday night at the Harmony Woods apartment complex on the outskirts of Junction City—known locally as Fort Riley West. Pulowski was reading over an article on Fourier transform pairs describing how certain wave forms naturally correspond to each other despite being in different domains. McKutcheon had switched off his cell, jammed a snowboard into his Subaru, and headed to Colorado for the weekend. Fowler was away, her apartment windows dark across the snowy dimple of the complex yard, probably off doing some sort of extra brown-nose work for Hartz, and so Pulowski had been expecting . . . well, nothing. No visitors for the evening. He had his sweatpants on, wool socks, a pair of fleece-lined slippers mailed to him by his mother, and he was sitting at the kitchen table with a blanket over his legs, reading and occasionally glancing up at the apartment's flat-screen, which he had, in an attempt to feel adult and responsible, tuned in to the *NewsHour with Jim Lehrer.* He shifted his gaze to the sliding black pane of his living room's glass door, seeing a reflection of himself, blanket tucked neatly around his knees, Diet Coke open on the table, and then, looming up just behind his reflection, so that their faces mingled in the glass, Fowler in a black stocking cap and parka, her gloved hands beckoning for him to let her in. "Come on," she said, her voice still muffled by the glass. "We got to go get Beale. Let me in."

Beale, as far as he was aware, didn't *need* getting. Still, five minutes later, Fowler stood inside the sliding door, her hair haloed by the static of her removed cap, waiting for him to get dressed. No information on where they were going, except that he was to wear civilian gear: parka, jeans, gloves, hat, boots. No ACUs. There was something mischievous and off-center in the way Fowler made this request—an energy, a confidence. The kind of self he saw in bed. Even so, as he tramped out the back door of his apartment, he'd experienced a small jolt of fear and displacement as if, however much he might have agreed with the spirit of this adventure, he wasn't sure that he belonged with her as a part of it, whatever it might be. "Tunes," a voice growled as he climbed into Fowler's truck, and he was surprised to see Dykstra lying on his side in the backseat, dressed in a red-and-black checked woodsman's jacket, his jowls caked with camouflage face paint. "Hey, welcome to special operations, Lieutenant," he said, cuffing Pulowski on the shoulder. "See if you can coax some music out of the LT."

They pulled through town, past the Casey's General Store, past the strip mall where he and Fowler sometimes ate Chinese, past the mournful city hall, with its wind-stripped tinsel. Then the highway ran straight and flat, eddying with snow beyond the pickup's headlights, and beyond that the white fields glossily and ghostly lit. Pulowski scanned the truck's radio dial, picking up scratchy stations from impossibly far away: WGN in Chicago, a pastor preaching from Vancouver, a weather report from Arlington, Texas, and the news. The signals that brought their voices down through the truck's antenna and into the cab were the very thing he'd been reading about back home, safe in his apartment. At one point, the scanner landed on a velvet-voiced news announcer, who said, "The Department of Defense has confirmed three more deaths in Iraq today. Private William O'Connor died when his Humvee was hit by an improvised explosive device in Anbar Province." For a moment, this signal sent a chill down his spine, like the snow that had fallen into his collar on his way to the truck, foreign to the warmth that the three of them generated in the small cab. The next channel was country music, and Fowler reached out and punched the button, ended the scan, and they drove together listening to Garth Brooks without complaint.

About ten miles out of town, the truck trundled off onto a gravel road, unplowed, the double ruts of tire marks obscured by the smooth-faced slopes of drifted snow. She downshifted into four-wheel drive, then gunned the truck, cresting the first drift, Dykstra in the back shouting, "Yee-ohah!" in a Philadelphian imitation of a hillbilly yell. Fowler beat back a grin and thumbed her stocking cap down over her forehead, shoulders hunched with matching intensity, and for a moment he forgot the road, forgot his curiosity about the purpose of their errand, forgot the forbidding darkness of the fields outside the cab, forgot the radio, forgot even that they were moving, and instead watched her, downshifting, then upshifting, eager, certain, and surprisingly calm despite the violent shaking of the cab.

Behind them, three more vehicles pulled up, all of them civilian: a hulking black Suburban, from which Sergeant Waldorf descended, a white Ford F-150 with chrome pipes that belonged to Jimenez, and lastly Crawford's car, which was a Honda CRV and looked like a toy compared with the rest. There was a brief blatting of bass that accompanied Crawford's car as it chugged up uneasily, loud enough for Fowler to turn around and glance, but her expression wasn't angry—Pulowski knew all her signals by then, even in the dark—more like ardent, even amused, and the music died as soon as the car shut off, and the rest of the platoon struck out after them through the field of snow, not exactly with murderous efficiency, since Pulowski could see Crawford and McWilliams horsing around together in the snow. But unified, at least.

There was a chain-link fence about a hundred yards across the field, and as they climbed the small berm that led up to it, Pulowski could see the watchtower tall enough that it had been fitted with red lights, to warn away small aircraft. Then, just beyond, banks of lights erected every quarter mile, shining down on rows of snow-covered tanks and Humvees, on flatbed trucks, and on the tents where every company commander in the battalion had stationed guard details to watch over their equipment as it waited to be loaded into the trains. The DRIF.

Dykstra was already kneeling, calmly cutting an opening into the links of chain. "Why in God's name would we want to break in there?" Pulowski asked. In response, Dykstra tilted his heavy, cold-pinched face toward Fowler.

"We've got to borrow a couple of Captain Masterson's things," she said. Why? Pulowski wanted to know. Borrow what? Didn't she know that this was totally illegal? Didn't she know they had guards down there? What the hell was she thinking? Wasn't the whole problem with her platoon that they didn't have respect for the rules? Fowler squinted her eyes thoughtfully against the snow until Dykstra had finished cutting a seam in the fence, then lifted one corner with her gloved hand. "Beale's getting smoked off-site by some of Masterson's goofs," she said. "He's a dickwipe, but he's my dickwipe, and it is *my* conviction *my* dickwipes don't get punked like that. So we need some leverage, and you, Lieutenant, are here to be our guide. Besides, isn't it your conviction that getting court-martialed *now* might not be such a bad thing?"

"Well, since you put it that way." Pulowski shimmied through the opening, elbows pulling his body forward, the powder flaring up around his chin, and then they body-skied down the berm, sliding and falling, cushioned by the snow, so that the descent felt like an interesting mixture of something that was truly dangerous and something that was not. The DRIF resembled an immense city whose residents thought primarily of murder—or so Pulowski had described it to Fowler, largely to get her goat, but also because, in his opinion, it felt that way. Spooky as hell, especially if you tried to mentally put together the video he saw, say, on *Lehrer*, of the moment when an IED hit—the *thoom* sound of the tape, the way the camera always twisted and joggled with the report, and then the inky black column of smoke coiling up. And then you walked around the DRIF and saw about five hundred Humvees and wondered which one of them would be hit that way. But now it wasn't scary. Not on this particular trip.

They huddled on the back edge of the lot, against a row of Bradleys, their armor fringed with icicles. Everybody hated the DRIF. Pulowski had worked several night shifts there, twelve hours in the command center, freezing his ass off in a poorly heated tent; in there, the DRIF was a giant algorithm, paperwork upon paperwork, lists of gear, every piece itemized, presented to him and then entered into the computer program that kept track of their logistics. But out here, in the actual open, alone with Fowler and her platoon, there was a perverse kind of freedom to it. Security was light. The forklifts weren't running. Most of the officers had given themselves the night off, along with most of their underlings. The intruders rested, listening to the growl of generators and dusting off their pants, then Fowler peeked down one of the long central aisles, and said, "So, where does Delta Company keep their shit?"

Pulowski crept up and crouched beside her. Every so often, the lines of vehicles were broken by a passageway running perpendicular to the main aisle, and at each of these intersections—a solution that had been thought up a week into their time on the DRIF—was an orange cone that labeled the contents of that area. The next sign read HUMVEES. He fed this into his mind. He had a picture of the grid in there, the map of the whole DRIF, which hung in the command center and which, by now, he'd seen a thousand times. The key was to picture it clearly, as you might an equation. Somewhere out there was a long, snow-covered aisle with stacked containers filled with every company's gear. He nodded when he had the location, pointed down the aisle ahead of them, then showed Fowler two fingers, and pointed to the left. Then Fowler stood and waved her platoon forward, repeating the sign that Pulowski had just made, and they all hustled down the snowy alley, Fowler charging out ahead.

"What in the world are you doing?" Pulowski asked.

Beale was holding a black trash bag and picking up beer cans from the side of an unplowed county road, twenty miles outside of Fort Riley and the DRIF. Beale's nose had a clear drop of snot suspended from its end. "Policing the area," he said.

"For whom? Why?"

"Orders."

"Come on with the fucking orders, Beale. Where were you last night?"

Beale glanced back down the road. There was a plywood

structure in the milo field there—a cross between a building and a Hollywood western set.

"You stayed here?"

Beale nodded. His nostrils were ice-crusted and he walked splay-footed through the roadside snow, his upper lip trembling.

"Well, that was fucking genius. How'd that go for you?"

"Loud," Beale said.

"Really."

"It was very loud."

"That wasn't the answer I was expecting."

"Wolves," Beale said. "Other things."

"Wolves? I didn't know they had wolves out here." Pulowski scanned the open field. Cut corn stalks poked up through the snow.

"Oh, yeah, man. It's fucking badass out here. These guys have seen a bunch of wolves. Bear. No fucking around. Band of brothers, man."

"No lions?" Pulowski asked. "No tigers?"

"Fuck you," Beale said.

There was a stir outside the plywood building, figures in ACUs, standing out checkered brown against the snow-cropped field. "No fucking help," one of them shouted. The sound was shredded up by the wind that cut through Pulowski's jacket, and he dug his hands into his pockets and reminded himself how little he liked the country, in any form. "Mouth, Beale. Get your mouth into it. Show us your mouth."

Another made what sounded like a pig call: *Sooey*.

Beale responded by getting down on all fours in the snow and rooting around in it with his nose. He pulled up a broken bottle, holding the neck of it between his teeth, and when he emerged this way, snow flecked on his nose and eyelashes, he held up the bottle for display for the soldiers who'd yelled at him and they cheered—though, even with the wind, Pulowski could hear higher notes of laughter. If Beale noticed these, he didn't show it, but instead pumped his fist and made a show of dropping the bottle directly from his mouth into the bag. "So this is your band of brothers?" Pulowski asked.

"It's SERE training, buddy," Beale said. "Closest thing you can get to Ranger training and still be regular Army. All these guys have it."

"*This* is SERE training?"

"Survival, evasion, resistance, and escape, dude."

"Yeah?" Pulowski squinted. "What part are we working on now?"

"*We* aren't working on shit," Beale said. "*You* are standing there waiting to get ass-raped by a bunch of hadjis."

"Really? That doesn't sound like very much fun," Pulowski agreed. He was slightly bored.

"Hey, to each his own," Beale said. "But when the ass-rape team comes calling for Carl Beale, Carl Beale intends to have a little training."

He picked up a second bottle with his teeth and deposited it in the trash bag, much to the enjoyment of the soldiers—one of them was Lieutenant Anderson, judging by his size—at the far end of the field. Then he stood up again and lumbered along beside Pulowski.

"You got a real nervous thing about this ass-raping," Pulowski said.

"Nervous." Beale blew air between his lips and shook his head sadly, staring up at the brilliant winter sun overhead. "Nervous. Fuck. You seen the reports we've been getting on IED traffic? You seen that shit on YouTube."

"I seen a lot of shit on YouTube," Pulowski said.

"Yeah, well, you want to fight the monster, you got to *be* the monster, dude."

This was the kind of moment, the kind of argument, the kind of discussion that was not very valuable to have with someone in the Army. In his experience, this was the time you walked away, which he would have done with Beale, except for the fact that he found him funny. "Fowler wants you back."

"Yeah, well, she was the one who kicked me out."

"Because you let the captain steal her shackles."

"She kicked me out because I let the captain steal her shackles," Beale said. "She kicked me out because I let the captain steal her shackles. Shackles, sir. Fucking shackles."

They were close enough now to the plywood structure that Pulowski could see it resembled a cross between a deer stand and a boys' clubhouse. It had two stories and had been constructed out of rough wood studs and plywood walls into which windows had been cut, unglassed and unframed. Up in the shadows of the second floor, Pulowski could see paint cans wrapped with black gauze, like cheap Halloween effigies, attached to a T-shirt stuffed with hay. "Hey, Beale," Lieutenant Anderson said. "Drop."

This kind of bullshit was the reason that Pulowski spent as much time as possible avoiding the infantry. It didn't have to exist, it didn't always exist, but it could. The main problem that he had with it was his first instinct was always to laugh. "Come on, you don't need to smoke this guy, Anderson. He's good. He never did anything to you."

"He's good?" Anderson said. "You think he's good?"

"Okay, what—you want to go with medium? He's medium?"

Lieutenant Anderson smiled at this joke in a way that seemed to Pulowski clearly learned from movies. The smile that wasn't a smile. The response he gave wasn't much more original. "Yeah, well, it is what it is."

"Maybe it is what it isn't," Pulowski said before he could stop himself.

By then Beale had dropped into the snow and was doing push-ups, grunting lightly, and one of Anderson's subordinates had come over to put a boot beneath his mouth, making kissing sounds and shouting out, *Sooey*, each time Beale's mouth touched it. Pulowski could smell Anderson too, smell his heaviness and his weight, and it wasn't going to be enough, in this particular situation, to simply cancel out his signal, refuse to receive it, and walk away. There was something bad here, he could feel it, whether or not he knew how to translate it exactly, and he wanted somehow to enunciate a different principle. It was the first time he felt absolutely sure of that.

Pulowski withdrew his hand from his pocket and, glad that he was wearing gloves, tossed a lavender wad of satin into the snow at Anderson's feet.

Anderson lifted a boot in the air, as if he'd stepped in something foul. "What the hell is that?"

"Your underwear," Pulowski said.

"That true, LT?" one of the nearby soldiers said. "Shit, check that out. You got some fucking downtown taste there, man."

The soldiers clustered around the tiny wad of lavender, hands on knees, inspecting it, one of them making a joke by poking at it with a stick. Anderson swept off his stocking cap and pushed them away. "Get up and get in my car," Pulowski whispered to Beale. And then he started to walk backward, eyes on Anderson, who bent down quickly, stuffing the purple tuft of fabric into the pocket of his ACUs.

"There's more where that came from," Pulowski said. He was

listening for Beale's retreating footsteps behind him. He hoped he heard them.

"Give it," Anderson said.

"You want your stuff back, Lieutenant Fowler wants hers. You give us Beale, we walk away. You don't need to be smoking this guy anyway."

"Fowler? The fat chick?"

"She says she likes a man in briefs."

Anderson heaved the football he'd been carrying at Pulowski's chest and Pulowski tucked a shoulder, so that it glanced off his back—still painfully.

That was the end of his tough-guy routine. He turned and made a break for the Celica, where he had a bag of personal items that they'd stolen from the Delta Company lockers out at the DRIF. Signal officers never did shit like this. In signal processing, the primary goal was to take the analog world and make it something that a machine could understand. Take light bouncing off white snow crystals and make it ones and zeros; take motion and make it pixels. You could store motion, store sound, store position, fold it up inside an equation, then an algorithm, imprint it on a wafer of silicon—and then re-create it, anywhere, on any machine. It was like stealing the world, except safely, cleanly. Nobody ever got hurt, or was actually cold, or got drilled with a football because of a digital file, and so, if you really thought about it clearly, you could see that signal processing was the future—hell, he could probably see this dumbass "secret" field of Masterson's on Google Earth if he wanted to and, in a way, what you saw there was more real, to more people, than the actual field that he was running through would ever be.

Meaning that signal work did not normally involve cranking the engine of an old Toyota, or stamping the gas pedal and hoping it would catch—and when it did catch, shouting, *Fuck, motherfuckerrrr!*—and pulling a U-ey through the snowy field while Waldorf circled Fowler's red pickup around beside him and Fowler herself, standing up in the back, tossed personal items out into the air—baseball caps, toothbrushes, boxers—and Anderson with his huge head and his beetle-black eyebrows high-kneed it down the frozen roadway after them, shouting, *Hey, you two fucking worms, get back here. Get back here with my fucking shit, Pulowski. I'm not done with your sweet ass, Beale!*

11

ARMY OF ONE was the motto that hung over the mirrors in the Fort Riley weight room, right next to the porny photographs of competitors for the Mr. and Mrs. Fort Riley competition flexing and oiled up in their bathing suits. Fowler was in her regulation ARMY T-shirt and black gym shorts wondering what the hell Pulowski was seeing when he praised her body in bed. After three solid weeks of paperwork and overseeing the packing at the DRIF, she looked like an Army of about fifteen. Her shorts felt a size too small and the small bung of soft flesh that drooped over the waistband was visible when she kept her shirt tucked in (as regulations required), giving her the profile of a deflated gray balloon, so she strove to keep her eyes on *SportsCenter* as much as possible instead.

Who had told her that she belonged here? Pulowski. Who had convinced her that she had convictions? Pulowski. Who had given her the ridiculous idea that she should act on them, even if that made her different? Well, she definitely looked different enough here—as did Dykstra, who at the moment was gamely struggling to do sit-ups on an inflated ball. Meanwhile, Fowler rocked her feet on the elliptical paddles, swinging them in a vague waddling motion that definitely wasn't going to intimidate anybody.

"He's here," Dykstra said. He'd wandered over from the bouncy ball with a towel around his neck, his bald head beaded in sweat. As a protective measure, he'd put on a hooded sweatshirt and standard-issue old-school cotton sweats (speaking of porny) and black Converse high-tops with green socks.

"Feel strong, be strong," Fowler said. They were watching Masterson as he worked his way through the free weights, in an ARMY shirt that seemed to have been deliberately chosen to be one size too small. He carried a small leather pack from which he withdrew a towel, an iced bottle of water, a pair of weightlifting gloves, and a sheaf of papers, sat down on the end of a bench press that two significantly larger sergeants had been using, and began Velcroing on his gloves while reading the papers, which he set between his feet. The soldiers who'd been using the bench, though larger, moved silently away. "I got a different motto," Dykstra said. "Never risk good health bennies."

"Really?" Fowler gave Dykstra the up-and-down.

"Hell, yeah. Working the deli at Wawa don't cover kids, you know what I'm saying? Soon as Jenny peed on that stick, I'm out doing roadwork, wearing a garbage bag. Drop forty pounds, sign up, pass my physical—and bam, that's it for me on the workout thing." Dykstra scrounged a cookie from the pocket of his sweats.

"That's a great story, Dykstra," Fowler said. "Excellent example for everybody. Remind me to put that in the company newsletter, okay?"

"Hey, I ain't supposed to be an example." Dykstra pawed his belly affectionately, then tapped her on the shoulder with his cookie. "That's your thing."

Squats were what Fowler decided to try, her legs being the area of her body where—in Pulowski's estimation—she had the most productive mass. She'd seen it done a couple of times from right there on her elliptical trainer and she doubted that there was any kind of intensely specialized knowledge that went with lifting weights—in fact, she suspected that, like most male things, the more men acted like there was some sort of specialized body of knowledge that she was unable to acquire, the less likely it was that that knowledge amounted to anything. She knew people as well as Masterson knew people. She could train and run her soldiers as well as he did. The whole hard-ass aura that he gave off, the weight-lifting gloves, the dark and silent intensity, the gloom, his special little campground out in the woods—all of that was just sleight of hand.

But that was only her best self, the new self that Pulowski managed to bring out somehow. The old self still believed that appearance mattered and, what's more, was *always worried* about looking the part, having never really looked the part in high school, or as Harris's stand-in mom, or as a lieutenant. That self believed that the hard-ass Masterson was real and deeply impressive and would've preferred to remain invisible to him.

Masterson began a set on the bench press. Little peeps of effort escaped his lips, and his arms shook in what she saw as a reassuringly human way. She slipped two thirty-five-pound weights onto the squat bar, tightened up her back belt, positioned the bar behind her neck, gripped it with her palms, blew out (like she'd seen other lifters do), then stood, lifting the bar off the rack, feeling its weight press down on her shoulders—and squatted. Once, twice, three times, feeling easy straight through five reps. Not bad.

She propped the bar back on its stand with a satisfying clank. "How ya doin', sir?" she said. "You need a spot with that?"

Masterson sat on his bench, breathing hard, and stared at her for longer than it should've been possible to stare at somebody without speaking. Then he reclined, legs splayed, with the sad whitefish belly of his inner thighs and his package visible at eye level. "What do you want, Lieutenant?" he asked.

"I thought you might need a spot."

"I doubt it."

It was a difficult and unnerving response. Did he mean that he doubted that was what she wanted? Or that he doubted he needed help?

What would've been wrong with saying thanks?

"Sorry, sir, my bad." Fowler gave a wholly unconvincing laugh. "I just thought that we were sort of working here on the same team."

"Foster!" Masterson said. A giant sergeant set down a barbell and, with a nod from Masterson, tossed Fowler a plastic water bottle.

"Thank you, sir," Fowler said. She drank. Then dropped it down quickly, eyes tearing, and choked down a mouthful of warm beer.

"I don't want you on my team," Masterson said.

She clenched her fist and deliberately drank again. "Even so, sir," she said, wiping her mouth, "I would like to talk to you about Sergeant Beale. And some shackles he might've given you. I apologize, but I'm going to need both Beale *and* those shackles back."

"Apologize?" Masterson said. "Hell, I should be thanking you. Who would the Packers be without the Vikings? Who would the Chiefs be without the Raiders? You want to talk about teamwork, Lieutenant—the most important ingredient in teamwork is the other team. And it really helps if they are a prissy pain in the ass."

She considered this theory during her second set. When

she'd finished, she walked over to Masterson again. "Who exactly are the Raiders in this equation, sir?" she asked. "Because I don't really see how there's a hell of a lot of things you've got to fear from my unit. Or from Beale. He's not Charles Woodson. He's just my platoon sergeant. Or he would be if you'd tell me where he is."

"Charles Woodson," Masterson said, smiling approvingly. He nodded over at the hulk, Foster, who'd resumed his curls. "That's fucking nice, huh? Chick knows her old-school football. We should get you on the Delta fantasy team."

"I watch a lot of TV," Fowler said.

"The circle of brotherhood only works if there's somebody on the outside. You and your man Beale are good candidates until we get to the Iraqis. Hell, anybody who has the nickname Family Values Fowler—that's an outsider to the universe. I mean, personally, I'd make an effort to get that changed."

"It wasn't my first choice."

"It's not *my* first choice to drink beer on Saturday mornings, but the guys like it because they feel like we're getting away with something. It wasn't my first choice to steal your shackles, but the fact that you got your panties all in a bunch about it is amusing. You should try it, Fowler. Have some fun. *Dislike* someone. Find an enemy. All this happy talk about reconstruction and helping the Iraqis stand up and saving them for democracy? Not happening. Even if it's real, which I sincerely doubt, it's bad for the mind. All I really need for unit cohesion is a shithead. Beale's an excellent shithead. I don't think that you really *are* a shithead. But you keep acting like this, and hassling me about a bunch of shackles, then I'd be happy to put you on my list."

The anger was good for lifting. She grunted through a set with ninety pounds on either side of the bar. No twinge in the back. No pain. She clanked the bar back in place, dusted her hands off, and walked around to the weight rack, slamming on more plates, not even really caring what weight they might be.

Masterson racked his weights for the bench press—including the clips Fowler would've liked to use but was afraid to steal—and shifted over to a vertical press just beside her. He tucked the sheaf of papers he'd been reading under one thigh and paged through them thoughtfully. "So what you're saying, sir," she said, "is that in order to be a good lieutenant, I need to take the biggest shithead in my platoon, the weakest person, cull him out, make his life miserable, and crap all over him."

They were now in what Fowler considered to be a classic male position, side by side, but not facing each other. Maybe she should have tried talking to Beale that way. "Pretty much it," Masterson said.

She was glad, given the curtness of his tone, that she could not see his face. "Seems convenient," she said.

"That's my thing," Masterson replied.

"You got your things, I got my things, sir," she said. "Or really, actually, I've got a lot of your things, too. All your Bradleys. All your Humvees. All your transmissions. All your fuel lines. A maintenance platoon is like the equipment manager, sir. We're pretty quiet but we do get our hands on a lot of important gear."

"And?"

"And so I'd love to help you as a teammate. But I'm going to need my soldier and my shackles back first. Otherwise, things might get out of place."

"That's it? That's your battle plan? Help people?"

"If you're strong," Fowler said, "you help the weak."

That was it, pretty much. It wasn't exactly a complicated thought. Wasn't likely to win any Nobel Prizes. But yes, that was pretty much it when it came to her convictions. Like most things, it sounded stupid once you'd said it, but at least now she had.

Or at least it seemed stupid, until she had waited on the bench long enough for the second thought to occur to her: *That's exactly what you did with Harris. You cut him out when he was weak.*

"Let's try it my way once," Masterson said. He ambled over to the squat station and, lifting the bar one-handed, carried it out from the frame that surrounded it and set it on the rubber-padded floor. Yet again, Fowler wasn't sure whether he was referring to his command style or to the weights. "I think you are a practical woman, Fowler. And I don't think you're all as goody-goody as you play. So I tell you what. Every guy in my unit is required to be able to squat *at minimum* twice their weight. I think you can do it. Moreover, I think you want to do it. I don't think you have any interest at all in being weak. And I think you understand exactly why I've got your Sergeant Beale out at my camp and have been abusing him like a lame puppy."

"One-thirty," Fowler lied, standing up. "That's what I weigh."

"How about we say one-fifty and you don't have to get on a scale?" Masterson said, grinning. He peeled two of the largest plates off the weight rack and added them to the bar's end. "Peer pressure, it's a wonderful thing."

"One lift," Fowler said. "Two-eighty. What do I get out of it?"

"You do it, you get your shackles back." He'd finished adding weights by then. The bar had three forty-five-pound weights and a five-pounder on each side. It looked like something from a Tom and Jerry cartoon. "Hey, fellas," Masterson shouted to the entire free-weight section of the gym, fifteen guys, all of whom, she would've guessed, could've qualified for Mr. Fort Riley, and all of whom, she was sure, were infantry. "We got a bet here. Lieutenant Fowler here believes that we have committed the grave sin of stealing some of her platoon's shackles, which I know is a deeply offensive accusation for all of you honorable Christian men." Laughter now, more clearly audible. Even Fowler thought the line wasn't so bad—made a note of it, as if it might be something that she herself could use. "So, because I am committed to the principle of equal opportunity as much as the next guy, I'm going to bet the lieutenant that if she lifts twice her body weight"—here Fowler heard what sounded like a lowing sound, deep and guttural, which caused her to flush and focus on the shiny textured grip of the bar between her feet—"then I will give her all the shackles she could ever want."

With her head bowed and her knees bent, Fowler lifted her hands up beside her shoulders and allowed Masterson and another soldier to set the bar into them, until its full weight rested against her back. She could feel the full horizontal press of it along the vertebrae of her neck and both shoulders, as if the wall of a building had been set down there. She almost fell forward once, light-headed, but Masterson was right about one thing: the mooing had helped her focus, the opposition and scorn and distrust of the soldiers in the room did give her something solid to press against. She blew out a breath, focused all her energy, and drove up, huffing and groaning—sounding, she was sure, completely idiotic, but at this point who gave a shit—until her vision blurred and she felt her legs extend and lock at the knees and she stood there quivering and triumphant, hearing nothing but the silent defeat of Delta Company. Then she blinked once, twice, and saw that the free-weight room was empty, the barbells still out at their stations, but the soldiers gone, including Masterson, and she was stuck, without a spotter, unable to take a step. With great effort she managed to turn her head to the racks of elliptical trainers and stationary bikes at the far end, where a few other support soldiers like herself were pedaling quietly, none of them in the slightest bit interested in looking her way. "Little help here?" she said.

12

"I can't believe that my own platoon sergeant would let another officer waltz right into our equipment locker and steal our shit," Fowler said.

"Maybe Beale didn't think of it as stealing," Pulowski said. "Maybe he figured that Masterson would bring the stuff back."

Fowler didn't answer this. "I fucked up," she said. "My whole life, my whole career, the most relentless suck-up you've ever met. Oh, jeez, I want to be a good officer, sir. Please like me. And then, when I gotta make an actual decision, I gook on my shoes. I fucking can't take care of people. I can't protect these guys. I'm good at *pretending* that I can take care of people, that I know what I'm doing, but I don't, okay? Maybe Harris is right. We are two months out from going to Iraq. I think we're trained. But maybe all I'm doing is checking off boxes of what I think I'm *supposed* to do, Pulowski. I don't have any convictions! Beale at least has some convictions. Masterson has convictions! They're fucked-up convictions, but they still exist. Even Seacourt and Hartz, they at least presumably believe in the way we've been getting trained!"

"But you don't?" Pulowski said.

"No, that's your conviction, Pulowski."

"Hah, that's just my pose."

"Oh, really?" Fowler propped herself up on her elbow. Pulowski was spread-eagled atop the motel bed's sheets with a bag of potato chips on his chest, a small flap of coverlet flipped over his groin. "I thought this was your pose," she said.

Pulowski glanced down at his own body wryly, his head cocked at an angle by a folded pillow. He wriggled his toes where they rose up into the lower corner of the TV, where they obscured the legs of Tom Hanks as he sat talking to Jay Leno. Then he reached out and gently cupped a hand beneath her breast.

"How do you suppose you can tell the difference?" he asked.

"What, between a conviction and a pose?"

Pulowski rumpled his lips and shrugged, as if this were a choice that she had defined on her own, rather than something he'd led her to—though of course he hoped he had. "That's a pose," he said, nodding at Jay Leno, and then, rolling onto his side, he kissed her breast, right atop the nipple. "And this is a conviction," he said.

How the hell did he come *up* with crap like this? He'd had a knack for it ever since Fowler had first crossed the lawn between their apartments, knocked on his door, and stood there, looking actually angry as she said, "Would you like to go to lunch?" and he'd said—he'd somehow known to say—"Well, if you're going to ask me out, you could at least look like you think I might say yes." He'd never specifically said that self-doubt was a bad habit of hers, but every time she tried to get him to admit to some flaw that she had—as opposed to discussing his flaws—he'd twist and turn and evade the question, turning it into a joke, as if there couldn't be anything more ridiculous than taking such talk seriously in any way. Part of her appreciated that. He felt it, a little click.

Fowler reached down and circled his penis with her fist. *Click.* "Yeah? And what kind of conviction do we have here?"

"That's a tired conviction," Pulowski said.

"So you do have them," Fowler said.

"Horniness, love of beautiful women, love of television." He held up the bag of chips. "Ruffles. These are the things that make our society great."

"You forgot baseball," she said.

"I suck at baseball," he said. "Remember that."

"So, what, you can only have convictions about things you enjoy?"

"I think convictions *are* the things you enjoy," Pulowski said.

"Those are called temptations," Fowler said.

"Really?" This time it was Pulowski's turn to sit up in bed. "You seriously believe that?"

"That's what I always told Harris," she said.

"We're skipping that," Pulowski said firmly. "You raised a sociopath. Welcome to America!—where, by the way, you started parenting at age *eight*. It's not some life lesson you're doomed to repeat."

"That's your conviction."

"It is."

"Wish I could say the same."

"You got plenty of convictions, Fowler. Don't short yourself."

"Yeah? What the hell are they?"

"Convictions are the things that you do without thinking about it."

After they made love, he lay on his back in the dark, with his arm curled beneath her neck. He would've liked to point out that *that* was one area where Fowler did fine without thinking. But he could feel her thinking now, their prior conversation drifting back down over them like a mist, lighter, he hoped, than the way that her brother, Harris, talked to her—though in essence, he and her brother were recommending similar things. Ease up. Stop worrying about the rules so much.

“I cannot believe Masterson stole those shackles,” she said. “Right there. Right in my face. He stood there and told me that I didn’t know what I was seeing.”

“But you did see it.”

“Yup.”

“Sounds like a conviction to me.”

“Yeah, well, the problem is that Captain Hartz’s conviction is that there’s nothing more important in the Army than chain of command. Know your place. Keep your head down. And if you’re a support lieutenant, don’t fuck with the infantry. All of which I can live with, so long as somebody convinces Beale to do the same thing with me.”

“How do you intend to do that?”

“I don’t know, Pulowski,” she said. “That’s how we started this whole conversation, okay? I don’t *have* any convictions, that’s the problem with me. I thought that I joined the Army because it was going to clarify shit. Make things simpler. You got rules, you got responsibilities. One person owes another a certain respect. You don’t have to define how things are supposed to work. It’s all clear. There’s rules for how to cut your toenails, for chrissake. You’re not supposed to sit around and worry about convictions. Right? Beale disobeyed my orders. He screwed up. So forget him—let him pay.”

Jesus, how could he be so nuts about a woman who was such a mess? Maybe because he had a conviction that she wasn’t, really. He lay there grinning in the darkness, enjoying this. “I don’t think that’s your conviction,” he said.

“No? Why not?”

“If it was, you wouldn’t spend so much time explaining it to me.”

13

The motor pool hangar was a lonely place, far from the parade grounds, or the firing range, or anything that seemed remotely immediate in a way that Fowler, over the past few months, had come to appreciate. Thorny locust trees had been left to grow along the edges of its vast parking lot, filled with rows and rows of vehicles, the boring and forgotten kinds: front-end loaders, diesel container trucks, backhoes, even a road grader—along with her favorite, the Hercules, which she'd tucked back into the shade of a cottonwood. Which was why, as she parked her Ford, she was surprised to see Captain Masterson pushing out the hangar exit into the pallid sunlight, a pair of lieutenants flanking him on either side, lugging duffel bags that clanked and seemed oddly heavy. Though Fowler saluted, he did not salute her back. "Too nice a day for the office, Lieutenant," he said. "We're going to have a turn in the weather here just about any second. I've been out here three straight years, and once that cold air starts pouring across the mountains, it's game on. So enjoy it now, that's what I say."

"I grew up here, sir," Fowler said.

"Oh." Masterson seemed unflustered by this correction, or at least uninterested, his eyes a bit vague and out of focus, as if smiling through Fowler at his Humvee. "Well, congratulations on *that*."

"You guys find what you need?" she asked. The storage lockers at the motor pool generally held a company's most valuable and delicate electronics equipment. Not stuff that clanked, like these bags did. Not stuff you'd *want* to put in a bag.

"This?" Masterson waggled one of the bags in front of her nose, as if inviting her to sniff it. "This is our baseball gear. Isn't that right, fellas? We're going to head out and take advantage of this last little bit of warm weather. You want to come, you can."

"Naw, I got to work," Fowler said. She glanced back regretfully at the hangar. "I'm the unit movement officer. I need to get all our vehicles and containers inspected and ready for staging at the railhead. We've only got another week."

She felt proud of herself saying that. Proud and official. You almost never got to talk to infantry commanders about supply work, especially not one who'd nearly screamed her off the training course six months back.

"Excellent," Masterson said. He opened his Humvee's door and gave her a smart salute. "Hell of a job, isn't it?"

"We got to move this whole lot," Fowler said. "Plus a bunch more, sir. I timed it out. We've got to be able to load a vehicle on a railcar in thirty minutes. You count up every vehicle on our list, and you look at the window we've got to do the work, you want to make sure everything's inspected and squared away. No time for snags."

She flushed. Why was she *talking* so much? Probably because she'd been staying up till all hours of the night, running through spreadsheets listing every vehicle they needed to prepare, where their tools had to be packed, how their containers should be loaded—none of which she'd been given even thirty seconds of training on, either in ROTC or at Fort Lee. And so it was painfully satisfying, like having a deep, unreachable itch scratched, to have an actual company commander like Masterson notice that she had done this. Masterson whistled between his teeth and surveyed the motor-pool yard.

"All this stuff?" he asked.

"Well, sir," she said, "everything that belongs to our company. Of course, I'm not going to be bringing my truck. Or any of the other civilian vehicles you see here."

"And why the hell not?" Masterson asked. "If I was the unit movement officer, I'd sure as hell pack up my truck. Maybe strap on a couple of ATVs."

"I guess, you know, I could think about it," Fowler said, squinting and surveying the motor pool, happy to play along with Masterson's banter. "Those railcars do carry a lot of weight. We could probably figure out how to add a little old two-ton pickup. It'd be like the cherry on top."

She was well aware that her answers had gone on too long, that she'd been geeking out on details—exactly the kind of thing that Beale tended to hate.

"Fascinating," Masterson said. "Fascinating stuff, Lieutenant. Nothing like Army logistics, huh?" He gave a sideways glance at his lieutenants, who might have been derisive, but when his expression returned to meet Fowler, it seemed harmlessly amused. With her, not at her. "Keep it up," he said. "I'm sure you're doing just great."

Inside the hangar, she found McWilliams driving a forklift with a cigarette clenched between his teeth while Beale balanced on the lift's front tines, clutching a half-inflated basketball against his chest. "Let's go, White Chocolate!" McWilliams shouted.

"Throw it down!" Immediately the glow of Masterson's words curdled—he hadn't been complimenting her. He'd been laughing at the goofballs under her command. Like Beale, who at the moment clutched the ball against his overly ample belly, as McWilliams steered him toward the basketball rim that had been erected at the hangar's end. Fowler judged that he had never dunked—or even probably played organized ball. It was a fantasy. A dream. By then, still hooting and hollering—and being too stupid to notice that their commanding officer was present—McWilliams had swung the unsteady Beale, with his bright red hair and his flushed face, by the basketball hoop, and Beale, setting up for his dunk, slipped at the last minute and came up short, the ball jamming against the rim, and the entire basket tipping over, its metal pole banging against the hangar floor with an enormous *thongg!* "Beale? McWilliams?" she shouted. "What the fuck are you doing?"

McWilliams, at least, seemed mildly ashamed of himself. He was high-cheekboned, with long sideburns, the top of his crew cut platinum blond—a pretty boy with rough and brutal edges, a fairly heavy drinker, but not a soldier troubled by any grand illusions of what he might be. "Um, shooting hoops, ma'am?" he said. Beale, however, was another matter. Even if he wasn't what you'd consider an athletic specimen, Beale was at once bigger and more boyish. And the smirk on his face—he'd pulled his upper lip down over his teeth, his green eyes bright—destroyed every good feeling Fowler had taken from her encounter with Masterson. "You think that's funny?" she asked.

"No, ma'am," Beale said. "Nothing is ever funny. We know that."

"Did you see Captain Masterson walking through here? Do you think he was particularly impressed with watching you play grab-ass?"

"No, ma'am," Beale said sullenly.

"Because I was just out front talking to Captain Masterson and he was telling me how much he appreciated the work we're doing here."

She immediately regretted admitting her pride in this, seeing the ripple of amusement that passed over Beale's features. "I'm glad to hear it," Beale said.

"Are you?" she asked. "Because I don't know about you, Beale, but I take some pride in what I do. This is my platoon. I am not embarrassed to be organized. I am not embarrassed to do things right. That's why we're here. And if you don't think that this job is important enough to take seriously, then why don't you go right up the chain of command and check? Ask Captain Hartz if he doesn't care if we do things right. Ask Captain Masterson. Ask the colonel. And what they're going to tell you is that the Army is not about acting cool. It's about getting the job done. It's about being precise. It's about completing your mission, okay? You get no points for style."

A fantasist, a dreamer. That's what Beale was. Somebody imitating what it meant to be a soldier—Pulowski had been right about that, at least. Not long after Beale had been assigned to her platoon, she'd met his mother at a battalion-wide "family weekend" picnic on post. Beale had been off playing horseshoes and smoking a cigar and Fowler had sat in the wilted food tent with his mother—a small, fretful woman with ragged blond hair, dressed in jeans, with tiny, oddly delicate ballet slippers on her feet. What it was that caused this woman to begin speaking so frankly about her son, Fowler couldn't say. Maybe it was a warning, or maybe Beale's mother had believed that this was information that could be exchanged only female-to-female, as if Fowler's sex put her more in the category of a chaplain, rather than of Beale's boss. Whatever it was, the woman had begun a vague discussion of her son's childhood that quickly found its focus in her ex-husband and the effect his departure had on Beale. Her son had been a risk taker ever since. And she had always, in some ways, thought that Carl's interest in joining the service (this was how she'd phrased it, as if the word "Army" frightened her too much to say) had been in a sense a way for him to find another father, or at least a different series of fathers—first his high school Army recruiter, then the sergeant who'd put him through basic. And that (so Beale's mother said) Carl had been deeply disappointed, after his vocational aptitude test, that he'd graded out as a fuel handler, rather than infantry. Meaning, Fowler knew, he'd scored incredibly poorly. *So,* she had thought, giving the woman her best party smile, *in other words, your son is a reject.*

Traditionally, a platoon sergeant was supposed to be a father figure for the men, not to mention a bridge between them and a rookie lieutenant like herself. Having daddy issues appeared to be a bad ingredient for either job; so far, rather than learning from Beale's supposed wisdom and experience, she'd felt nothing but impatience at his immaturity—he was like a stuck wheel on a shopping cart, causing her whole platoon to veer and shift in inexplicable ways. Like now, when, instead of sulking after she'd yelled at him, Beale instead became mysteriously generous, offering two or three times to get the gear all out for her, even suggesting that she go get lunch while he took care of the rest. Or at least it seemed like he was being generous—like maybe she was making progress—until she dragged out the crate of shackles that she'd stored against the wall and began to inventory them. The box was supposed to hold eighty-seven shackles, each nearly impossible to replace. She counted only fifty now. "Beale, come here for a second," she said. "McWilliams too. You got any explanation for this?" she asked, nodding to the box.

"It's a box of shackles," Beale said. But his smirk was missing.

"You got a better answer, McWilliams?"

"No, ma'am," the private said, looking at his boots.

"So you have no idea why there are fifty shackles in this box, instead of eighty-seven? Which is how many there were this morning?"

Beale flinched and swiveled his shoulders, as if he couldn't believe he was going to be called to the canvas for something so trivial.

"What, you don't care about thirty-seven shackles?" Fowler asked.

"Doesn't seem like the biggest loss in the world to me."

"How about your weapon? How many rounds in your magazine?"

"Thirty."

"So why don't we take, what, forty percent of that away? You want to go outside the wire with eighteen rounds in your magazine instead?"

Beale muttered something.

"What?"

"I said," Beale spat, "that I'd be a hell of a lot more worried about some missing shackles if I thought they'd keep me alive. Or if we ever got to go to the firing range instead of sitting around here practicing how we're going to load a Humvee onto a train car, which isn't even going to happen for another month."

"You want to be in the infantry, Beale?"

"Sorry?"

"I said, 'Do . . . you . . . want . . . to . . . be . . . in . . . the . . . infantry?'" She could see Beale's mother, sitting there at her kitchen table, disliking the woman intensely for having saddled her with such an idiot. "Or maybe it's me. Maybe you just have some kind of problem taking orders from a woman. Isn't that what you really mean?"

It wasn't like she hadn't worried this might happen. Hell, if she'd had a mother like Beale's—which she'd once had, in a way—she might've thought that a woman couldn't run a platoon. But what she hadn't expected was how raw and explosive her own direct reference to her sex would feel, the way it would suck all the air out of the hangar. The way she could hear her entire platoon listening.

"Because if you *were* in the infantry," she said, "if you *were* with Captain Masterson, who just now walked out of here, I can promise you that he would feel exactly the same way that I do about some lost gear."

"I don't think you understand."

"I think I do." Here she was on firmer ground. "This is my platoon. I am not embarrassed to be organized. I am not embarrassed to do things right. That's why we're here. And if you don't think that this job is important enough to take seriously, then why don't you ask Captain Masterson? Because what he's going to tell you is that the Army is not about acting cool. It's about getting the job done. It's about being precise. It's about—"

Halfway through, Fowler felt her firmer ground dissolve. She was repeating herself. Beale had dropped into a squat, his head tucked, gazing off to the side, his raspberry lips mashed against his sleeve. "Captain Masterson *took* the gear," he said.

"What are you talking about? I just—" She glanced toward the doorway of the hangar. "He was just here. He was *complimenting* me . . . us."

Then she remembered the "baseball" bags. Their heaviness. Their metallic clanks.

"Stand up!" Fowler shouted. "Stand up and look at me."

Beale did stand. He had to, which in her mind was supposed to be one of the benefits of the Army. But this time it didn't feel that way.

"Why didn't you report it to me?" she asked.

"What would you have done if I did?"

Out of the corner of her eye, Fowler saw McWilliams and a couple of other soldiers laugh at this. "Report it myself," she said.

"Oh, that's great, ma'am. That'd really work out."

"Why not? He's not immune to the rules. If a captain's doing something wrong, it's no different than anybody else." The moment that she said these things, she realized that she sounded exactly like his mother. Talking about how unfair the world had been to her poor Carl. Taking refuge in how things were supposed to be. "If he's wrong, he's wrong. That's the end of it," she added, as if to convince herself more than anybody else.

"Yeah, well, then I'm wrong, aren't I, ma'am?"

"So?"

"So you won't defend me. But he might."

It wasn't what Beale said that set her off. Beale could have accused her of a lot of things, plenty of shortcomings—poor organization, bad people skills. Impatience. Quickness to anger. Lack of self-confidence. It was how she sounded when she was responding to him. Her shrillness, her brittleness. She could hear the humorless flatness of her voice spanking off the upper rafters of the hangar, with their leaky fiberglass tiles, and returning back to her, and whoever *that* person was, whatever she might be saying, however true it might have been, she sure as hell wouldn't have been convinced.

"You're out of here, Beale," she said. "Until I get you reassigned, I don't want you near anybody or anything that involves me or my team."

14

"Cancer," Pulowski was saying. "Psoriasis. Mumps—which can make you sterile, if you're a guy."

"I think that's chicken pox," Fowler said.

Her brother, Harris, had had chicken pox about six months after their mom left. For a moment, in the rattling cab of her truck, Fowler could smell the skin of her brother beneath his pajamas. The best solution to the itching had been cold baths, peeling Harris out of his clothes, slipping his bony shins down into the tub, both of them examining with a certain admiration the red bumps on his chest.

"Really? What the hell would you know about it?"

Pulowski had spent a good portion of their two-hour drive to Kansas City compiling a list of diseases that he might contract to avoid deployment.

"My brother had them," she offered.

"Before or after your mom left?"

"After."

Her pickup rattled through an unfamiliar, leafy residential maze in the city's core. A school bordered the park off to her left, identified by a white signboard and about twenty girls in sweatpants and cleats swinging hockey sticks out on a thatched and yellowed field. As they descended past hotels and high-rises and crossed a bridge over a creek, entering a crowded shopping area, Pulowski's GPS entered into a state of panic. *Turn Right. Recalibrating route. In one hundred yards, turn left.* For once, Fowler could identify with the machine. The wealth of the surrounding shops, the vaguely familiar names—BCBG, Dolce & Gabbana, Ann Taylor—swirled around the truck in dizzying confusion. Pulowski stared at her cockeyed as she wrenched the Ford down a side street, flaring a pack of women who all seemed to be wearing high black leather boots with extremely pointed toes—a style she'd managed to somehow miss entirely. "So you did, like, take care of him occasionally, didn't you?" Pulowski said. "There might conceivably be some good memory that he has of this."

"That's not how Harris works," Fowler said as she parked and climbed out.

"How do you know?" Pulowski scooted over to the driver's window, sticking his head out.

"Because I lived with him," Fowler said. "Because he's my brother. Because we are both very stubborn people and we have different views on shit."

"And you don't think people change?"

"If I say yes, would you actually feel better? Or would you just go back to pestering me about the chicken pox?"

"Do *you* have chicken pox? Because if that is actually deferment-worthy—" Pulowski closed his eyes and lifted his chin as if for a kiss.

"Pulowski!" On the far side of the truck, she noticed people had paused along the sidewalk, gawking. "See? I'm not encouraging this," she said. "There's no point in fixing one worry, if you're just going to replace it with something else."

"See what?" Pulowski asked. He kept his eyes closed and

smiled goofily. "I got a hard-on. But I'm not *seeing* anything, really."

She rounded the corner, past a shop that sold, apparently, only women's jeans stacked on racks of white shelves, all of which looked far too skinny for her to be able to actually wear. Mom jeans. That was what Harris had called the pants she'd gravitated toward back in the day, none of which appeared to be on sale here. Harris himself had always been much quicker, much more decisive, much more original in what he chose to wear. No uniforms for Harris. Nothing that would have suggested that he came from the place that he actually had come from, whereas for her, the uniform, from the moment she'd put it on, had been a relief. Better than mom jeans, since mom jeans were still pretty tight in the crotch. But similar, since mom jeans meant that you had a husband to come home to, which implied (she assumed) that the women who wore them had negotiated some sort of cessation of hostilities, wherein the mom might be said to have value for something other than the fit of her jeans. For what she did. That was what the uniform meant to her, at least.

Maybe it was a weakness, wanting to belong so badly. Harris certainly had seen it that way. And there were times, like this morning, when she wore the uniform as protection and as a warning, even though by regulation she should've probably been in civilian gear. She was passing a restaurant with tables set out on the sidewalk behind an iron railing, and the patrons were out in wire-backed chairs, every one of them eating something different—salmon, salad, fruit, a plateful of pasta. She tried to imagine herself as one of the women there, tried to imagine herself holding a job, maybe living in one of the glassy apartments off to her left, up the hill. Tried to imagine not having a platoon, not knowing Dykstra, not knowing Crawford, not knowing

Hartz, not having to go to PT, never having replaced the hydraulics on a Hercules, or signed her commission, or given a briefing, or fired an M4.

She'd reached the bank building by then. The windows along the sidewalk were clear and oversize and the décor inside was, if anything, retro compared with the shops she'd passed: broad red carpet, teller window of newly stained wood, potted plants, a set of three very large and very heavy-looking desks with nameplates, brass lamps, and translucent green shades. It had been two years since she'd last seen her brother, and nearly seven now since their fight over the Ryersons' car, and as she paused outside the revolving glass door, buffeted by women in their high, unsteady heels, she wished, if only briefly, she'd worn something that would make her seem as helpless as she felt.

"Hello! Can I do something for you?" The girl who approached her could've been one of the ones from outside on the street: glossy black hair cut straight across her forehead, a pencil-thin skirt, two-toned shoes.

"Yeah," Fowler said, "I'm, uh . . ."

"Are you wanting to open an account?"

"No. No—I mean, I have a bank account."

"Looking to finance a mortgage?"

"That would be, um . . ." She was still scanning the room, past this woman's silk, pin-striped shoulder, searching for . . . what, she wasn't sure. A patch of curly ginger hair (I kissed that once; I combed it; I washed it with soap and water). *Yes, I'm here to see my little brother, but I have no idea what he does here. No idea how he got here. No idea how long he's been here. Or why he didn't tell me.* "That would be a little premature," she concluded, folding her arms so that her briefcase covered the name tag on her blouse. "I'm afraid. Unless, you know, you got something outside Baghdad."

It was a joke—at least Fowler had intended it that way. But even though the woman seemed to understand this, there was no corresponding laughter. Only a reshuffling of possibilities behind her plucked eyebrows, her wide-eyed, mascaraed face.

"We have a federally funded program for servicemen and -women," she said, thrusting a brochure into Fowler's hands. "I can prequalify you at a rate of five-point-six percent for the first five years of your mortgage. I can fold your closing costs and your down payment into the loan, so you can walk out of here with immediate access to a couple hundred thou in equity. Plus"—the woman came around so that she was shoulder to shoulder with Fowler, her perfume sharp as spoiled wine—"we will actually pay off, in cash, your title fees. It's our way of saying thanks."

"For what?"

"For your service," the woman said. She nodded at Fowler's fatigues.

Fowler handed the brochure back. "Do you think you could help me find Harris Fowler? He's supposed to work around here someplace."

Speaking her brother's name out loud caused Fowler's legs to go wooden, and her hands seemed cottony and distant, as if her blood sugar had suddenly dropped. For the woman, however, it seemed to have the effect of a slap: her face dimmed without changing expression, like a phone screen that had shifted to sleep. She stepped off briskly to her desk, pushed a button, spoke into her phone's intercom, then savagely rifled her drawers before returning with her business card: Rachel Nystrom.

"I know that Mr. Harris has a good reputation," Rachel said, "but I can really use the business—and I can pay better attention to you too."

She hadn't considered the possibility that Harris would have a reputation of any kind, certainly not one that would intimidate a woman like Rachel; she'd imagined that he'd still be wearing a hoodie and a faded T-shirt promoting some deliberately obscure band—Echo and the Bunnymen, the English Beat—that had been popular before they'd been born, and even then not very. His "ironic" Budweiser cap. But instead he exited an office at the far end of the room dressed in a starched white shirt and a flashy yellow tie with a gold clip. His tightly curled brown hair was now cut short along the sides, he was taller than she'd remembered (was he still growing?), but the expression on his face—a studied and carefully arranged lack of focus, an overstudied calm—was familiar. It was the same expression he'd worn when she'd confronted him about the Ryersons' car, as if he knew exactly why she'd come, how she'd found him—though in fact Pulowski had done it on the Internet. "Well, look who's here," Harris said. "This is a surprise." He appeared to be evaluating the room to see if anyone else would notice their meeting.

"I was just in the neighborhood," she said, then stuck her hand out at Rachel Nystrom, rather than hugging Harris, since she wasn't sure what sort of reception she'd receive. "Lieutenant Fowler. I'm, uh—well, I grew up with this kid."

Immediately Harris stiffened, and a slight warp lifted his lip. But when he turned toward her previous host, his voice seemed artificially loud, designed to draw the attention of the tellers and the other employees. "You learn anything interesting from my sister, Rachel?"

"No," Rachel said, in a tone that seemed to imply that she hoped that Fowler wouldn't repeat anything she'd just said.

This seemed to set Harris at ease. "No? You're kidding me. You let a client walk in here and don't get a read on her? Come on, haven't I taught you anything?"

“Hey, take it easy,” Fowler said. “I was in the neighborhood. I came by because I’ve got some family business. If you aren’t free, I understand.”

“Now, there’s a revealing comment,” Harris said. “Do I have a choice about this meeting? Or does the lieutenant really mean that because we’re *family*, she can show up out of the blue and expect me to take off work? *That*, Rachel, is information you can use. Rule one, make sure you know what your client values most.” This was spoken while Harris executed what looked like a series of community-theater stage directions: return to the last, largest desk on the bank’s open floor, adjust your name tag so it’s visible, hunt busily for props. “Rule two, pay more attention to what they do, not what they say.”

“What’s the third?” Rachel asked.

Harris came beaming around the desk, swinging the briefcase, a golden moleskin coat over his arm. It was an impressive sight—as if he’d finally arrived in character, a banker who looked just exactly like a banker. He gave Fowler a dry peck on the cheek, slipped Rachel’s folder from her hands, and waved it as he headed for the doorway. “The third rule is if you want to *steal* a client, never let them go to lunch with me.”

The skating rink had been Pulowski’s idea. He’d called it a tactical move. The fact that neither he nor Fowler nor Harris actually knew how to skate was the point: here would be an opportunity for Fowler and her brother to encounter each other on neutral ground. It also revealed a helpful chink in Harris’s man-about-town armor, since Pulowski was the only one who’d googled the rink’s name and saved its address—it was farther downtown, in a large shopping complex, and thus Fowler got to drive all three of them in her truck, following the chirps of Pulowski’s

GPS. The soundness of this plan felt less evident twenty minutes later, however, when Fowler found herself at a white steel-mesh table with a pair of beige rental skates bound about her feet, feeling about as comfortable as an amputee. Pulowski had already wobbled out onto the ice while Harris sat across from her, paging through the forms she'd brought that named him the beneficiary of her estate. Tactically, the papers were her excuse for *why* she needed to see her brother, but all she'd really wanted to know was how Harris was doing and the answer—as the rink's boards thumped with the toes of other skaters and Justin Timberlake pulsed from speakers overhead—appeared to be fine. Better than she'd expected. Definitely better than in San Antonio, when she'd tried to bail him out of jail for a DUI. So why didn't she feel more relieved? "So you didn't have any trouble with your record?" she asked when Harris finished reading. "I mean, I'm glad you've got a job, I'm just trying to make sure you didn't have to lie to them or anything. Make sure it's secure."

"Fuck," Harris said warmly. "Lying's practically the job description."

"What's that supposed to mean?"

"How much do you make?" Harris asked. He handed the folder of papers back to her across the table.

"What?"

"You heard me." He jabbed a finger at the paperwork. "You show up and claim you want my approval to make me your beneficiary. What am I supposed to say? 'Oh, cool, I'm your beneficiary'? Because it doesn't feel cool to me. Imagine I gave you some paperwork whose primary takeaway was that my job put me *at risk of being dead*—"

"Forty a year," she said. It had never been an embarrassing number to die for until now, sitting on the terrace of an ice rink, in the middle of what appeared to be an urban shopping center—

tall office buildings looming around, a fifty-foot Douglas fir set out amid brightly painted nutcrackers—watching Harris raise his pale eyebrows in a wince.

"There's good benefits," she said, trying to make a joke out of it. She reached under the table and touched his knee. "If I make captain *before* I bite it, you'll get an extra bump. Sorry, sorry—" She waved her hands as Harris reared back. "Look, the paperwork is just a technicality. Nothing is going to happen to me. I got a good team. I came out because I wanted to see you. The only real thing I need is your address."

"You know what's great about the mortgage industry?" Harris pushed the papers back without writing anything. "No team. Straight percentage. Don't have to worry about anyone walking away."

"I didn't walk away from you, Harris."

Harris assaulted the pocket of his suit and retrieved a pack of Camels—one of the few habits he'd picked up from their father. Despite his last jab, he seemed mollified by her decision to frame the paperwork as a ruse. "Maybe you're right," he said. "Maybe running a platoon in Iraq will be a good educational experience for you. Come back down to earth with the rest of us fuckups. Provided you survive."

Fowler laughed, genuinely this time. "Oh, come on, Harris! Jesus Christ, talk about the Fowler morality hour. Next you're going to be telling me that you want to join Greenpeace and vote for fucking Kerry. I'm sorry. For bleeding hearts, I know plenty of officers who've got you covered. Along with about half the guys in my platoon."

Harris seemed mildly surprised at this. "Well, that's fucking great. I don't know, does it improve things when you know you're doing something stupid?"

"Depends on how you define stupid."

"Did Rachel run over our 'Thank You for Your Service' plan when you came in?"

"I rent," Fowler said.

"Well, at least you've got some sense," Harris said.

"Yeah?" Fowler said. "What's so bad about what Rachel offered?"

This was the Harris that she remembered. In the old days, she'd imagined his arguments like a snare. Fowler was always trying to defend something—school, grades, not getting stoned at three p.m.—that put her in the position of sounding impossibly square, impossibly naïve. The more she tried to avoid being pushed into that position (who didn't recognize that there were arguments against going to school, who didn't know the world wasn't fair?), the angrier Harris got and the more he'd argue, until finally she'd step into the snare. Once it happened, she imagined a loop circling around her ankle and her body being dragged suddenly upward into the air by a bent tree, until she dangled helplessly upside down, so that Harris could lecture her on her stupidity.

"First of all," Harris said, leaning forward in his seat, "how much of a loan did she say she could set you up with? Three bills? Yeah? And how the fuck are you going to fulfill a mortgage payment on three bills while making forty grand a year? The answer is you're not. And we don't even care if you do. We're going to sell that thing, securitize it, and it's out of our hands. You guys, the blacks, and the Latinos—our triumvirate of morons. And do you know what you all have in common? You all are stupid enough to believe that you actually *deserve* something. Because you're good Americans. Because you like to feel that you're morally superior. Hey, I'm a good soldier. Hey, I'm going off to war to save my country! Aren't I awesome! Don't I deserve to be thanked? No! You *volunteered* to get screwed. Okay? And at some level, you know that."

Fowler relaxed back into her chair. She felt some guilt for having egged Harris on, but there was also a certain relief, proof that her brother was the person she'd claimed he would be—especially for Pulowski, who'd swung up to the boards beside them, close enough that he'd likely overheard the whole thing. No hope here. Nothing to see.

"You guys coming out?" Pulowski said, tugging at the wrist of his right glove with his teeth. "You pay for the skates, you gotta skate. Come on, now, it isn't possible for either one of you to be worse than me."

Harris's green eyes flitted between the two of them, as if an ally were the last thing he'd expected. "We're having a conversation," he said.

"That's not what it sounds like to me," Pulowski said. "What it sounds like to me is that you are passing off garden-variety, bullshit MSNBC skepticism as actual opinion. You're going to have to do better than that or I'm going to have to start thinking that Fowler here may have actually fucked up your childhood as badly as she imagines."

"Pulowski is one of those bleeding hearts I was talking about," Fowler said. "He'd probably agree with you on the whole volunteering-to-get-screwed thing."

"Maybe," Pulowski said. "But, hey, going to Iraq isn't any *more* ridiculous than lecturing people on the ways of the world because you're making eighty grand a year selling mortgages. If that. Imagining that somehow you're not getting used. It's a multi-billion-dollar industry, slick. Where do you think *you* stand in the fucking pecking order? You are right there on the bottom with the rest of us idiots. We're all getting used."

"Yeah, well, at least I'm not going to get killed while it's happening," Harris said.

"And if you were going to get killed, who'd you want to be with?"

"I wouldn't want to get killed at all."

"*Now* you're making some sense, dude," Pulowski said. He clopped over to their table on his skates, his pants smeared with ice chips. "Fortunately"—he stuck his hand out to Harris, waggling his fingers, as if to pull him from his seat—"getting killed is not a risk while skating. The only risk is looking like an idiot, which, you know, comparatively isn't any worse than, say, stealing some asshole's car."

The entire argument embarrassed her. Even if she agreed with some of Pulowski's points, the car issue was supposed to be buried territory between herself and Harris—his job to bring it up, his job to apologize, since who else in the universe other than Pulowski would claim that somehow stealing a car wasn't wrong? And yet here was Pulowski defending her by using language, principles, and ideas that seemed every bit as bleak as Harris's. So far as she was concerned, the snare was still wrapped around her foot and she was dangling up in the air, battered by both of them now—though Pulowski's argument was being made in her favor, which counted for something, at least.

"I'll go with him," she said. She stood, a bit wobbly, and took her brother's hand.

"You've got to keep your weight *forward*," Pulowski said. He gave her a sly look that said, *Forget the argument. This is going better than you think.* "Don't lean back. You just kind of glide and push. Just focus on what's *ahead*."

"Shut up, Pulowski," Fowler said pleasantly. And then, in the moment that her blades left the rubber mat and she could feel the greasy uncertainty of the ice underneath her, frictionless, like outer space, she squealed in a very un-lieutenant way and grabbed Harris's arm. "Holy shit!"

"Okay, okay," Harris said, concentrating. He'd reached a hand out instinctively, as if to pacify her. "We can do this." This she remembered about Harris: his concentration. The small jut of his lower lip, bright scarlet, the way his nose wrinkled up, rabbitlike, when he was really concentrating. They tottered silently through a quarter turn of the rink like this. Even his grand unified theory of the idiocy of her trip to Iraq was itself a form of concentration. He must have thought of it ahead of time, worked it all out, imagined what he would say. And what was concentration but a form of love, no matter how it came out? It was his best attribute, the thing he had to give.

He was quiet now beside her, absorbed. You could have called it meditation, save for the occasional spasms that ran through his limbs when his balance faded away. He skated just exactly like she did: determined not to look the fool. And now, steadying herself, bending her knees as Pulowski had suggested, reaching that state of glide which, oddly enough, seemed to be largely composed of not trying to glide, she tried to work out what Pulowski had told her about her brother, the complicated riddle that she was not responsible for how her brother had turned out and yet, *at the same time*, was and always would be. "You trust him?" Harris said. He was still holding her hand.

The question was a surprise. It appeared to be genuine, no pose, no implied criticism. She wobbled, overcorrected, clutching Harris's sleeve. "Who, Pulowski?"

"Yeah. I kind of like the guy. Is he gonna stick?"

"He's okay," she said.

"Not like Mom?"

"You mean not like me," she said. She was blinking her eyes more than usual, as if the wind had scalded them. "I'm sorry about the car," she said. "All of that. I mean, we never even talked about it. I don't know why I have to be such a hard-ass."

Harris shrugged, as if he wasn't entirely sure he would've wanted things to be different. "You were never like Mom," he said.

"Do you really think so?"

Harris raised his shoulders as if he didn't care. "You were worse."

"No, I wasn't!"

"See?" Harris said cheerfully. "It's useful to have someone be absolutely sure you fucked up. Gives you something to define yourself against." He slid his cigarettes back in his jacket. "You ought to try it sometime."

Instead, she glided through a forest of memories as fleeting and as finely detailed as the backs of the skaters that they trailed. She had wrestled Harris on the Indian rug in her father's living room, and argued over her willingness to defeat him. "Try harder," he'd insisted. "It's no fun if you *let* me win." And in the passenger seat of the Ford, a teenager with nervous hands and the experimental outline of a pack of cigarettes in his breast pocket, arguing with her over Vincent Foster, who she refused to admit had been murdered by the CIA. Everything had to be questioned; every position she took, examined, checked for flaws—or maybe just dismissed for the sake of it. A waste. But who said it had to be? She and her brother had argued enough to fill fifteen of Pulowski's laptops, and yet it was only now that she had ever considered that maybe he hadn't really meant to trap her in a snare. Maybe Harris's jutted lip and wrinkled nose were attention, directed with all his soul, her way. "It seems a little academic, doesn't it," she asked, "which one of us has the true view of the shittiness of everything?"

Harris was silent after she spoke, watching as Pulowski, up

ahead of them, fumbled for his stocking cap. "I'll do the next-of-kin thing," he said. "Okay? I'll give you my address. But that's as far as I go. And you gotta promise to do one thing for me."

"What is it?"

"Find somebody to be your Emma over there."

"What's that supposed to mean?"

"Let somebody else do the work, for once," Harris said. "Let somebody else worry about what's supposed to be true but isn't. That way you can figure out what you really believe. It works. Or anyway, it worked for me." His coat buzzed, and, pulling out his phone, he held a finger up and said, "Sorry, I gotta take this."

They had reached the open gate that led off the rink. Harris murmured into the phone and then, with a sharp and amused glance at Fowler, one that implicated her in his amusement, he let go of her and glided rather stylishly for the exit, stepping over the scarred wood plank and onto the black rubber mat and into the crowd. She watched him go. Without her, he fit in, looked as organized and citified in his moleskin coat and his yellow tie as anybody there—a part of whatever was happening here. The first club he'd ever wanted to join. Then she swung around awkwardly to find Pulowski.

15

Fowler was in the kitchen. Pulowski sat with her father in the low-ceilinged gloom of her ancestral TV room. A decent-size flat-screen illuminated a knitted throw rug in red and black Native American patterns, old enough that he suspected the threadbare patches nearest the TV had been put there by Fowler's elbows. Her father, Donny Fowler, was slight, dressed in a denim shirt and with thinning black hair that he wore combed straight down in a bowl. His skin had drawn into a tight little bunch of wrinkles up under his neck, and his eyes were brown and mobile. When he'd briskly shaken Pulowski's hand a half hour ago, Pulowski had been surprised to find a flash of timidity in his gaze—a groping quality, as if he were begging the lieutenant to accept him, his house, and his friends for what they were, despite whatever deficiencies might exist. "Lieutenant, this is our resident bullshit artist—I'm sorry, cousin, Bob Summers. My advice is don't let him touch anything that you're hoping to see ever again," said Donny Fowler, introducing a man in a purple Kansas State fleece and a pair of khakis, who was examining the Pinot Noir that Pulowski had carted in. "Now, see that, Bob? That make you feel better? Bob is always dissatisfied with the wine list over here. But what the hell do I know about it anyway? That's officer business, not mechanic territory. What I can do, what I *will* do, is get you another beer—"

"No, I'm fine," Pulowski said.

"That is not fine," Donny Fowler said. "Not fine at all." He turned then away from Pulowski, handed an empty bottle to the kid who'd accompanied Pulowski inside, and said, "Ronnie, you go get your mother to pull out a Corona from the fridge for the lieutenant here. We're gonna sit him right down and have him relax."

Like his father, who, once the football-watching started in their own family, tended to quietly excuse himself and drift away to his study, Pulowski had never been particularly comfortable in the company of a large group of men. He didn't know how to sit. Had never chewed or smoked tobacco. He could drink just fine—and he was glad he'd pregamed with some beers up by the Ryersons' place—so once young Ronnie Summers came back to him with a Corona Light, he focused intently on that.

"So, I guess you guys have been training pretty hard to get ready for all this," Bob Summers said. "Ol' Donny here tells me that he's been hearing all kinds of artillery, last couple of weekends. Isn't that right, Don?"

"Shoo," Donny Fowler said. "I think that might've been why I chose to put money on the goddamn Lions." He spun a circle by his ear. "That stuff's loud enough for me to get out on PTSD. Man, I'd hate to be underneath it."

"I heard some of those rounds are spent uranium," said a wiry blond in a Peterbilt cap. "You know Steve Roebuck? He's got a cousin down at Fort Hood. He says when this is all over, there's gonna be soldiers ending up with exactly the kind of health claims they had with Agent Orange in Vietnam. Lawsuits all over the place."

Pulowski's battle plan for this particular family gathering was to keep his head above water, float along, remain present but unobtrusive. Stay detached. Avoid politics. But a silence followed this observation and Pulowski realized that it had been left for him. "Well," he said, "that might've been true with the invasion, but we're not going to be in a real artillery-friendly situation over there. Or at least that's what it looks like to me."

"So why the hell you all practicing so much?"

"'Cause it makes people feel good," Pulowski said. "I mean, look, we've got enough satellite coverage there, we can *see* the muzzle flash right out of a mortar. And now that we've got bases set up, our response system's mechanized—automatic fire. Soon as that mortar's in the air, they got coordinates and ten seconds later you've got four or five rounds on the way. It's a programming problem, mostly."

The head-bobs that followed this explanation seemed to suggest that in this room of men, he was, shockingly, an authority. The women in the family bustled in the kitchen, and the prairie wind buffeted the house outside, and as the network cut to videos of the turkey-eating soldiers, shot against the dune background of tents or bunkers, Pulowski began to say whatever in the hell came to mind. True, Fowler would've called him out on some of the bullshit he came up with—and it seemed odd to him that they hadn't already asked her about these same issues. But Fowler wasn't there. "Did your daughter ever tell you the story of how our battalion commander got the nickname Bucky?" He glanced up at the men's expectant faces, then hesitated theatrically. "I probably shouldn't tell it. I doubt she'd approve."

Donny Fowler wheezed and coughed in the chair beside him, waving his hand as if to suggest his outburst should be ignored.

"So you *do* know it," Pulowski said.

It was Bob Summers, sprawling back and observing the scene with a milder, wiser grin on his face, who filled him in. "Naw, son, it's just we all have had a little experience with the lieutenant"—he said this in ironic quotes—"disapproving of something. Ain't that right, Donny?"

"I don't think she disapproves of cursing, does she?" Pulowski asked. "'Cause that's what Colonel Seacourt does."

The men considered him through the haze their cigarettes left in the living room—it was the first real case that Pulowski had seen of indoor smoking—as if he'd just declared that the colonel had two heads. Donny Fowler was still coughing, his eyes wet with amusement from Bob Summers's joke. "Come again?" he said.

"No cursing—that's how the colonel got his nickname," Pulowski said. "I mean, he can't outlaw it, exactly. Not in the entire Army. But he did have everybody on his personal security detail sign a pledge that they would quit."

"I would sign a pledge to kick his ass," Bob Summers said.

Pulowski lowered his voice to a whisper. "So one day the colonel's got the base commander, General Nunce, out for troop review. We're going to do a convoy-protection exercise for him. The one thing Colonel Bucky tells everybody to do is make sure they keep enough distance between their vehicle and the one in front. Don't speed. Don't rush it. Don't cowboy anything. You know, just keep in line."

"Uh-oh," Donny Fowler said. "I think I've seen this movie."

"That's right. First thing, first thing that happens—right in front of the grandstand, which is where we're doing this—"

"Because," Bob Summers put in, "they've got a whole lot of grandstands in Iraq, don't they?"

"Right in front of the grandstand, a private pops his clutch and runs his Humvee right up under the back of an Abrams tank. Bumper gets pinched, immediate traffic jam. End of the exercise. But get this, get this." Pulowski was waving his hands now, leaning in. He had his audience, he could feel that. "The colonel, he's standing off to one side of the grandstand, and you can just see his face." Pulowski made a drooping motion with his fingers along his cheeks. "I mean, he is furious. Head's about to blow off. He stands there for a second, then he does an about-face and heads off under the grandstand. The guys around him wait. He doesn't come back. Finally, this major—a guy named McKutcheon, he's my CO—he goes after him, and he finds Bucky just whaling away on one of those I-beams with his boot. Just kicking it. And you know what he's saying? "*Buck, buck, buck*—"

The kitchen of the wood-frame house was tiny, a cramped hutch—nothing at all like the place his mother had refinanced back in Clarksville, with a granite counter and a bright and shiny Sub-Zero refrigerator. The wives of the men in the front room were gathered there—including Bob Summers's wife, who introduced herself as Aunt Carla—all wearing similar combinations of sweatshirts, massive purses, tennis shoes.

The back door crashed open and Fowler charged in, dressed in a pair of jean shorts and flip-flops, her hands black with soot. "All right, Aunt Carla," she said, "I got the coals going." She gave Pulowski a flickering glance that he had a tiny bit of trouble trying to interpret: partly accusatory, partly worried, mostly flighty, as if she wasn't quite sure what to make of him standing in the kitchen. It was uncertainty, he realized. Divided purpose. That's what made it seem unfamiliar, enough so that he enjoyed standing there.

"Your father was going to do that," Aunt Carla said.

"Well, do you see it happening?" Fowler asked. "Are there

coals started? I've got fourteen people to feed, and I've got three birds to make, and salad to get started, and—"

She grabbed one of the three chickens that Aunt Carla had lined up on the narrow counter. "Hey, hey, don't touch that," Aunt Carla said. She pointed at three black smudges that Fowler's fingers had left on the bird's skin. "You got to wash your hands before you're handling the meat."

Fowler held her hands up, splaying her fingers. "We're cooking this on a fire, right, Carla? Am I right about this?"

"*On* a fire," Aunt Carla said, her head bent stubbornly, her thick fingers parting a clot of chicken innards. "Not in."

"What I'm saying is it doesn't matter. The whole thing gets cooked anyway, right? It's not like this is bacteria or something—it just burns off. It's a little smudge. Right, Pulowski?"

"That's sort of a false dichotomy there, if you ask me," Pulowski said. He edged his way past Aunt Carla's ample rear end, removed the chicken carcass from Fowler's smudged hands, and carried it to the sink. "Think of it like a weapon," he said.

"She's in charge of weapons?" Aunt Carla said.

"The better question would be, what weapons isn't she in charge of?" Pulowski said. "Squad automatic weapon, fifty-caliber machine gun, M4, that cute little Beretta she walks around with all the time."

"Is that right?" Aunt Carla said. She was shuffling over to the oven disapprovingly, showing them her wide back. "So what you're saying, Lieutenant Pulowski, is that Emma's good enough to play rifle with her soldiers, but not good enough to remember to buy a Thanksgiving turkey for her family?"

He followed Fowler out back a few minutes later, carrying two of the chicken carcasses that he'd cleaned, stifling any further argument. The plan was to make beer-can chicken, a recipe that Pulowski had heard about but never seen prepared: A rub, he thought, possibly. Or a marinade. But he had a hard time paying attention, with Aunt Carla's jealous sniping still floating about his head, a fart-scented mist of stupidity.

Fowler reached into a cooler, pulled a can of Busch Light, opened it, and set it on a cutting board, the circular top of a cable spool that appeared to be serving as a cook space beside the grill. "You can either hold the can or hold the bird," Fowler said, nodding at the three chicken carcasses that Aunt Carla had given them.

He picked up a bird. It felt clammy in the warm November air.

"And?" he said.

Fowler cracked the beer and assumed an odd position, half in a crouch, holding the can with both hands. "And put it on here," Fowler said.

"Put it on there," he said.

"Put it on there." While he stood there blinking, examining the chicken, turning it over in his hands, Fowler watched him dryly. "Where the hole is, Pulowski," she said. "Come on, you ought to know how to do this."

Pulowski chose to hold the bird. It was not exactly the kind of thing he could've imagined doing with his college girlfriend, Marcia Widemann, in the backyard of her parents' Tudor in Bucks County. No head-tilt or coquettish smile as she worked the Busch Light up into the chicken's chest cavity. Instead, her features, her slightly charcoal-smeared cheeks—there was a war paint element that suited her—were simply open, neutral, her eyes slightly widened and her brown forehead tweaked as if to admit her awareness of the possible sex jokes on hand, and also to suggest that he move on to better material. "You got a better recipe?" Fowler asked.

"I might have gone with chicken piccata," Pulowski said. "Make a little roux to go with it. Maybe grill some peppers."

"Oh, we're a cook now."

"I know how to read a cookbook," Pulowski said. "Although I have never personally read about Busch Light chicken in a book—but hey, maybe it's like a family tradition? Something passed down through your history?"

He'd almost said mother—that was the one person whose picture he noticed wasn't anywhere in the house—and he felt a slight tightening in the air. *Steer clear, keep it light*, he told himself. *No need to get involved in a family mess.* He had definitely clear memories of his own father, in the house they'd lived in before the divorce, but his mother had moved almost immediately—a good choice, in his opinion. Leave the past in the past. Something his parents had agreed on, anyway. Nothing absolutely had to be permanent. "What, you don't like family traditions?" Fowler said.

Politeness. That was the word he would've used to summarize and quantify nearly all of his failures with women, all his faults. There had been Betsy Greyson, with whom he had spent one terrifically awkward evening at the Clarksville Country Club, on pasta night, very politely ignoring the fact that Betsy had at least three times told her parents that he would be "following in his father's footsteps" into medical school. Also a trip to Bucks County with Marcia Widemann: a Kappa, a member of the student senate, an alternate on the cheerleading team. Oh, God, he'd been polite to Marcia Widemann in her yoga pants and her ballerina flats. Polite enough to spend an entire weekend at her parents' house in Bucks County, not having sex. Polite enough not to "mind" as Marcia also invited her "good friend" from high school out to lunch, while Pulowski played eighteen holes of golf with her dad. Polite enough that he did not mind getting smoked by Mr. Widemann to the tune of two hundred dollars, and polite enough—so perfect, so polite—that he'd merely nodded in agreement when Mr. Widemann had shown him the picture he'd taken with Dick Cheney at a Rotary Club luncheon. Polite enough not to dispute the heroic motives that Mr. Widemann attributed to him, while beating the living crap out of him on every tee, all of which Pulowski had been too polite not to accept.

But of course he was not polite, not really. Back in the kitchen, when Fowler had hung her head and silently submitted to Aunt Carla's stupidity, he definitely hadn't felt that way. "There's a difference between family and family traditions."

"Such as?"

"Such as you could serve chicken piccata to your family even if it wasn't a tradition and it would taste okay," he said. "Or you could stop letting a battleax like Aunt Carla intimidate you. What's she got on you anyway? You murder somebody?"

Fowler's legs had a tethered musculature, the long curve of her thigh muscles tapering and gathering in above her knee. In shorts and bare feet—Pulowski gave a brief thanks for the unseasonably warm weather—this was visible in a way it never was in her ACUs, along with the strange, dolphin smoothness of her skin. As she knelt, cupping her hands about the brim of her ball cap and peering in at the charcoal, her pale, untanned soles peeled up from her flip-flops, revealing a line of tendon that extended from the ball of her foot to the heel. "Your parents are separated, right?"

"Divorced. My dad's passed away."

"So how happy were you when he left?"

"I wasn't thrilled about it." He could feel where the conversation was going. Somehow this was really about her brother. If there was one thing he should know better than to bother with in this relationship, it was this missing brother of hers.

"Did you talk to him much?" Fowler asked.

"Nope."

"And you joined ROTC because you didn't want to take any of his money to go to school, right?"

"Fucking stupidest decision of my life, but yeah."

"Why was that a stupid decision?"

The answer to this was that if he hadn't done that, he wouldn't be in the Army, stationed at Fort Riley, about to go to Iraq. But he also wouldn't be standing here with Fowler. "Because he is an independent person. Because he didn't have some kind of special responsibility to stay married to my mom if he didn't want to stay married. I mean, I didn't like it, necessarily—but that's not a good enough reason not to take his money." By now they both knew this was a parallel commentary, heading off any attempt Fowler might make to beat herself up about her brother. Or at least he knew it.

"Still, you told him to piss off," Fowler said.

"That's my right too. He's got a right to bag a hot nurse and move down to Florida before he kicks it. And I got a right to be an idiot and join ROTC."

"Yeah, well, that was pretty much my mom's theory. Which was a nice one for her, but it didn't work out too good for the rest of us."

"So what's that got to do with anything? *You* stayed. Your mom didn't. What the fuck right does Carla have to be riding your ass?"

"I *didn't* stay. Not completely."

"Which is exactly what she's jealous of," Pulowski said.

"No, she doesn't think that I'm holding up my end of the bargain," Fowler said. "I should've stayed back, taken care of my brother. If I had, he'd be here."

They fixed the other two chickens and got them on the grill, a short, uneasy truce, during which Pulowski evaluated the backyard of the Fowlers' place. It wasn't exactly what you'd call poverty-stricken, but it also wasn't something you'd see out back of a doctor's house in Clarksville, or Bucks County. An unpainted chicken coop. The metal remnants of a clothesline. Bare and severe-looking, purely functional, the kind of place most people *wanted* to escape. The same went for the backhanded comments about Fowler's "disapproval" back in the living room, any fool could see that. Except Fowler, who seemed oddly vulnerable around her family, unarmed, eager to please . . . if not wounded already. And what had he done in her defense? Been polite.

"What the hell kind of bargain is that?" he said, deciding to press the argument. "All the guys sit around and watch the Lions game, Carla and her mommy cohort take over the kitchen, you work all week training fucking Beale, and—"

"Jesus, Beale," Fowler said, rolling her eyes and laughing. "He'd fucking love it over here, wouldn't he?"

"You're saying to me that you think this is a fair and equitable system?"

"Hey, it's family, Pulowski. You know this. Rules are rules. Traditions are traditions. If Aunt Carla was having the dinner at her house, she'd be the one who did the shopping. She'd have coals ready. I'm head of the household."

"That's terrible logic." Pulowski was surprised at the decisiveness in his voice, at the vehemence of his anger. "But fine: You follow your rules. I'll make mine."

"Such as?"

"Such as, if anybody complains about having beer-can chicken for dinner—without coming *out* here to help you cook—I get to kick their ass."

Pulowski yanked the chickens around the grill barehanded, imagining a very unlikely scenario in which he was tough enough to kick Aunt Carla's ass. Imagining some better version of himself, one that would actually get mad at the people who deserved it, instead of yelling at a woman who didn't. When he turned, expecting Fowler to have disappeared, to have run inside, he nearly trampled her. She was standing close to him, close enough that he could feel her breasts against his elbows. He tried to walk around her but she stepped, slyly, in front of him. Her chin was up and he could smell her shampoo. "You, Pulowski," she reminded him. "You'd be the person who complained."

What would happen if he met a woman who did not require him to be polite? Or even want it? At a loss, he leaned down to kiss her, his hands covered in grease.

This, apparently.

16

Fowler's mother had picked her up from school early, the day she left. The feeling Fowler remembered was one of derangement. Not mental derangement (though her mother, on that particular day, probably qualified), but deranged as in rearranged, out-of-phase; Deirdre Fowler was not dressed in her usual khaki pants and a belt and an oxford shirt, but instead had shimmied into a dress, an actual evening dress, short-cut in turquoise blue, which seemed a strange choice for the middle of the day. And also she could not, or would not, engage with her daughter directly; only when Fowler stopped asking questions about their destination—"Can we go to the pet store?" "Are we going to a movie?" "Don't we have to get Harris?"—and instead mooned out the window quietly did she feel her mother's abstracted, fluttering caress. Even these touches were ill-timed, somehow off-beat, arriving when her mother was busy making a turn so that the wheel slipped and she had to quickly grab after it, and when Fowler turned to try to catch her mother's eyes, to get an actual answer, she would find instead her mother's face quickly averted, as if the only circumstance in which she felt comfortable looking at Fowler was when her daughter wasn't looking back.

"Why are you all dressed up, Mama?"

That had been her last question. She'd asked it again as they were heading down the corridor at the White Haven Motel. She had never forgotten that motel, the strange time warp of that specific corridor, the ceiling whose plaster had been teased into swirls, the stained, nearly black woodwork that, despite the darkness of the dye, still seemed light, insubstantial, the doors hollow-core, the frames a cheap white pine. Their flimsiness lacked the compensating familiarity of a Motel 6 or a Days Inn, and the rooms she glimpsed as they strode along had seemed oddly old-fashioned, out of time. They had dressers made out of gray carved wood; they had faded, embroidered chairs.

If one thing haunted her thinking during her first few months with her platoon, it was this last encounter with her mother. Not that she made the connection immediately: the actual conversation itself, which she had never spoken about to anyone, had long ago become an event she'd "dealt with" but rarely thought about consciously. A man had been sharing her mother's room at the White Haven Motel. He wasn't there when Fowler arrived, but his things were, commonplace objects that, set amid her mother's things, stuck out with unnatural clarity. The T-shirt draped over a chair's back, a line of yellow around its neck. The smell of spice, a different, fruitier smell than her father's, that leaked out when her mother bustled her past the bathroom. And in the bathroom, a leather dopp kit on the toilet's back, a rusty pair of barber's scissors, a shoe tree, upended, with its carved wooden sole facing her way. She could sense that her mother didn't care at all what the room looked like. That it would feel shameful; that its shame would be legible to Fowler in such a clear way. She was talking confidently now, unzipping and zipping bags of makeup, knuckles close to her teeth. "I just want you to promise me, Emma, that you are capable of handling your brother. Of, uh, well, basically giving him some structure"—her eyes darkened here, as if the word "structure" stood for some deep emotional event (or, as Fowler thought later, because the word seemed so cheap)—"because Harris is a lot more fragile than you. He's more like me."

"How do you know that?" Fowler had asked. It was not really a question. Everybody knew this about Harris. But her mother's claim left her flushed, marked, her right leg bent and sliding up against her left beneath her skirt, as if she wanted to strip herself naked there. To show her mother everything.

"Harris?" This at least caused her mother to laugh. "Oh, my God, honey—it doesn't take a world of observation to see that you two are different."

"But why aren't I like you?" she demanded.

Her mother's eyes were compressed into slits by the pressure of her hands and then snapped back to their almond shape. "Trust me, honey," she said, "you really should be thankful for that."

"How do you *know* I'm not like you?" Fowler said. She was propped against the desk, a pad of White Haven stationery under her left hand, which she was crumpling, crumpling, crumpling. "You're my mother. Aren't I supposed to be?"

Did her mother know that she imagined, right now, this clump of stationery bursting into flames in her fist? She imagined showing her mother this: See? See? But as she squeezed, the stationery only grew soggy with sweat.

"Honey—okay, look. Could you hand Mama a Kleenex?"

"No," Fowler said. Though she did. It was an excuse to stand beside her mother, right between her knees, squeezing that ball of stationery until it burst into flames.

"I'm leaving," her mother said. "Surely you see that. Here's the thing. You know I'm different, and you're only eight. Your father knows it, everybody knows this. I want to do things I'm not supposed to do, which is why it was a mistake for me to get married to your father in the first place. A mistake, okay? And do you know what else? I *make* mistakes. I think too much. I don't know what I want. I'm not organized—or I'm too organized. Or I organize the wrong things. All of these things that your father says are true, exactly true. It isn't that hard to be happy. It shouldn't be hard, but I'm not happy, and it isn't fair for me to take it out on you and your brother. Or your father."

These were exactly the things that her father had said. Fowler had been hearing them over dinner and down the hallways of their house for over a year.

"But what if that's like me?" she asked.

"But it isn't, honey," her mother said. She wanted her mother to grab her, to crush her to death, but instead she stood and unlocked her suitcase, her skirt trailing away against Fowler's wrist. "It isn't, honey, because, see, you are a good girl, and your mother—I am—well, really basically when you get down to it, I have violated all the rules. I don't keep rules, I break rules. That's not what you do."

"So what?"

"It's not so what," her mother said. "You're a good girl. A beautiful smart girl. You really are. And your brother is going to need someone who can give him rules. Here, take this, will you hold these for me?"

These were the blue books that her mother had pulled from the suitcase. They were embossed in gold: PASSPORT. The first showed a picture of Emma at age six. The second was Harris as an apple-cheeked four-year-old.

"I want to go with you," Fowler said. "I don't want to stay with Harris and Daddy. I want to leave."

"Oh, no, honey, really—trust me—you're much better here."

"I don't want to stay here. I don't want to. I won't do it."

"Yes, you will," her mother said brusquely as she opened the door. "That's just who you are. That's what you'll do."

Fowler was thinking about this as she listened to Captain Hartz lead a discussion of Colonel Hal Moore and his efforts in the Ia Drang Valley. It was Hartz's view that officers must be noble, that they must care deeply for their soldiers, that they must never complain down the ranks, that they should never ask their soldiers to do anything they wouldn't do themselves. Since nobody but Pulowski would've argued this, Hartz ran the leadership seminar as something of a film and literature appreciation course, a gut in which the best traits of an officer could be confirmed by film clips, passages from the field manual, information from Petraeus's counterinsurgency manual, object lessons taken from previous deployments, pamphlets on the rules of engagement.

During most of the fall, Fowler had kept her mouth shut. The seasons had changed outside the wooden casements of the battalion's briefing room, which was where they'd held their class. But on this, the final day of lecture, Hartz had cued the movie *We Were Soldiers* to the scene where Hal Moore addresses his troops as they depart for the Ia Drang Valley, and then settled down in his rolling chair behind his desk and gave the class a very long and knowing stare—or at least a stare that Fowler believed was meant to appear knowing, while twiddling a pencil in his small, neat hands.

"Every damn Hollywood movie got the Vietnam War wrong," Hartz said. "That's what the real Colonel Moore said before he made this movie. Why did they get it wrong? What did they get wrong? Why should it matter to you that four hundred Americans held out against four thousand Vietnamese soldiers one November day in the Ia Drang Valley, on a mountain that was of no clear military value? And more than that, why did so many people see this movie?"

Fowler knew the answer to this question. Everybody in the room did. The answer was that Hal Moore represented all the good qualities in an officer: he loved his wife, he prayed with his kids, he refused to abandon his troops in the heat of the battle, he swore and promised that he would never leave anyone behind, and he was always the first one off the helicopter. Anderson, an infantry lieutenant from Delta Company, raised his hand and said, "Because he's a badass, sir?"

There was laughter here, some snickering; all along, during the entire fall, there had been an undercurrent of resistance to the class, a consensus that the good-hearted and noble points that Hartz had been assigned to make were so boring and so preordained that the only interesting thing for anyone to do was to make fun of them.

"You think that's it?" Hartz said. Since they'd watched the movie, Hartz had taken to emphasizing his Oklahoma accent, in imitation of the actor who'd played Mel Gibson's loyal sergeant major before going on to narrate *The Big Lebowski*. "You think that the thing that makes an officer great is being a badass?"

"It was pretty sweet when he shot that dude who was coming at him with a bayonet," Anderson put in, grinning thickly for the benefit of the room.

Her guess was that Anderson imagined himself as the fierce and courageous sergeant, who'd buried himself in the ground and saved his lost platoon.

"That was luck," Hartz said. "I'm looking for principles."

"He was nice to that one guy," said Lieutenant Weazer, a whey-haired lieutenant in Delta, who was the youngest of the group.

"Which guy was that, Weazer?"

Weazer stuttered and flushed. He was shy, she knew, and

religious—and married, with a five-year-old kid—though he was also, at the same time, sleeping with Shoemaker. She'd already guessed the character that Weazer had identified with. "The guy he prayed with," Weazer said. "In the church that time."

"Yes, well . . . ," Hartz said.

"You mean the guy who got his face shot off in the end," said Anderson. "The principle there is don't be a fucking weak-ass."

Fowler faded out from the discussion at that point—or tried to, anyway. She glanced at Pulowski, who was sitting in the back, with his laptop open. He'd convinced Hartz that he took notes that way, but Fowler knew for a fact that he generally gamed. She'd slept with him the night before and now she imagined his penis, how unguarded it had looked when she wrapped her hand around it, or when it flopped back against his belly on the bed. There hadn't been any shots of Mel Gibson like that.

"I think people like the movie," she said, "because it makes them feel better that there's someone perfect around like Mel Gibson to fix everything."

"Sorry? What's that, Fowler? Did you say something?"

Instead of imaging herself *as* Mel Gibson, worried and obsessed with duty, poring over pictures of Custer at his dining room table, she tried imagining herself and Pulowski someplace else entirely, doing something completely frivolous . . . Skiing. In the French Alps. But the vision wouldn't jell completely. "I'm just saying that Colonel Moore lost a bunch of men in that battle," Fowler said. "So if I'd been in a battle like that, and lost that many people, I wouldn't write a book about it."

"Are you saying that he did something wrong tactically?"

The movie involved four hundred men fighting to hold a single clearing on a mountaintop against four thousand well-armed fighters, who were living underground in a fortified position. Tactically, it was about as useful to her as learning Chinese. "Sir, I guess I'm going to leave the tactical assessment to the big boys like Anderson here," she said. "I was thinking that we were watching the film more as an instruction manual for how an officer should act, and I'm just saying that it's interesting to me that Colonel Moore wrote the book and he comes off as being pretty perfect, generally. If he'd really been all the things he says he was, he wouldn't have needed to, I think."

"That doesn't even make sense, Fowler," Hartz said. "He either did those things or he didn't. Are you denying that he stayed with his men? He never lied to them. He risked his life to bring the bodies of his men back. Or are you saying those aren't good examples of how to lead?"

She thought of the nice clapboard house with a big screen porch that Mel Gibson and his hot wife had lived in during the movie. This time, she imagined Pulowski in a nightgown coming in to pet her cheek, while she stared at Custer's massacre. Pulowski having tea for Waldorf's and Dykstra's wives. These daydreams were funny and arousing, good dreams, far more interesting to her than anything she'd seen in a movie. "Actually," she said, "I don't see why everybody seems to think he's just a badass. I mean, who the hell doesn't know that you're not supposed to abandon your men? Or that you ought to be the first in, first out? It's not exactly rocket-science principles of leadership, sir." She riffled through her notebook of Hartz's handouts. "You gave them to us on the first day of class. Besides, if you asked his wife how to take care of his kids, she probably would have said the same thing. What I'm saying is that he seems conceited to me, sir. He says he cares about his men, but if that was true, then his men would've been the subject of the movie. Instead, we get all this stuff about how he went to Harvard, and how many books he has, and how nice and sweet he is to all his children—I mean, I don't know about you, sir, but if I had a commanding officer telling me how perfect he was all the time, I'd get a little bit tired of that, don't you think?"

This was not meant as an indictment of Hartz—more like a compliment, since she knew that he'd previously been divorced, that his kids from his first marriage lived in Cleveland, and that his ex-wife had remarried a consultant, who made twice what a captain's salary could ever be. But she could also tell that Hartz was not going to take it that way. She glanced over at Pulowski. He'd had an outbreak of acne and his shoulders looked bony and un-Gibson-like, but the skin along his neck was as soft and milky as the skin of Mel Gibson's wife in her negligee. "Why conceited?" said Hartz.

Pulowski gave her a smirking grin. They were in their manicured backyard, Fowler tending the grill with a cigar in her mouth, Pulowski wearing a checkered apron, carrying out a silver tray of condiments. "Because he's not really leading," Fowler said. "He's putting on a display. I mean, the guy loses a bunch of soldiers. What about that scene where he has his helicopters buzz by his men in the hangar—"

"Which was awesome," Anderson said.

"—which was totally unnecessary. Why didn't he just take them out to the landing pad? Why? Because he's acting. He wrote the movie, right?"

Pulowski yipped laughter. She loved the sound of it—even if she was really just talking about herself. Who wouldn't want to lie to make themselves look better than they did? Hartz was close enough then that she could smell the coffee on his breath, see the small bright tears along his cuticles. If anybody deserved an Oscar in this room, it was him, for patiently putting up with crap like this. *I'm going to be a fake and a coward my entire life*, she thought angrily. *I'll lose control of my platoon. I'll be court-martialed for incompetence.* "All right, Fowler," Hartz said. "Let's say you were leading four hundred infantry soldiers into the Yo Drang Valley. Who would you want to act like?"

Ia *Drang Valley*, she thought. She was also trying to think of the name of even one woman who'd led an infantry charge, anywhere, in the Army's history.

"Eisenhower," she said.

This name produced an almost physical contraction of boredom in the room, as if a great shadowing cloud had passed overhead. Hartz licked his chapped lips and glanced up at the ceiling. "He was a general, Fowler. Not a colonel."

"Yeah, well, before any of that, he lived around here," Fowler said. "We had to take a field trip to his house when I was a kid." It was actually a field trip she'd taken twice, once for freshman history, and then again when Harris had been in the same class and he'd missed the field trip bus so she'd driven him up to Abilene personally—a good excuse to spend the afternoon together. But instead she'd been pissed off because he'd tried to ditch the class. A three-hour round trip, on a sunny fall day, during which she had not spoken—time that now she'd give anything to have back.

"Well, then," Hartz said, "maybe you should tell us a little bit about what made the general so great."

This time, instead of Pulowski in a negligee, she imagined Harris, acting just as loving and well-behaved as all of Mel Gibson's kids. Harris waiting for her on the screened front porch of her perfect officer's digs. No cigarettes, no dope, no Black Sabbath shirts, no angry resentment at her rules. Eisenhower had five brothers, and one of them had injured and eventually lost an eye when Ike was taking care of him. He never forgot his failure to protect someone who was weaker than him, who relied on him. And then later, when his family ran out of money, Dwight let his older brother Edgar go to college while he worked night shifts at the local dairy. "The thing about Eisenhower," she said, "was that he never sat around thinking about how he was going to look to somebody. He didn't try to impress people. He didn't act. He wasn't showy. He was boring. He would've thought boring was good."

"That's an interesting perspective," Hartz said

Way to go, Fowler, she thought, now that she'd finished speaking. *Nothing like speaking up in class to inform your commanding officer that you don't really want to be interesting.* "Think about it this way," she said. "How many people have seen any movies that Eisenhower made?"

"If there wasn't any movie," Anderson asked, "then how the hell do you know so much about this?"

"I read a book about him for a class," Fowler said, flushing now, humiliated. Goodbye to Pulowski in his negligee. *Forget about backyard barbecues and adoring children. Forget about fitting in. There's a beat-down on the way.*

"Sir," Anderson said, his wand waving in the air. "I think that the lieutenant had a good point, sir. I think we need to spend a lot more time reading, sir. That's one of the real mistakes that I felt that Colonel Moore made in the Io Drone Valley, sir. I kept looking for it, sir, but during the entire battle, nobody read a single book. It was shocking, sir, if you ask me."

"There's nothing wrong with a soldier being interested in history," Hartz said. "I'm sure the colonel would appreciate your thoroughness." His tone was odd, not a warning, exactly, but the opposite of a compliment.

In other words, he had no idea what to do with her—the

exact conclusion that she most feared, particularly from the men who were in charge of things. *I got a book you should read*, she thought, and imagined Anderson in a miniskirt and heels and tried, desperately, to inject this thought clear across the room into Pulowski's brain.

17

In September, four months before their deployment, Fowler disassembled and rebuilt the hydraulic system on the Hercules, having ordered new hoses through the requisition office. The pattern of the hoses, as they branched and divided through the interior of the machine, was a reassuring puzzle, complicated but never contradictory, the return lines and outgoing lines perfectly balanced, like the arteries in a heart. By the end, each was flagged, the pattern fully memorized by herself and by Sergeant Eggleston, whom she had chosen to command this machine, and all the rest of her NCOs. Having made the Hercules whole, they would soon have to break it all down again for transport to Iraq, but before they did, they spent weekends trundling the great big squat machine patiently out into the soybean fields, a deeply unsexy, dowdy beast waddling up to creek beds and hauling out logs, clanking out to the motor pool and hooking its tow cable to decommissioned tanks, to truck cabs, to Fowler's beater F-150.

Now, lying beside Pulowski in the La Quinta Inn, she guiltily compared the puzzle of the Hercules to the puzzle of the signal officer she had now slept with four times. Physically, things clicked just fine, though she was beginning to worry that the other parameters of their relationship weren't going to be as cut-and-dried. "You gonna ever tell me anything about yourself?" Pulowski asked, rolling over on his side. "Or are these meetings going to be just, kind of, a refreshing form of PT?"

"What do you want to know?" She slid one leg over Pulowski's skinny midsection and sat up high atop him, so as to feel less vulnerable.

"What about your family?"

"Divorce," she said. "Mom remarried, like, fifteen years ago. Lives in Oregon. So not really in touch. And I got a brother, Harris, who"—she poked him in the nose with her finger; playful, but also reminding him that he was an outsider to this whole thing—"is not a big fan of my joining the Army."

"Sounds like my kind of guy."

"I thought you had a sense of humor."

"I do." He craned his neck to catch a glimpse of the TV behind her, where Leno was talking. "Speaking of which—"

"Yeah, well, Harris isn't much into jokes. Harris is a very serious guy. Or at least he is when it comes to me."

"Maybe it's the way you talk to him," Pulowski suggested.

"Maybe. Although he also gets mad when I *don't* talk to him."

"Sounds like what you might need are some lessons in male psychology."

"Yeah? This from a guy who tells me I need to make a fool out of myself. I *always* find that useful when I'm dealing with my platoon."

"Maybe you ought to try it."

"Have you been a woman in the Army?" she asked. "Like in some previous life?"

Pulowski had his head propped up against a folded pillow and he gave her a beaky, acned smile, as if in fact he had. Or was intending to try it out.

"I know that if my nickname was Family Values Fowler, I might consider the possibility that I needed to lighten up. Especially since, you know"—he gestured to the room with a sweeping wave that included, in a final underhand curl, her crotch where it pressed against his belly—"there's so much excellent evidence here to the contrary."

She'd not heard the name before and she felt immediately self-indulgent and foolish, talking about herself. Self-indulgent to even *be* here. She slid easily off Pulowski's belly and padded over to the table and chairs that sat before the motel room's window and found her panties and, sitting down on the rough woven wool of the chair, fit her feet through the leg holes. Pulowski may have been right to make fun of Seacourt and his proscription against smoking, his rules, his habit of dropping down to do fifty push-ups during meeting breaks, his focus on PT. None of it, she admitted, was going to necessarily help anybody in a firefight. But there was still something clear and clean to it that she liked; if you sat in a chair in your office and pored over the roster of your platoon and you learned to be thinking only *of* them and knowing that you yourself needed nothing *from* them, it helped with the nerves. And in moments like this. "Really?" she said. "That's what they call me?"

"That's what I heard," Pulowski said, pushing himself up on his elbow so that he could watch her dress. "So is it true?"

She'd finished pulling up her panties and sat back in the chair, otherwise naked, testing out how this felt under the beetle-black gaze that Pulowski gave her from the bed. It felt good. "No," she said. "I was *bad* at family. Or at least that's what my brother seems to think."

"Why does he think that?"

"Because he thinks I abandoned him," she said.

"Did you?"

"No," she said.

Pulowski waited for a further answer—or no, that was wrong. He accepted her answer, without any further comment, which was not, she realized, quite the same thing. She was curious about how he knew that she preferred it.

"He stole a car," Fowler explained. "When he was, like, sixteen. It was our neighbor's, right down the road. The Ryersons. He hid it in our barn out back, which was totally insane, naturally." She laughed, thinking about it now, trying to imagine what might have been going through Harris's head.

It was a funnier story when you said it out loud. Funnier too when she said it to Pulowski. If she'd tried it with Hartz, or Seacourt, they would've spent too much time trying to figure out what professional lessons could be drawn from it.

"Sweet," Pulowski said.

"Oh, yeah. It was sweet, all right."

"So what did you do?"

"I fucking turned him in," she said. This too she found herself unable to say without a guilty smile.

"You're kidding me!"

"What the hell else was I supposed to do?"

This was not a question she liked to ask. In fact, the best way she'd found to get over the past was to accept the present, to *take it one day at a time*, as Hartz would've said, which was one of the things she loved about the Army, that you could actually try. The present was always there. Tomorrow, there would be M4 qualification at ten a.m. Then a PowerPoint on tactics for observing IEDs. Then vehicle inspection. Then at 1600, a five-mile run for PT. All of that she felt perfectly capable of handling. It was the stuff that had to do with the future or the past that frightened her. And yet she had been dying to ask somebody this question about Harris since the first moment when she'd stood the soldiers in her platoon up for roll call and listened to them blurt out their names. Their trusting faces had terrified her in exactly the same way Harris's had.

"You could've let him go," Pulowski said. "Got him off—or at least let him sneak the car back. Did anybody else know that he'd stolen it, other than you?"

"No," she said. "Nobody else did."

"So why didn't you do that?"

"Because I was angry at him," she said. "Because I thought he needed to learn a lesson. It *is* wrong, you know. It is not a good idea for a sixteen-year-old to steal a car. Did you steal any?"

"No, I was too much of a pussy."

"Okay, and plus it was bad for the family."

"What?"

"There's rules for a family, just like there's rules for a platoon. Or a company. You don't fucking run out on people. You don't break the law. You don't lie—or at least not to the people who are supposed to be on your side."

"That's it? That's your whole philosophy?"

"It's what I'm working with currently."

"You don't think it's more complicated than that?"

"Such as?"

"Such as if your brother decides to steal a car, that's his problem, isn't it? Why should you care one way or the other about that?"

"Because he's my brother. He did something wrong. If I don't say something to him about it, if don't tell him that it's wrong, then who will?"

"I think it's probably not that simple," Pulowski said.

"Yeah, well, why don't you talk to him, then?"

"Maybe I will."

"What would you tell him?" She'd crawled back on the bed

by then, sitting up this time, watching the TV between her knees. Pulowski had told her, early on in their relationship, that Leno was the inferior late-night host, especially when compared with Letterman. Largely, in his opinion, it was because Leno was unwilling to be genuinely unpleasant. He was a glad-hander. He tried so hard to get his audience to *like* him that he could never be quite as funny as Letterman. He pulled his punches instead, refused to humiliate his guests. The comparison had been, she guessed, a proxy for Pulowski's own views on how she dealt with her platoon—or, in the current conversation, how she dealt with Harris. The implication was that she was more complicated than she pretended, a flattering criticism, especially since nobody in her family had ever suggested it.

"I'd tell him it's possible for somebody to be more than one thing," Pulowski said. "Like maybe he might consider the possibility that you could be wrong and right."

"Why both?"

"Because everybody is," Pulowski said. "The possibility that you're just like everybody else is something he probably hasn't considered yet."

"But I didn't *do* anything wrong," she said.

Pulowski turned his chin and looked at her with a squint, as if he'd never heard such a ridiculous assertion. "Then how did we end up here?"

It was a fair question. At night, during the previous summer, when she left Fort Riley and returned alone to her apartment in Harmony Woods, she had developed a habit of drinking beer on a small porch outside her bedroom. It was just a slab of concrete, marked off by an iron railing, that led onto a poorly tended patch of grass—an imitation of something real. Pulowski had lived in the apartment across the way. He'd normally be up and about in a T-shirt and a pair of what Harris had referred to derisively as "tighty-whities," drinking a glass of orange juice and firing up his computer, alone at his kitchen table, unaware of his existence in her head. The alone part had interested her. So she'd continued to investigate. He was from Tennessee but had no accent, no visible interest in football or sports, drove a Toyota Celica, and did not hang out with the other southerners in the battalion, which made him less of a risk. On the rifle range, she noticed that he showed no visible interest in even attempting to look proficient with his weapon, but instead tended to choose a shooting station as far away from the other soldiers as possible, and quickly run through his shot selection without any real concentration, as if firing a weapon were somehow a shameful or embarrassing thing. In terms of avoiding complication, these were all good things. Relationships between officers of equal rank were legal, technically, in the Army. But the gossip they engendered was more toxic for female officers than any technicality. Just the news that she'd been slutty enough to ask someone out, much less sleep with them, was enough to obliterate all the respect she'd worked to achieve. Pulowski, however, had had no one to tell. So maybe her decision to ask him out *was* just a crime of opportunity. Maybe it was just being selfish, her body knowing that she liked having somebody to touch when she got home from work. Maybe it was just her own mind entertaining itself and there was nothing special about this guy.

And yet it didn't feel that way. Here on a queen-size bed in the La Quinta Inn, drunk on the beer she'd brought, the room lit by the blue glow of Leno's set, she was pleasantly aware of Pulowski's increasing complexity.

"Sorry to disappoint you, Pulowski," she said. "But knowing that I sleep around is unlikely to make my brother happy."

"I thought we'd just established that he's an idiot."

She sat up and whomped him with a pillow.

"What the hell was that for?"

"This is my brother we're talking about," she said. "I'm the one who gets to say whether or not he's an idiot. Not you."

Pulowski got a curiously amused expression on his face. "Okay, then what do I get to say? What areas am I fit to comment on?"

"Yourself."

"And you?"

"No, not me. Just you."

Snorting, Pulowski scooted toward her along the bed so that they were shoulder to shoulder and he swiveled his hand down along her pelvis, and as she leaned her head back, she could smell the soap he used. His nose brushed her neck. "Then maybe *I'm* the idiot," he said. "Because I am very, very happy"—his touch was like an electric current grounded through her body—"that you've done wrong with me."

In the morning she got up early, before Pulowski did. It had been a mistake to sleep with him, she was sure of that. In her sleep, she'd had vague dreams about her company commander, Captain Hartz, leaning over her and telling her to get her shit in a pile, effective immediately. The scary thing was, in the dream she'd had the sensation that her shit was in a pile, at least everything that she understood her shit to be. Her files were all in order (in real life, a rarity). Her Beretta had been cleaned. She had a to-do list written up for the day. She'd even emptied out her email in-box entirely. It was a common dream of hers, one that she'd been repeating fairly frequently since she'd received her commission. There had been a frost overnight and the windshield of her truck was opaque. She searched through the bed and found her frost scraper and cleaned the windows off, then put her gloves back on and headed across the parking lot toward the Gas 'n Go, where she intended to buy some coffee for the ride back to Fort Riley. Halfway there, she turned around and walked back to Pulowski's Celica and peered in through the windows to see if he had a scraper. He did not, though the inside of this car was extraordinarily clean and neat, far more than hers.

She returned to her truck, grabbed the scraper, and carried it back to his car, where she began scrubbing off the frost and dusting it away. Who was he to tell her how to be a lieutenant? Who was he to tell her how to talk to her brother? Of course, it was early enough in their relationship that she could break things off and no one would complain, least of all Pulowski. There had been no commitments made. No rules at all to govern their relationship—nothing that explicitly held them together or determined how they should act. It was just an affair, neither good nor bad. There was no group, no platoon, no company, no family, no blood, no country. No expectations. No structure to tell either of them whether they were doing things right. And thus, no way to judge it, no way to guess how it might turn out, or where it might possibly lead.

And yet she was out here in the cold at six a.m., scraping the frost off his windshield and feeling happier about it than she had any right to be.

PART FIVE

EPILOGUE

THE FIELD

The police station in Bini Ziad, a small town west of Baghdad, is in a long cinder-block building that has been painted white with a blue stripe. It's early June. Lieutenant Emma Fowler follows an Iraqi constable and her company commander, Captain Hartz, through the front entrance and down a dank hall to a makeshift interview room, its walls constructed of sheets hung from wires overhead. The mother of the Iraqi whom Fowler shot that morning is there. She refuses to take Captain Hartz's hand and then, checking her chair as if something might have climbed up on it, sits down with a sweep of her hand beneath her black skirt. She wears a Western blazer with gold buttons, a black scarf about her head, her mouth drawn prim and fierce. None of the humor that Fowler remembers in Pulowski, no self-deprecation, no eye turning inward. Instead, the woman speaks offhandedly to the Iraqi officer, her gaze askew, and moments later, a hand pokes through the sheets with a glass cup of chai. Money is what this says to Fowler; here's someone who's used to getting what she wants in this place. Captain Masterson is already there, seated at the table, his body armor piled in the corner. Fowler strips down too, but Hartz chooses to sit down in full gear, so that he appears swollen, like a giant pumpkin, the skin of his neck flushing scarlet. "This letter, ma'am," he says as he unfolds a piece of stationery, "constitutes an official condolence for your son's death from the coalition forces and the United States Army. This letter is not an admission of guilt. Your son was present during an attack on coalition forces, during which three soldiers were killed. We believe our soldiers acted properly to defend themselves." He casts a hopeful glance at Fowler, which she does not match. "Unfortunately, these actions appear to have resulted in your son's death. It was an accident, which doesn't make it less of a tragedy."

While these words are being translated, the woman rolls her eyes and grimaces at the curtained wall off to the interpreter's left. But when the interpreter stops, and a silence falls in the small room, the woman's face crumples in on itself, as if her resistance to the ridiculousness of Hartz's monologue has been the only thing keeping her features in place. She begins to sob.

"I'm sorry," Hartz says. He pushes the letter forward with a gloved hand.

This at least gives the woman something to do. She flinches and flares away from his advance, striking out and swatting the letter to the floor. Relieved, Hartz bends over to retrieve it, is stopped by the resistance of his body armor, and, grunting, scoots his chair out and drops to a knee.

"Can you even say his name?" the interpreter is asking by the time Hartz regains his seat. "Ayad. My son is Ayad al-Tayyib. Do you think a letter brings him back? Do you wonder why people are not happy in the way George Bush has freed our country? For what? So my son can die and bandits can drive me from my own house?"

"Yes, about these bandits," Hartz begins.

"Why don't you shoot *them*?" This the woman says in English.

"That's what we'd like to do, ma'am," Masterson says. His back is to Fowler, who has stationed herself by the beaded door. She can feel the whisper of the room's sheet wall against the back of her head like a shroud. Hartz laughs nervously, as if his fellow officer is a crazy uncle, friendly but given to overstatement.

"The reason we're asking you to help us," Hartz continues, "is that there were five bombs found buried in the field right behind your house, which we believe is your property. Is that correct, that it's your property?"

The woman nods, almost imperceptibly.

"If so, these are very troubling charges, ma'am. Very troubling. If we were to find out, for instance, that you knew that your son—or anybody else—had planted those bombs there. And you did not come forward. That would be a very serious offense. And, well, I'm sorry to say we believe that an American soldier's body has been hidden there. Buried, I mean."

"Sorry to say!" Masterson bursts out. He opens a manila folder. From it he retrieves two sheets of yellow legal paper covered in handwritten Arabic. There's a photo clipped to each page.

"These are sworn affidavits that your son was involved in an insurgent group dedicated to the resistance of the coalition forces. Can you explain to me why these Iraqi citizens would say your son was involved in the insurgency if he was not?"

"Hold on a second here—" Hartz says.

"Why would I do that, Captain?" Masterson says. "These documents are proof that this woman's son engaged in anti-coalition activity."

As soon as Fowler sees the affidavits, she knows they're fake. One is from Masterson's former interpreter, Faisal Amar, who is conveniently dead. The other is accompanied by a photo of a sheikh she recognizes, a man in his fifties, with a heavily lined face. She and Masterson had interviewed him at the schoolhouse in Bini Ziad the day of Beale's abduction. He knew nothing about Beale—though at one point he spread his hands, a bargaining man, and explained that perhaps he could be more helpful if the captain told him whom *he* wished to blame. But the affidavits don't matter. What interests her is the woman's reaction to the files, the way her gaze slides contemptuously off to the side. Fowler wants a confrontation, wants her anger, wants the woman to dare to challenge their legitimacy. She leans forward until the woman meets her gaze.

Immediately, the woman speaks, abruptly, haughtily.

"These people are nothing," the interpreter says.

"Nothing in what way, ma'am?"

"Her son was educated," the interpreter says. "These are village people. They can't even write. It's an insult to bring her this testimony."

The woman speaks with pure contempt, a clear, high-octane cook-off of hatred, which Fowler finds herself more than ready to meet.

"So you know them, then?" Fowler asks.

"Who is this?" the woman asks.

"Ma'am," Hartz says, halfway rising, "this is Lieutenant Fowler, one of my subordinates. She was in the field when your son was . . . received his injuries. She lost three soldiers herself . . ."

But the woman has no interest in Hartz. She's locked on to Fowler now.

"My son was deaf," the interpreter says while the woman, loosening her scarf, pulls her ear as if she intends to rip it off and hand it to Fowler. "He was deaf. He was deaf. You are a woman. You tell me, what kind of animal would kill a man like that?"

"Ho now!" Hartz says. He's up and out of his chair, sweaty and red, waggling his pale palms in her face, as if he might rub her away. "Let's take a break, okay?"

"No," Fowler says. "I'll speak to that. I shot your son." Hartz has collared her now, hauling her away. "But if I'm an animal, then maybe you can ask her where she was when I came looking for him. Why don't you ask her that?"

The interpreter dutifully begins, but Hartz waves him off. "No, no. I don't think that's a good idea."

"Why not?" Fowler says. It's ugly what she's saying and she knows it, but she can taste Pulowski's death in her mouth, choking her, and she will say anything to get it out. Even animals have to breathe. "Single males living alone are the people most likely to be targeted by insurgents. That's the profile. She knows that. You leave a kid out there alone, with no clue what's happening, nobody to speak for him—ask her what kind of animal does a thing like that."

The backyard of Ayad al-Tayyib's house is a mess of men. The Explosive Ordnance Disposal Team is rigging charges to clear the remaining IEDs from the field so that Fowler and her platoon can safely dig out Beale's body. She exchanges nods with these men, brief waves. Pulowski's body is long gone, on the first transport out the night before. Coming through the side yard, she has a couple of flashes of him scrambling away from her, as if she has become a person whom he does not know, or cannot see. It feels like she's peering through the wrong end of a telescope at a universe from which she had been barred, passport revoked, papers out of date. She goes into the living room to get Eggleston, who's watching TV. "Eggy, come on," she says.

"I can't believe those guys are dead, ma'am," Eggleston says.

The video is of a cricket match, a sport she doubts the sergeant has ever seen before. Or cares about.

They watch it together as a memorial to the dead, the vast glowing park of green space, somewhere in Pakistan. No stranger than the fact that Crawford, McWilliams, and Pulowski have gone away. "You get any intel from the mother?" Eggleston says.

"Enough to make me sick," she says. She's moving already to the back of the house, through the parquet-floored hall in front, past a varnished, spindle-legged table, a nice one, whose front drawer has been opened, spilling papers, bills. "Look at this shit. It's like a fucking country club around here. Fucking lady, you should've heard her." She paws through these bills listlessly, recognizing the stationery, but seeing Crawford's peppercorn eyes. "Fucking sob story. Calls me an animal for shooting her kid. Meanwhile, she's fucking sitting around watching cricket while Beale rots in the backyard."

"That's bullshit, ma'am. I'm sorry."

"And then the captain shows her sworn testimony that her son was running with bad guys, and what's she do? She attacks the witnesses. Hear no evil, fucking see no evil, huh, Eggy? You can't help people if they act that way."

Someone had carried down Pulowski's camera system from the roof while she was away and placed it just inside the front door of the dead man's house. A cord runs out of a hole Pulowski had bored in the side of one of the Rubbermaid tubs, and up into the hollow base of the camera's metal stand. She traces it with her finger to the smoked bulb of glass at the curved end. A black glass eye. She stares into it, but it's just a camera. Unlike Pulowski, it doesn't flinch or shy away. But his last signal is somewhere inside. "Where are the guys?"

Eggleston jerks his chin, indicating outside.

"How are they holding up?"

Eggleston has a fleshy, baggy face with violet bands beneath the great big hooded globes of his eyes, a face that belongs inside, overfleshed and heavy, like a guy you'd see on a subway in New York City. "Waldorf's having a hard time with it."

"Why's that?" She's hot with embarrassment. She realizes what it is now. She's embarrassed at how happy she was to bring Pulowski here. How fucking naïve it was to wish even for a second that they could've ever returned to anything.

"He feels like it was his fault that we left the compound. He should've stuck with your orders instead of listening to Pulowski."

"Yeah? And who was the genius who brought Pulowski out? And then left him behind with you guys to whine about some fucking dog he saw on TV?"

Now its Eggleston's turn to be embarrassed. He shuffles his feet.

"Answer my question, Sergeant."

"You were, ma'am."

"So you can tell Waldorf to quit crying about it, then. I don't have time for everybody to be running around crying today. That's how you make mistakes."

It's hot and still in the dead man's house. She does not want whatever Eggleston is trying to give. "I do think Pulowski was legitimately trying to help, ma'am," the sergeant says. "For what it's worth."

"Well, it's not worth very fucking much, Eggy, is it?" She has a little problem with voice control at the end of this. "You tell Waldorf this. Pulowski made the call to go out, not him. I've known that guy a long time. I should've known he wouldn't follow orders. He has no concept of orders. I'm sorry he's dead, but *he* made the mistake."

She finds her platoon outside the north wall of the compound, sitting with their backs against the stone and looking out at the field. There's a tiny strip of shade along the base of the wall. They are sitting with their heads in the shadow and their boots sticking into the sunlight. Waldorf's hands cover his face. Dykstra has wrapped his arm around him. Others, like Jimenez, have their eyes closed, trying to sleep. Down below them, in the wheat field, a lieutenant from the EOD Team walks out of the field, away from the abandoned hulks of her Humvee and Eggleston's Hercules, back toward the compound gate. He carries a great spool of copper wire under his arm, unrolling it as he goes, the wire flashing and gleaming as it bucks and falls into the grass, like a string of fire.

"All right, guys," she says, crouching down into a squat. "Come here, gather in with me. Waldorf, where are you?" He's off to the left, hunched over, at the far end of the line of faces, and she reaches a hand out to him and pulls him in closer, so that he has to squat beside her. She drapes an arm around his neck.

"I just met with Captain Hartz." She looks up. "He told me specifically to relay to you his pride and gratitude for the bravery of your actions here, recovering the body of Sergeant Beale. The two guys we killed in that field were our enemies. I have the testimony here to prove it. They killed Carl Beale. They buried him in this field like an animal. They would have left him to rot here permanently."

Dykstra snorts and shakes his head.

"All right, maybe he didn't say that," Fowler admits. "So fuck him, then, I did."

When she glances over her shoulder, she sees the EOD lieutenant, his goggles flashing, waving with both hands like a priest for her to kneel.

"What the fuck is wrong with him?"

"I think he wants us to take cover, ma'am."

"Oh, for chrissakes, we're too far away. He can't hurt anybody."

"Fire in the hole, I need you to take cover, please!"

This time the lieutenant is pointing at her directly, and Fowler stands and waves him off and squats down again. The harsher instructions she's given to Eggleston will be transmitted in their own way. Now what she wants is control. She will give them a story and they will accept it and she will drive away the laggards who attempt to tell it a different way. "Six more months," she says. "That's all we got left. You did what I trained you to do. The men who died here did not die because of you. They died *for* you, and it's you who are going to bring the truth of what they did back." She waits for an argument but there is none, and so they bow their heads, waiting for the blast.

Even in the worst circumstances, there's usually something funny about a controlled detonation. Amusement at the power of the explosives, relief that the bombs were friendly and their power would not be directed at them. This time, though, when the charges rip, Fowler and her men pull in together, touching the brims of their helmets.

They stay there for a while longer, after the all-clear. Nobody's saying anything. When she looks up, she can see everybody's eyes. Who here will be the dissenter? Who will be her Judas? Who will dare report her murders? What breaks the tension, relieves the awful interrogation of her gaze, is the rain of dirt from the explosion, pouring down out of the sky. It rattles on their Kevlars. "Fucking typical," Jimenez says.

Then she stands and leads them all into the wheat.

ACKNOWLEDGMENTS

The author gratefully acknowledges the support of the Hodder Fellowship at Princeton University's Lewis Center for the Arts. This book could not have been written without the help and advice of many soldiers who served in Iraq, especially members of the 1st Battalion, 22nd Infantry, and the 36th Engineer Brigade. A sincere thank-you to all of them. Specifically, I would like to mention these servicewomen and servicemen: Stacy Moore, Travis Parker, Angela Fitle, Nate Rawlings, John Sabia, Sam Karr, Edwin Melendez, Elizabeth Harmon-Craig, Sarah Apgar, David O'Donahue, Erin Kennedy, Sammy Sparger and Jennifer McDonough. Their kindness and expertise was invaluable. I would also like to thank Khaldoun Ahmad, who advised me on Iraqi life, and Flagg Miller, who consulted on the Arabic in this book. The following friends, writers, editors, and institutions provided crucial input and support: Andy Wright, Tom Shroder, Deborah Clark, June Thomas, Ed Quigley, Susi Cohen, Margot Livesey, Michael Knight, Michael Pritchett, Crosby Kemper III, Shannon Jackson, Daniel Woodrell, Frank and Sandy Terrell, the R&S Artspace, the Kansas City Public Library (thanks, H.F. and C.C.!), and UMKC. About halfway through this book, as I was wrestling with its reverse chronology, my colleague Michelle Boisseau recommended Charles Baxter's marvelous novel *First Light*. I second her recommendation. Sarah Scire, Nora Barlow, and many other wonderful people at Farrar, Straus and Giroux have worked tirelessly to introduce this novel to the world. A final and enduring thanks goes to my agent, Warren Frazier, and my editor, Sean McDonald. They believed in this project at the most crucial moments, and without them, I wouldn't be writing this.

A NOTE ABOUT THE AUTHOR

Whitney Terrell is the author of *The Huntsman*, a *New York Times* notable book, and *The King of Kings County*. He is the recipient of a James A. Michener–Copernicus Society Award and a Hodder Fellowship from Princeton University's Lewis Center for the Arts. He was an embedded reporter in Iraq during 2006 and 2010 and covered the war for *The Washington Post Magazine*, *Slate*, and NPR. His nonfiction has also appeared in *The New York Times*, *Harper's Magazine*, *The New York Observer*, *The Kansas City Star*, and other publications. He teaches creative writing at the University of Missouri–Kansas City and lives nearby with his family.